BOOKS BY

MIDNIGHT IN SCOTLAND SERIES

The Making of a Highlander (Book One)

The Taming of a Highlander (Book Two)

The Temptation of a Highlander (Book Three)

The Wickedness of a Highlander (Book Four)

The Love of a Highlander (Book Five) – Coming soon!

Right Place, Wrong Duke (A Midnight in Scotland Novella)

RESCUED FROM RUIN SERIES

Ever Yours, Annabelle (Prequel)

The Madness of Viscount Atherbourne (Book One)

The Truth About Cads and Dukes (Book Two)

Desperately Seeking a Scoundrel (Book Three)

The Devil Is a Marquess (Book Four)

When a Girl Loves an Earl (Book Five)

Twelve Nights as His Mistress (Novella – Book Six)

Confessions of a Dangerous Lord (Book Seven)

Anything but a Gentleman (Book Eight)

A Marriage Made in Scandal (Book Nine)

A Kiss from a Rogue (Book Ten)

Once Upon a Midnight Kiss (A Rescued from Ruin Novella)

The Oddflower Series

The Secrets of a Moonlit Night (An Oddflower Novella)

COMING SOON:

The Rake's Rules for Deception (Book One)

The Earl's Rules for Seduction (Book Two)

The Scoundrel's Rules for Marriage (Book Three)

The Duke's Rules for Scandal (Book Four)

Standalone Titles

Once Upon a Haunted Knight (Novella)

Want to know what's next? Visit **www.elisabraden.com** and sign up for Elisa's free email newsletter, so you never miss a single new release! And for more frequent updates and other fun stuff, be sure to follow Elisa on social media:

Facebook: @authorelisabraden

Instagram: @authorelisabraden

Twitter (X): @trueelisabraden

ELISA BRADEN

This is a work of fiction. Names, characters, places, and incidents are products of the author's imagination or are used fictitiously and are not to be construed as real. Any resemblance to actual events, locales, organizations, or persons, living or dead, is entirely coincidental.

Cover design by Dar Albert at Wicked Smart Designs

For more information about the author, visit www.elisabraden.com.

ISBN-13: 978-1-950805-13-6

Chapter One

July 3, 1827
Inverness, Scotland

Beneath her oversized umbrella, Sabella Lockhart squeezed the rose she held until a thorn punctured her glove. She scarcely felt the wound.

"I didnae ken him well," said the earnest young constable standing on the opposite side of the grave. "But he had the lads' respect."

Mr. Gillespie was only a lad himself. He'd removed his hat in an attempt at fine manners. Rainwater rolled off his pomaded hair like oiled glass.

"Thank you, Mr. Gillespie," she said softly. "The sergeant would have been pleased to hear it." She wasn't certain the sergeant had ever spoken to the man, but if he could be here now, he'd be far from pleased. Oh, the upbraiding he'd deliver to one of his constables for attending a burial rather than attending his duties. She could almost hear that barrel-chested bark. It *almost* made her smile.

Still, the lad was the only one who'd come to pay his respects. Sabella, at least, was grateful. The sergeant's gruff manner hadn't won him many friends.

The constable departed. The downpour heaved, pounding her umbrella so loudly that she couldn't hear her own thoughts. So much the better. Her head wasn't a pleasant place to be.

Rivulets turned the mounded soil into mud, spattering the stone marker she'd purchased. Eventually, the mound would flatten, she told herself. The stone would weather and stain. Given enough rain, enough time, his marker would match the other two bearing his name.

Munro.

She glanced over her shoulder at the couple she'd hired to help her transport Sergeant Munro from Edinburgh to Inverness. The McCabes were rosy-cheeked and ruddy, small but sturdy. Kindness poured from them like the sweetest honey. Indeed, the instant they caught her looking in their direction, they tilted their heads sympathetically and rushed forward in unison.

"Let me hold that umbrella for ye, Miss Lockhart," said Mr. McCabe.

"Aye, dearie," Mrs. McCabe seconded. "Mustn't dirty yer hems whilst payin' yer respects."

Sabella handed him the umbrella and smiled her thanks. She'd managed to keep the lavender *gros de Naples* spotless all morning thanks to the McCabes. Such goodhearted people.

Carefully gathering her skirts, she laid her rose atop the mound. "You're home, Sergeant," she murmured, resting her hand upon the gravestone which, along with their passage from Edinburgh, had swallowed a quarter of her remaining funds. Her eyes flickered across the three names now lying side by side: *Sergeant Neil Munro, Eudora Munro, Isobel Munro.* Tears burned her throat. "You're with yer lasses again. Rest easy, now."

The McCabes hummed their sympathy. "Poor, wee dearie. Here." Mrs. McCabe handed her a lace-trimmed handkerchief. "Nae rain on yer silk, nor rain on those fair cheeks."

Sabella dabbed discreetly and accepted Mr. McCabe's offered arm as they exited the cemetery and made their way toward the inn. Halfway to their destination, Mr. McCabe withdrew a watch from his pocket. "We'd best hurry, miss. Cannae have ye missin' yer coach. Next one for Glenscannadoo isnae for a sennight."

The McCabes were even more generous than she'd thought. For the few shillings she'd been able to pay, they'd accompanied her and Sergeant Munro on a lengthy journey, repeatedly helped load and unload her trunks, and recruited four strapping lads to carry Munro's coffin. Mrs. McCabe had even acted as Sabella's lady's maid during their travels.

All the while, Mr. McCabe carried a fine gold timepiece in his pocket. Clearly, they had no need of her shillings and had taken the job purely out of compassion.

He urged her on faster. Faster. They were nearly at a run by the time they entered the courtyard. There, the muddy mail coach waited, piled high with a teetering mass of trunks, packages, and passengers.

She slowed to catch her breath, trying to determine where she was meant to sit. "Oh, dear. It's quite full, isn't it?"

A lady and two gentlemen sat behind the driver's bench, snug, damp, and miserable. Behind them were canvas bags stuffed full to bursting and five valises of varying sizes.

Mr. McCabe glanced skyward then closed the umbrella. "Would ye look at that? Rain's stopped." He opened the coach door and urged her forward. "In ye go, Miss Lockhart. Dinnae mind the smell. Ye grow accustomed to it."

Good heavens, the inside was more crowded than the outside. She apologized to the gentleman on her left before stepping up and wedging herself between the coach's wall and a woman with three visible teeth. Mr. McCabe started to close the door.

"Wait!" Sabella craned her neck to scan the top of the coach for her trunks, but the load was covered in canvas. "Are you certain the gentleman you hired loaded my belongings?"

"Oh, aye," he said, closing the door with a firm shove. "They were the first trunks strapped in place. That's why ye dinnae see 'em. They're in the center 'neath all the others."

Despite the wheezing pressure on her lungs, she breathed a sigh of relief. "Thank you, Mr. McCabe." She stretched a hand through the carriage window. He tried to return her umbrella, but she shook her head. "There isn't room. Keep it. I've another in my trunks."

The driver called out a warning: "Aw fer Glenscannadoo, Drumnadrochit, and Invermoriston! Departin' now."

Smiling at the couple who'd been so wondrously kind, she pressed the lace handkerchief into Mrs. McCabe's extended palm. "I wish I could repay the kindness ye both have shown me."

"Trust me, dearie," the woman said with a pat and a gleam. "Ye have."

The coach rocked into motion. Sabella waved goodbye to the McCabes then squeezed her arm back inside. Drawing a shallow breath, she nodded to the woman whose elbow wedged uncomfortably against her side. "Good day."

The woman sucked noisily at her three teeth. "Nah. 'Tis a *dreich* pisser."

Sabella might have tried to translate whatever language she spoke—Gaelic, perhaps?—if it weren't for the sudden and overwhelming nausea. She turned her head away. Outside, the air smelled like the back end of six overworked horses. Infinitely preferable.

Three hours later, she suspected her stays had punctured an organ. Her stomach waged a revolution against her sense of smell. Her bones had jarred loose to rattle about freely like spoons in a soup tureen.

And her foul-breathed companion would not. Stop. Talking.

She couldn't even understand her. At some point, the woman had told Sabella her name, but it sounded like throat-clearing after a lung complaint. Privately, she'd dubbed her Mrs. Foulbreath instead.

When Sabella realized Mrs. Foulbreath was speaking English—of a sort—she made an honest effort at comprehension. Some terms remained foreign and garbled. Others, she realized, were vulgarities she encountered too rarely to be familiar. Eventually, she gave up, pasting on a polite smile instead.

Sabella was a Lowlander. She'd spent her life in Edinburgh, apart from a few years attending schools in England and France. She didn't know what *"skelpt ma doup"* meant, and, God willing, she wouldn't be in the Highlands long enough to find out.

She'd begun with three tasks: Settle her brother's debts, bury Sergeant Munro, and speak to the MacPhersons before leaving Scotland for good. The first two had been hard. The third would be harder.

It wouldn't change what her brother had done, of course. Nothing could mend that. But the least she could do was face them.

The MacPhersons lived near a remote Highland village nestled at the juncture of two mirrored glens:

Glenscannadoo and Glendasheen. Having visited on two previous occasions, she'd once found the wooded mountains, shimmering lochs, and wee, humble village enchanting.

But that was before she knew Kenneth had gone mad. Before the nightmare from which she couldn't awaken.

The mail coach descended along a bone-rattling road toward the village of Glennscannadoo. As leafy birches ceded to grass and brambles, she caught a breathtaking vista of the place she remembered. The steep, misty mountains. The long, steely loch. The thick pines blanketing the foothills. The near-magical slant of light across the water.

She drew deeply of pine-tinged air. Memories flashed like vivid paintings, quickening her heart. She shook them away.

A cluster of rough stone structures stretched three lanes deep along the northern end of Loch Carrich. The village square consisted of a few small shops, several taverns, and one ridiculously large statue.

As they passed the silly thing, a gull splatted something foul on the statue's head. She remembered Annie complaining about the man who had erected the thing, Laird Glenscannadoo. "Laird?" the fiery redhead had scoffed. "Wee tartan peacock, ye mean. That statue is naught but an eyesore and a repository for bird shite."

Annie did not suffer fools gladly.

The coach rocked to a halt outside one of the taverns. The gentleman across from her snorted awake and threw open the carriage door while mumbling about "a pint and a piss."

Sabella followed him out, sucking in her first real breath since departing Inverness. Mrs. Foulbreath elbowed her aside. The other passengers poured toward the tavern door while the driver and guard began unloading packages. Without the McCabes, she'd need help with her trunks.

A pair of freckled lads exited the haberdashery arguing over whose turn it was to muck out the stables. "Laddies!" she called. Digging into her carriage dress pocket, she offered her last two coins. "There's one for each of you if ye'll help me transport my belongings."

The pair eyed her silk skirts and white kid gloves. After a glance at each other, the taller one asked, "How far ye goin'?"

The shorter one nudged him. "Nae matter. We'll assist ye, m'lady."

"Oh, I haven't a title. You may call me Miss Lockhart."

The shorter lad lifted his cap, dusted it against his leg, and grinned. "And ye may call me Mr. MacDonnell. This is my brother. He's Mr. MacDonnell, too."

She smiled at the boy's cheek. He couldn't be older than ten. "Well, *Misters* MacDonnell, I'd be grateful for your help. Do ye ken where Glendasheen Castle is?"

"Oh, aye. Our da works there."

Relief flooded in. She'd wondered if she'd have difficulty finding the place. Perhaps her luck was changing for the better at long last. Annie wasn't expecting her, and Sabella hadn't been certain about this visit until last night. Her courage was more of a sapling than a well-rooted oak, bending with every twisted gust.

The boys took the coins from her fingers. "Which bag is yers, m'lady?" asked the taller lad.

She turned to watch the guard tossing two valises down to the driver, who placed them on the ground. "I have three trunks, actually." She frowned as two bulky canvas bags dropped into the driver's waiting arms. "They should be here."

Wandering closer, she cleared her throat. "Sir?"

Another valise sailed past her head. She sidled toward the rear of the coach, searching for the distinctive green leather with brass trim. They had to be here.

A tiny flutter of panic rose in her chest. She rounded to the other side of the coach. The pile that had been strapped there was down to one brown trunk and a few canvas bags filled with letters. "Sir?"

"Aye," the guard grunted, wiping his forehead with his wrist.

"Where are the green traveling trunks?"

He gestured to the brown trunk. "That look green to ye?"

She frowned. "No."

With a shrug, he pulled out a flask and took a swig. "There ye have it."

"I don't think you understand. My companion hired men in Inverness to load them onto this coach. They would have been in the center. Three trunks. Green with brass trim."

"Only men loadin' this coach are me an' the driver. Too many swindlers and knaves lookin' for free fare these days."

"But my companion assured me—"

The guard hefted another bag down to the driver. "Left 'im behind, did ye?"

Frantically, she followed him to the front of the coach. "Would you be so kind as to check again?"

He swept a glance over the roof, which was empty of all but the brown trunk, a blue valise, and two canvas bags. "That's all there is, lass."

"No, no. You must be mistaken." She rounded the coach again to speak to the driver. "Three green trunks, sir. Please, you must have forgotten where you placed them." They must be here. Everything she had in the world—her clothing, her mother's jewelry, her umbrella, and, most importantly, the last of her money—lay in those three green trunks. They *couldn't* be lost. "Perhaps they were left in Inverness by mistake."

The driver and guard shared a skeptical glance. The driver began hauling the canvas bags inside the shop where locals retrieved their post. Meanwhile, the guard secured the remaining cargo and climbed down to tend the horses.

She dashed around to the front of the coach. "Please, I must return to Inverness."

He shot her a pitying glance. "Have ye the return fare?"

Blinking, she spun toward where she'd left the two lads. They were gone. She searched the square, her stomach twisting into a hard knot. Nothing but a splat-stained statue and a few kilted locals. Panic made her heart pound. "No," she breathed.

"I'm sorry, lass. Cannae take ye without pay."

"But you were meant to load my trunks in Inverness! Surely ye'll make an exception when the error was yours."

Another pitying frown. "Yer companion told ye he hired men to load yer belongings, aye?"

Her eyes fluttered as she scrambled to comprehend his implication. "Aye."

"Now they're missin'. And where is he?"

She shook her head. "But he wouldn't … Mr. McCabe is a very kind …"

The guard patted one of the horses. "Swindlers and knaves, miss. They're everywhere these days."

This couldn't be happening. It simply couldn't.

The driver returned, shouting toward the tavern, "Aw fer Drumnadrochit and Invermoriston! Departin' now."

Mrs. Foulbreath and two other passengers shuffled past Sabella to take their seats. The guard climbed onto the box seat. A moment later, the coach lurched into motion. She watched it roll away, her head swimming.

The McCabes had robbed her. What was she meant to do when everything she had in the world was gone? She glanced around the square. A few villagers went about their business, paying her no mind. A few more cast her stares ranging from curious to hostile.

Dizzy with encroaching panic, she called upon all the lessons she'd learned over the past year from Annie, Sergeant Munro, and even from Kenneth: Storms did damage, but they passed. Focus on the open doors, not the locked ones. Take shelter where shelter is offered.

And breathe.

She breathed, albeit tightly. She'd come here to visit Annie, who'd become an unlikely friend. Annie would help her.

Smoothing the creases from her *gros de Naples,* she entered the tavern. The interior was dim and smelled like sour sweat, musty ale, and burnt wood. It was small and uncrowded at midday, so she spotted the tavern keeper immediately.

Then her day went from dreadful to abysmal.

"Naebody I ken is headed to Glendasheen 'til tomorrow," he said, pouring another pint for a thirsty customer. "Who ye aimin' to see?"

"Lady Huxley."

"Be glad ye didnae venture all that way, lass. Annie's in England with Lord Huxley and his kin. They'll be gone all summer."

She hadn't considered the possibility that the Huxleys might be traveling. Annie had recently birthed her husband's heir, so it made sense that they'd take the future earl to visit Lord Huxley's family. But good heavens, this was a disastrous turn.

Among the MacPhersons, Annie Tulloch MacPherson Huxley was Sabella's lone defender. Annie's stepfather, Angus MacPherson, wanted nothing to do with the sister of the man who'd falsely imprisoned and tortured his beloved son. Sabella couldn't blame a father for such resentment. Neither could she blame Broderick, the target of Kenneth's evil misdeeds. Two of the three remaining brothers, Campbell, the eldest, and Rannoch, the youngest, were slightly less hostile. The fourth brother was … well, she preferred not to think about him.

Nevertheless, she'd come to Glenscannadoo to face the MacPhersons before leaving Scotland. Having Annie present to help facilitate an accord would have comforted Sabella immensely. But Annie wasn't here, all of Sabella's worldly possessions had been stolen, and her only other local acquaintance was Laird Glenscannadoo. Like everyone else in their circle, the laird had renounced all association with Lord Lockhart following Kenneth's fall from grace. Sabella considered her options and winced. The "wee tartan peacock" it was.

She cleared her throat to draw the tavern keeper's attention. "Do ye ken if the laird is at home?"

"'Tis summer. He's in Edinburgh 'til the Glenscannadoo Games next month."

Drat and blast.

She swallowed her nerves and asked, "What about Broderick MacPherson?"

"Nah. He traveled with Annie and Huxley to England. His wife's a Huxley too, ye ken."

Double drat and blast.

She asked about Campbell.

"England. Different part, though. Somethin' about his wife's inheritance."

She asked about Angus.

"Spends most of his time in Inverness of late."

She asked about Rannoch, the most charming of the four brothers.

The tavern keeper chuckled. "Ye're not the first lass to ask about that one. Lad's runnin' himself raw makin' deliveries for the distillery. Last I kenned, he was in Glasgow."

That left only one MacPherson—the one who hated her more than all the others combined.

"Ye look a wee bit peely, lass. If ye've a hunger on ye, we serve a fine venison stew." She started to thank him—until he told her the price. "'Tis only sixpence fer a bowl and a pint."

She didn't have sixpence. She didn't have a single farthing. Politely, she excused herself. While making use of the privy behind the tavern, Sabella assessed her options.

Shelter was the most important thing. She could go hungry for days. She'd done it before. But nights in the Highlands, even in summer, could be cold and wet. Aye, shelter first, sustenance second. Then, somehow, she must acquire sufficient funds to leave the glen, and more to leave Scotland. Nothing remained for her here apart from nightmarish memories and the scorched ruins of her family name.

Smoothing her skirts and sleeves, she surveyed the square and settled on an idea. Her first attempt was the tiny dressmaker's shop.

"Position?" Resettling a sprigged cotton skirt across her table, the harried dressmaker laughed. "Lass, if I could afford an assistant, I'd be employin' my sister."

"Oh, but it needn't be for long. Only until I earn enough for fare to Inverness. I'm a fair hand with a needle."

The dressmaker nodded to Sabella's gown. "That yer work?"

Sabella glanced down at the exquisite work of Madame Tessier. The Paris seamstress had spent weeks on the hem embroidery alone. "No," she answered, her stomach sinking. "This is French."

A dubious snort. "Aye. Both yer gown and ye are a bit too fine for my shop. Best ye try the haberdashery."

Sabella held out her gloved hands. "What will you give me for these? They're the finest kid. I purchased them in—"

The dressmaker grasped her fingers roughly, turning her hand to inspect the supple white leather. "They're stained. A wee puncture, there. That yer blood?"

Sabella looked closer. "Oh. I suppose it is. I was a bit careless with a rose stem—"

"Cannae offer ye coins I dinnae have."

Desperation soured her stomach. "What about my bonnet? Could you sell it for me?"

"Try the haberdashery, lass. Mr. Cleghorn makes purchases from time to time." She returned to her sewing. "Now, off wi' ye."

Sabella entered the haberdashery full of hope—and left defeated. Mr. Cleghorn said he didn't have any work available and didn't acquire "used goods from Lowland lasses." Then he disappeared into his storeroom to shout at his son, "That rope isnae fer gnawin', ye wee dafty!"

By evening, her stomach was too full of fretfulness to be hungry. The clouds hung heavy with waiting rain, and she'd failed to find work or accommodations after inquiring in every shop and all but one of the taverns. A few kindly women offered to provide lodging, but only for a fee. The taverns would feed her, but only for a price. Often, she received the same answer the dressmaker had given: If the villagers had aught to give, they'd give it to their kin first.

Now, she was down to the final tavern. It was the most popular tavern in Glenscannadoo, thronging and raucous even at this late hour. Perhaps they could use a barmaid, she thought. Sabella didn't know how to be a barmaid, but she could pour tea. How different could it be?

With a deep breath, she entered. Somewhere in the back of the room, a fiddler played. Everywhere, men crowded around tables, laughing and jesting, draining their cups of whisky, ale, and cider.

She swallowed against a dry throat and brushed her silk skirts. They were a bit dustier than this morning, but she'd been careful. By tomorrow, if she didn't find a solution to her very serious predicament, she'd be in a much worse state.

Bypassing three women singing drunkenly near the window, she sidled toward the grizzled man wearing an apron and pouring beer. "Sir?" He didn't seem to hear her. She squeezed between two sour-smelling gentlemen jesting about a lass's flat backside. "Sir!"

Again, he didn't hear her, laughing and shouting orders to a woman at the opposite end of the bar.

Sabella wedged closer, cringing as someone jostled her bonnet. "Mr. MacDonnell!"

Half the men turned in her direction. Drat and blast. She'd forgotten the glen teemed with MacDonnells.

To clarify, she waved to the barman. "Sir, might I have a word?"

He lifted his cap and gave her a once-over. "I'll offer ye more'n a word, lass, if ye take my meanin'."

A peculiar shiver raced along her neck. She rubbed it away and moved toward the barman. "I hoped to inquire about any positions you might have available."

"Positions?" His belly laugh boomed for all to hear. "Aye, there's one or two. Hope yer knees are sturdy."

The crowd erupted into uproarious laughter.

Sabella wanted to shrink until she was too wee to draw anyone's notice. Her neck turned ticklish, burning with a humiliated flush. Once again, she brushed away the sensation.

"Och, ye're pissin' in the rose garden again, brother!" called the throaty-voiced woman from the end of the bar. "Best ye proposition females who'll have ye. I hear Flora MacDonnell's sow is lookin' to breed soon."

More raucous laughter rang out as Mr. MacDonnell made a vulgar gesture to his sister. She returned the gesture and added a milking motion that Sabella didn't understand. Then she came toward Sabella with a sympathetic smile. "Dinnae pay Rab any mind, miss. He's nae the one to speak tae about positions, anyhow."

The tavern was called MacDonnell & Sons. "With whom should I speak?"

"That'd be me."

Sabella blinked. *"You're* the tavern keeper?"

Chuckling, the woman wiped her hands on her apron and leaned against the bar. "Aye. Joan MacDonnell, at yer service."

"A pleasure to meet you, Mrs. MacDonnell."

"Call me Joan, else I'll never ken which of us MacDonnells ye're addressin'."

Sabella attempted a shaky smile. "I'm Sabella Lockhart."

Joan's expression sobered into a frown. "Lockhart, eh?"

Perhaps she shouldn't have offered her name. Blackened as it was, it hadn't done her any favors in Glenscannadoo. The villagers were steadfastly loyal to the MacPhersons, who employed most of the glen's inhabitants.

Quickly, Sabella explained her very serious predicament. "I only require sufficient funds for fare to Inverness and lodging until the mail coach returns. Any tasks ye need help with, I shall do happily." She pointed to the pitcher Joan had placed on the bar. "I'm adept at pouring."

Folding her arms, Joan raised a brow and swept a glance over the crowd. When she returned to Sabella, her frown softened into pity. "Ye've wandered a bit far from yer pasture, lamb. Some here have long memories and sharp teeth. A few willnae hesitate to take a bite."

That much had become evident over the course of the day. Even Lowlanders weren't ordinarily treated so rudely in the Highlands. Of course, on her previous visits, she'd enjoyed all the protection and luxury her brother provided. They'd traveled in a velvet-lined coach and lodged in Laird Glenscannadoo's fine manor. Kenneth wouldn't have allowed a single drop of rain to touch her skirts, let alone permitted a barman to make lewd jests at her expense.

No stain or slight could be tolerated toward the sister of Lord Lockhart. Only he was permitted to punish her.

"Please." She swallowed the sick, leaden lump rising from her stomach to her throat. "I have nowhere else to go. Isn't there some work you can offer? Some way I may be of service?"

Joan shook her head. "Would that there were. But I just finished payin' for repairs after a nasty kitchen fire. My brother's helpin' mind the bar for free. If I could afford to hire anybody—"

"It would be your kin," Sabella finished softly. "Aye. I understand."

With a sigh, Joan gestured toward an empty table. "Have a seat there, lamb. Ye look fit to fall over dead."

Sabella gathered what was left of her pride. "I'm fine."

"Sit," Joan ordered, hefting her pitcher and shoving away from the bar. "Unless ye're eager to stand out in the rain."

Just then, the noise on the roof registered. The skies had opened. It was going to be a long, miserable night. She should never assume things couldn't get worse, she decided. Fate relished proving her wrong.

Avoiding the gazes of the women near the window, she took her seat and focused on the stained, scarred wood. Minutes later, a bowl of thick, creamy soup appeared in front of her. She glanced up.

Joan set down a basket of bread and a large cup of cider then nudged Sabella's shoulder. "Eat up, lamb. Cannae carry the world's troubles on an empty stomach."

Sabella's chest tightened. "Thank you, Joan."

Once the tavern keeper went back to serving her paying customers, Sabella tried to eat, but her stomach was knotted too tightly to settle, and the cider made her head swim. The bread helped a bit, but she only managed a few bites. Everything tasted like wet plaster. But she didn't want to seem ungrateful, so she forced down half of the soup and a slice of bread.

Two of the three women near her table staggered out into the rain. The third weaved between chairs to approach Sabella. "Couldnae help but overhear ye're seekin' work, lassie." The woman was older and appeared kind. Of course, Mrs. McCabe had also seemed kind. "Ye'll have a devilish time of it here. Many have left to seek employment in the cities or even in England. Dark times, indeed. Most here cannae afford to hire anybody, and if they could, they'd hire kin."

Sabella sighed.

"There's only one position I ken hasnae been filled." The woman scratched beneath her cap. "But a lass'd have to be mighty desperate to want that one."

Sabella glanced at the driving rain pounding the window. "What is it?" she asked as another shiver winnowed up her spine.

"Och, what am I sayin'? Fine lady like ye wouldnae consider such labor. Foolish of me to mention—"

She reached for the woman's arm. "Please. Tell me."

"There's a man livin' in the easterly braes in need of a maid."

"A—a maid?"

"Aye. 'Tis gruelin' work—"

"This man lives in the hills to the east, you say? How far away?"

"A few miles. Young lassie like ye can walk there in an hour if ye dinnae tarry." Her directions to the place sounded simple enough.

An hour's walk. Sabella glanced again at the rain pouring beyond the window. Darkness had settled in deep. It was late—past ten—and she was exhausted. But the chance at shelter and employment, a chance at extricating herself from this very serious predicament, was only an hour's walk away. Perhaps she'd been wrong about fate reveling in her misery. Perhaps her luck had finally taken a turn.

"Bessie!" Joan called sharply from behind the bar. "What mischief are ye up tae?"

The older woman flinched. Her kindly demeanor fell away, leaving disgruntlement. "Leave me be, ye harridan."

Joan came over to swat the woman with her cloth. "For the last time, ye cannae blame all Lowland lasses for yer son movin' to Edinburgh."

"They all think they're sssoooo grand. Too grand for my son, are ye? We'll see. When ye're smellin' like peat ash and piss, we'll see how grand ye are." The woman's slurring revealed how drunk she was—much more than Sabella had guessed. Then she started weeping. "He never writes anymore, Joan. She lured him to that rat-infested den of thieves and whores—"

"Edinburgh isnae that bad."

"—and he's forgotten all about his lovin' mam."

"I'm certain he thinks of ye from time to time." Joan caught Sabella's gaze and rolled her eyes. "Now, go home, Bessie. Yer grandsons will be wonderin' if ye drowned yerself in the loch."

Bessie nodded and patted Joan's shoulder on her way toward the door. "Right ye are. I love ye dearly, daughter. Even if ye're a harridan."

After she left, Sabella asked, "She's your *mother?*"

Joan chuckled. "Mother-in-law, aye. Bessie's harmless, but her youngest is the apple of her eye. She's bitter about him leavin' the glen." She flopped her cloth over her shoulder and crossed her arms. "What did she say to ye?"

"She mentioned a maid's position."

Joan cursed softly and glanced over her shoulder. "Ye dinnae want that job, lamb. Best ye forget it."

Sabella blinked. "You mean it's real?"

"Aye. But there's a reason it hasnae been filled."

"Is the wage dreadfully low?"

"No."

"Is the house dreadfully decrepit?"

"No. 'Tis a fine house."

"Then, why didn't you mention it? Perhaps I wasn't clear, but my predicament is quite serious."

Sighing, Joan shot another glance over her shoulder. Sabella frowned, trying to determine what she was looking at. The crowd had thinned, but the depths of the room were too dark to see anything clearly.

"Four lasses have taken that position," said Joan, low and quiet. "All four left after a week or two."

"Perhaps a week is all I require." Sabella stood and brushed at her skirts. "Your mother-in-law said I should follow the lane south along the loch then take the third road branching east. Is that true?"

Joan shook her head and clicked her tongue. "God preserve me from wanderin' lambs. Ye needn't go anywhere, lass. The man ye're seekin' is there." She pointed toward the darkest corner of the room. Sabella could just make out a pair of large boots, but nothing more. Joan began clearing the table. "I wouldnae provoke his temper if I were ye."

"Temper?"

Joan ignored her to carry away her dishes.

Sabella stifled a shiver as the strange, hair-lifting sensation returned. This time, it affected her whole body. Shaking off her nerves, she slowly made her way toward the farthest corner. Halfway there, the shadowy outline of a man took shape, but it was far too large to be real. She moved closer.

Closer.

The closer she drew, the more real his size became. Finally, she stood only feet away. And she knew.

She should not have done this. She should not have come to the glen. Rather, she should have taken the coward's path directly to London then onward to Paris. She certainly should not have ventured to the middle of nowhere seeking absolution from the MacPhersons.

Because the MacPherson who hated her more than any other was sitting before her now. And he was her only hope.

Chapter Two

The last time she'd seen him, she was soaked in his blood. Her hands. Her skirts. She'd cradled that dark head and begged a perfect stranger not to die.

Now, she could scarcely breathe. He was thinner yet still huge. Seven inches above six feet, to be precise. His hair was longer, nearly brushing his shoulders. That hard, hawkish face was half hidden beneath a dark beard. But the eyes were the same—black as night and twice as dangerous.

With one long, muscled arm casually draped over the back of his chair, Alexander MacPherson tilted his head. "Ye're a long way from home."

His voice, deep as an ocean, contained currents she didn't understand. As ever, she felt those currents ripping at her. She'd never known quite what to do about them.

Her mouth tried to form his name but only managed a puff of air. God, her heart was going to pound her to death from inside.

He poured himself a dram of whisky from the half-empty bottle near his wrist. After downing it in one swallow, he poured another. That one disappeared just as quickly.

She tried his name again. "Mr. MacPherson."

He poured another dram but let it sit on the table. Those impossibly long fingers turned the glass once. Twice. Thrice.

Schooling her breathing, she said, "I understand ye're in need of a maid." In truth, he was in need of a valet. Now that her eyes had adjusted to the darkness, she saw he wore only a dark shirt, deerskin breeches, and filthy boots. Beneath the beard, which wanted trimming, his cheeks were hollower than they should have been, his bones more angular. He'd suffered a long, slow recovery, according to Annie. Sabella wished his gauntness and lazy, sprawling posture made him less intimidating. The opposite was true.

He threw back the dram he'd been turning and poured another. All the while, his eyes burned the length of her like a torch.

She swallowed. "I came to the glen hoping to see Annie."

"Ye're a month late and two months shy for that."

Nodding, she dropped her gaze to her hands. Those coal-black eyes unnerved her, making her skin flush and tingle. "I wouldn't bother you, Mr. MacPherson. I know very well why your family despises me. After what Kenneth did to you—"

"He shot me."

She flinched. She could almost hear the crack of the gun, could almost see the bloom of blood on his shirt. "I don't expect you'll look upon me kindly. And if I hadn't been robbed of every earthly possession this morning, I wouldn't ask."

He turned his glass round and round.

Slowly, she gathered her courage and met his gaze. "If you require a maid, I—I should like to offer my services."

One corner of his mouth lifted. It was more of a sneer than a smile. "Where was yer *sergeant* while ye were bein' robbed?"

Cold, choking grief caught her off-guard. She thought she'd buried it along with him. How many times would she be proven wrong today? "I left Sergeant Munro in Inverness," she said tightly.

He stared at her for a moment, tossed back his final dram, then set the glass on the table with a sharp thud. "Have ye ever gone without a maid?" he asked quietly.

Panic rose, cold and fluttering. "When I was wee."

"I'd wager ye've never so much as washed yer own stockings."

She wanted to look away. The answer refused to leave her throat, but it didn't matter. He already knew.

"Yet, ye expect me to pay five shillings a week." He gestured insultingly to her gown. "For you."

She blinked. "Five shillings? Surely you intend to pay more than that."

He arched a sardonic brow. "How much do ye suppose a maid earns?"

"Several pounds a week at least."

He chuckled dryly. "Fly back to yer sergeant, dove. Ye're not safe outside yer cage."

She raised her chin. "If I had the means to return to Inverness, rest assured I wouldn't be here now. I have no funds, Mr. MacPherson. Not a single farthing. I've asked everyone in this village for employment or shelter. You are my last resort."

With a burning glance from her waist to her throat, he unhooked his arm from the back of his chair and shoved to his feet. His massive height and sudden nearness made her retreat a step. All the MacPherson men were enormous, but the way this one moved set him apart. She'd watched him pour an entire bottle of whisky down his throat, yet his motions remained ghostly smooth.

When she'd watched him perform in last summer's Glenscannadoo Games, he'd seemed otherworldly to her—impossibly powerful, lethally skilled, masterfully controlled. He'd dominated several events, including the loch swim, for which he'd gone shirtless. Watching water sluice over hard slabs of muscle and black chest hair had given her the strangest pain. Gnawing, restless pain. To this day, she didn't understand what it was. It resembled hunger, but for what?

Kenneth had accused her of secretly being attracted to the man. Having been pursued by many handsome suitors in her two London seasons, Sabella had known the warm, giddy excitement of attraction. This wasn't that. She didn't know what it was—fear? Obsession? Fascination?—but it wasn't anything so lovely as attraction.

Now, his muscular frame bore the ravages of a difficult recovery. He was thinner, to be sure. But his potency seemed greater, somehow, as if he'd been distilled down to his essence. And despite his haggard appearance, her body responded as if the past year hadn't happened. The low ache, the skin-lifting shiver, the pounding pulse of heat. All of it returned hungrier than before.

Dear God, he frightened her to death.

"Ye wish to be my maid? Very well. Two shillings per week," he offered.

Her neck stiffened. "Lodging alone is two-shillings-six. Mail coach fare to Inverness costs nine shillings."

Beneath his beard, a dark smile curved. "Nae need for lodging. I'll provide a bed."

"Two shillings per week is a pittance, Mr. MacPherson."

"For somebody more useful, mayhap. For you? It's generous." He shrugged. "Suit yerself. I'm certain ye'll find another sergeant to keep ye safely caged. That appears to be where yer skills lie."

Bristling at his insulting tone, she frowned. "What are you implying?"

He snagged his bottle by the neck and tipped it up to his lips, draining it to the last drop. Then he set it down, brushed past her, and strode to the door. The crowd parted warily as he passed.

Outside, the rain pounded harder. Joan approached wearing an "I told you so" expression. "Turned ye down, did he?"

"He offered two shillings per week," Sabella complained. "Can you imagine?"

Joan arched a brow. "That's surprisin'."

"I certainly thought so."

"I wouldnae have thought he'd be that generous."

Sabella blinked.

"Lamb, ye have nae skills. Even the good maids are happy to earn three shillings."

Sabella had seen how hard a maid labored. From sunrise to well after dark, the lasses who tended the fires, cooked the meals, cleaned her gowns, washed her bedding, and hauled her bath water could be summoned at any hour to do any task she required. She'd always assumed they were paid adequately, but she'd never asked. Kenneth had taken care of those matters. Following her brother's grisly death, Sergeant Munro had stepped in to help Sabella manage the destruction he'd left behind. Munro had dealt directly with Kenneth's steward on all budgetary matters. Sabella had been too busy burying her brother, selling their house in Charlotte Square, and paying calls to his many blackmail victims.

Drat and blast. If Joan was right, Sabella had just declined the only legitimate offer of employment she was likely to receive.

She rushed after her last resort, squeezing through the sotted crowd to the door. Beneath the eave, she searched for him in the dark. "Mr. MacPherson!" She inched toward the curtain of rain, holding her skirts carefully away from the splash. "Mr. MacPherson, are you still here?"

He emerged from the night like a phantom. Standing just beyond the edge of the tavern's glow, he stared at her without speaking for long moments.

God, he was huge. "I accept your terms of employment," she said.

"Do ye, now?"

"Aye. Though, I think you should grant an increase as my skills improve."

Deep, mocking laughter echoed through the dark. A horse's bridle jangled. "Is this how ye negotiate, lass? Not the slightest bit of leverage, just a *lady's* demands to a lesser man."

Lesser? If anything, he was greater. Certainly bigger. "I'm only asking for fairness."

She couldn't see his expression, but he ran a hand over his beard. "Are ye comin'?"

Her heart kicked. She glanced behind her at the warm glow of the tavern then turned toward the rain and darkness. Straightening her spine, she clutched her skirts briefly before letting them go. She stepped past the curtain of rain, wincing as the drops splatted onto her silk and pattered her bonnet's brim. She drew close to him, her heart pounding, pounding, *pounding*.

His horse's bridle jangled as he patted the animal's neck. "Up ye go."

It was her only warning before his hands gripped her waist and hoisted her onto the horse's back. If she'd had worries about him lusting after her, this erased them. She might as well have been a sack of flour. His hands didn't linger. His manner was perfunctory, as if he hefted lasses several feet off the ground every day.

Unfortunately, her reactions were less appropriate. When he mounted behind her, she couldn't breathe. That gnawing ache returned to plague her, along with embarrassing heat in more embarrassing places. She took a deep breath. He smelled like whisky and damp linen and rain. She leaned away, doing her best not to let any part of her touch any part of him.

He nudged the horse into motion, and she nearly toppled. She had to grip his thigh frantically to steady herself. The muscles had no give.

"Try not to fall," he said dryly. "I hear mud is a nuisance to clean from silk."

Glad for the darkness that disguised her flush, Sabella repositioned her hand and shifted her hips to find her balance.

"Bluidy hell," he muttered just before his arm banded her waist. "Be still, woman."

She sucked in a breath. His hand was so large over her ribs that his thumb brushed the underside of her breast. He pulled her tightly into his body, which felt like sun-heated stone against her back and shoulder.

When she caught her breath, she explained, "I'm accustomed to a sidesaddle. It has pommels to facilitate a proper seat." Why must he leave his thumb there? The tingling contact made her nipple humiliatingly hard. And every step of the horse rocked her against him. With his arm locked around her, it felt as intimate as an embrace. "The hour is late," she said as a distraction. "Will your housekeeper still be awake by the time we arrive?"

"I dinnae have a housekeeper."

"Your other maids, then."

"None of those, either."

Her voice thinned as realization set in. "Surely you have a staff of some sort."

"Aye, lass. I just hired her."

He had her. Sabella Lockhart had ruined his life, and he fucking *had* her.

He forced his arm not to tighten, his hand not to shift from her ribs. He ordered his body to remain relaxed, despite the vicious surge of triumph. The liquor helped. But he hadn't been this close to her since the day he was shot. His instincts were on fire.

Alexander remembered the first time he'd set eyes on her. She'd attended the Glenscannadoo Games with her brother last summer, and he'd spotted her staring at him after the loch swim. At the laird's ball later that evening, he'd seen the golden-haired beauty again wearing green silk and glittering emeralds.

His stepsister, Annie, had gone out of her way to befriend the lass as part of a strategy to lure Kenneth Lockhart into confessing his crimes against Broderick. Annie had described her as swanlike—beautiful, graceful, untouchable. The description was true but insufficient.

Sabella Lockhart had the purest white skin he'd ever seen. She moved carefully, as if dust were gunpowder and rain was fire. Every gesture was modest. Every glance from those enormous, leaf-green eyes was faintly bashful and sweetly alluring. Despite her height—five-and-a-half feet—her long, slender neck and thin frame lent her an air of vulnerable delicacy, which she used expertly to invoke a man's protective instincts.

Those instincts had gotten him shot. And after seven months of hell, he finally had the woman responsible in his control.

As he turned the horse down the road to his house, he noticed her shivering. They were both drenched to the skin, and with the heavy cloud cover, the air had a cold bite unusual for summer. There was no moon, no houses, no light. Fortunately, he'd spent his life in these hills and could have found his way home blind drunk and blindfolded. He also had excellent night vision, and his house was white, so it stood out amidst the inky blackness. He halted near the front entrance.

"Wh-why are w-we stopping?"

"We're here."

"We are? I hear water, but I can't see anything."

He forced his arm to release her, forced himself to dismount then lift her down. Her hands clung to his shoulders. Her silk clung to her curves. His body's reaction was galling but predictable. Clasping her elbow, he took her into the house, lit a lantern, and grunted, "Stay," before leaving to tend his horse.

When he returned, both she and the lantern were gone, but he glimpsed a glow from the stair hall. He found her frowning at the banister.

"Is my bed upstairs?" She swayed on her feet, her skirts dripping on the wood floor. "Perhaps I'll rest here for a moment."

"If ye expect me to carry ye, ye'll be waitin' a while."

She braced a white-gloved hand on the banister. The lantern in her other hand began to shake, making light dance against the walls. "No, I … no more touching."

What in bloody hell did that mean? It wasn't as if he'd groped her backside. He'd scarcely touched her at all. Of course, a nobleman's sister wouldn't want a rough Highlander's hands dirtying her unsullied skin.

Stalking toward the passage to the kitchen, he ordered over his shoulder, "Follow me."

The light bobbed as she lagged behind him. He led her through the kitchen and around to the quarters behind the hearth. "This is yer room."

"Oh," she breathed. "It's very near the scullery, isn't it?"

He withdrew a sheet and blanket from the wardrobe he'd crafted specifically to fit into the small chamber then tossed them on the narrow bed.

The lantern shook again.

Out of patience, he snagged it from her limp hand and set it on the washstand. "A sick maid is of no use to me. Change out of that wet gown before ye catch yer death."

She nodded. "I haven't anything dry to wear."

Indeed, her soaked gown fitted like a glove. He'd tried not to notice because noticing bloody hurt. But those slight breasts were sharply beaded, long thighs were clearly outlined, and narrow hips beckoned his rough Highlander hands.

He stalked to the kitchen, tugged one of his shirts from the drying rack in front of the hearth, and dropped it on the bed. "Day begins at dawn. Get some sleep."

Before she could reply, he left to find his bed. But even after stripping down to the skin, heat pulsed through every muscle, every vein, every damned inch of his body. He kept his bedchamber dark. He didn't want to look at what she did to him, but the relentless heat and hardness refused to be ignored. Throwing the window open, he let the rain cool him before pacing back to his bed. He gripped one of the posts and ran his palm over the puckered scar on his upper chest, digging the heel of his hand into the wound. The pain was only a faint echo of what he'd endured, but it was enough to remember what should never be forgotten.

Don't you wish to see him once more before he dies? The distorted voice of a damaged Kenneth Lockhart gloating to his sister.

He is nothing to me. Why would you assume otherwise? The cool, soft voice of an angel.

Last December, Alexander had been struck from behind while on a mission in Edinburgh with Broderick's wife, Kate, and his youngest brother, Rannoch. The next thing he knew, he was being hauled from a coach into a townhouse in the wealthiest part of the city. He'd feigned unconsciousness, waiting for his opportunity to strike. It came shortly after Lockhart reminded his sister that she was the daughter of a lord.

He is beneath you, Sabella. All the MacPhersons are, including the red-haired bitch you betrayed me for.

I didn't betray you.

Anne Huxley is still alive. Somebody warned her about the man I sent.

N-not I. Ye're my brother. I love you.

Her voice had remained conciliatory and, except for a tremulous moment or two, remarkably calm. He should have realized then how manipulative she was. It took a cold-blooded lass to maintain such composure while her brother prepared to murder a man in front of her.

Moments later, Alexander had struck with the *sgian-dubh* he kept in his boot. He'd aimed for Lockhart's eye, a kill shot. But his throw went wide, cutting the bastard's arm instead. In the Highland regiment, Alexander had been legendary for never missing his target.

This time, he missed the most important shot he'd ever taken. Because Sabella Lockhart had flown in between them like a bird defending its nest. The collision had jostled his arm, and when she'd collapsed, whimpering and gasping, he'd thought she was injured.

The bonnie wisp of a woman he'd surveilled from a distance for weeks aroused every protective instinct in Alexander's soul.

Christ, what a fucking idiot he'd been.

The instant he'd turned to help her, Kenneth Lockhart had shot him. He vaguely remembered the pain, a blast of unholy fire through his upper chest. Then nothing.

Months of bloody torment had followed. A long, grinding hollowing out.

Annie had defended Sabella, arguing that the lass had worked against her brother by sending subversive warnings in letters and meeting in secret with Sergeant Munro of the Inverness constabulary. When Alexander had demanded to see the lass, Annie had revealed that Sabella had remained in Edinburgh. But she hadn't been alone. The gruff, ambitious sergeant who only cared about his job—a man old enough to be her father—had stayed with her.

That was this woman's power over men. Alexander should know. He'd been obsessed with her from the first.

Sabella had everyone fooled: Annie and her husband, John Huxley. Broderick and his wife, Kate. Even Broderick's friend, Magdalene Cuthbert, who'd nursed Alexander through his wounds.

But he remembered what happened when she'd been forced to choose between her brother and one of his targets.

He glared down at his body, which didn't give two shites whether she was a spoiled, deceitful witch or an aristocratic mistress for any male willing to keep her in a pampered cage.

He should fetch more whisky, though it didn't help much.

Only one thing helped.

Pacing back to the window, he braced an arm against the casing and gave in. He closed his eyes, seeing her there in the dark. White skin. Wee, tightly beaded breasts. Long legs and those heartbreaking eyes. He pictured her lying in his bed, arching and eager for his mouth. As always, she was fully at his mercy, claimed as *his* mistress, *his* woman. He'd demand her nakedness beneath those silk gowns. He'd keep her wet and ready at all hours, pleasuring until she begged him to fuck her. Then he'd take her hard. He'd feed her hunger to satisfy his own. And he'd turn that untouchable angel into a devil's wanton.

Listening to the pattering rain and distant river, he took his cock in hand, wincing at the sensitivity. Seeing her again, touching her, riding behind her, all of it had him as primed as his rifle on a hunt. But having her under his roof, under his control?

He was a bloody cannon.

Perhaps that was why his mind fed him a different vision. This time, when he pictured her in his bed, begging for merciful release, she wasn't fully naked. Instead, she wore his ring, a brand that couldn't be removed.

In two strokes, the cannon primed.

His. Aye. *His.*

Three more strokes and the cannon readied.

Not a mistress free to seek out another protector, but a wife who belonged beneath his roof. Beneath him. A wife who *wanted* to stay so he could give her more of what her body craved, so he could fill her and claim her because it was his bloody right.

The cannon fired.

His hand gripped the window's frame. Growling and gritting, he pictured her milking him for every drop, surrendering with her hands, her mouth, her sheath.

Light exploded as never before.

His knees weakened at the blissful relief from a pain that never fully dissipated. Leaning heavily against the casing, he rested his head on his forearm and listened to the river's rush. Rain washed over him, cooling his skin.

Before long, the desire would return. It always did. No doubt he'd dream about her and awaken in the morning primed for another round.

Could he seduce her? Perhaps. She'd stared at him for an awfully long time after the loch swim, and her brother had outright accused her of an inappropriate attraction. But Alexander refused to fall into her trap merely to quench an incessant craving, even if it meant he'd never be fully satisfied.

Exacting a bit of revenge, petty though it might be, would have to suffice. He wanted to topple her from her perch, to watch her soil those pretty hands and dirty those pristine skirts. He wanted her to learn that nobody was beneath her, despite her noble bloodline.

A slow smile tugged. Starting tomorrow, Sabella Lockhart would begin her descent. And one day, she would concede that the man she'd once called "nothing," the man she'd put through the fires of hell, had brought her to her knees.

Chapter Three

"Miss Lockhart!"

The ocean-deep bellow awakened Sabella out of a dead sleep. She surged upright, settling a palm over her pounding heart. Her skin was bare. She glanced down to see her shift gaping like a man's shirt.

Because it was a man's shirt.

Drat and blast. It was *his* shirt.

"Dawn came and went an hour ago, woman! Where is breakfast?"

Breakfast? Was she meant to cook? She'd never made anything but tea.

She threw off her blanket and rolled from the bed. Parts of her ached—her hips and lower back, mainly—

and all of her longed for more sleep. Yesterday had been an absolute nightmare, from the burial to the final indignity of realizing she hadn't enough energy to climb a set of stairs. In the light of a new morning, things looked better.

She glanced around the tight, spartan quarters likely reserved for a scullery maid. Perhaps "better" was a bit exaggerated.

Three loud booms struck the door. "Are ye awake in there, woman?"

"Aye," she called breathlessly, turning to straighten her bedding. "I'll only be a moment."

A breeze struck her bare calves. She spun. A scowling giant filled the doorway. Clutching the gaping shirt closed above her breasts, she croaked, "Mr. MacPherson!"

Coal-black eyes blazed over her furiously. "I dinnae pay ye to lay about all bluidy day. Get dressed. There's work to be done." He slammed the door. Moments later, a more distant slam signaled his exit through the scullery.

Burning with humiliation, she glanced down. Her skin was nearly the same shade as the linen, so perhaps he hadn't noticed how exposed she was. Her nipples had remained covered—barely. But he would have seen how sharply her bones protruded, how wee her breasts were without her corset's shaping. Nobody apart from her lady's maid had ever seen her in such a state.

Once again, she wanted to shrink into nothingness. The longing reached for her with a soft, tempting hand. She closed her eyes, fighting the voice that promised oblivion. *So simple, Sabella,* it whispered. *Just like falling asleep.*

A noisy blackbird cawed and flapped outside her small window, jarring her from her dark thoughts. After slowing her breathing, she answered as she'd done before: *Not today.*

Peeking out to ensure the kitchen was empty, she hurried to the racks where she'd laid out her garments to dry last night. Her gown was still slightly damp, but her underclothes were much better. As swiftly as she could, she struggled into her shift, petticoats, corset, stockings, and gown then plaited, coiled, and pinned her hair. Maids wore caps indoors, not bonnets, so she went without a headdress. Sadly, her carriage dress was very much the worse for wear with the leaf-embroidered hem stained by mud. How she would ever restore it, she didn't know.

When she reentered the kitchen, she stirred the banked coals in the hearth and added a log before searching for a kettle. It took forever to find the thing. The kitchen was scaled for giants, with two walls of high shelving, three MacPherson-sized cupboards, a ten-foot-long center table, and a hearth large enough to house a fully grown cow.

The house itself was likewise shockingly vast. She didn't know why she'd expected Alexander MacPherson to live in a hovel. He and his family had one of the most successful distilleries in the Highlands, in addition to owning thousands of acres. The MacPhersons were far from poor.

Judging by what she'd seen last night, the place was thrice the size of her brother's townhouse in Charlotte Square. It also looked newly constructed with simple but handsome finishes: high beamed ceilings, white walls paneled with oak, numerous multipaned windows, oversized doors and archways, and floors of dark slate and polished oak planks. The scent of wood, stone, and varnish was everywhere.

So was the scent of dust. It covered every surface, including the floors.

The scale of her impending failure made her head spin. How was she meant to clean this place by herself? She didn't know the first thing about being a maid.

Sabella had been schooled toward a singular purpose—marrying a peer and bearing sons to carry on his lineage. Beyond that, she was utterly useless.

Eyeing the kettle in her limp grip, she trudged into the scullery, traded the kettle for a bucket, and opened the garden door. A cool, damp breeze greeted her. Thankfully, the rain had abated, but it had left a muddy mess. The mud squished around her boots as she stepped down into the yard.

Drat and blast, her hems would be a disaster before noon.

She searched the area that should be a garden—a forty-foot square of weeds surrounded on two sides by the house—but found no well. Venturing further, she spun to survey her new, temporary home.

The house was a white-stuccoed, two-storied T with a third-story attic. The kitchen and servant's quarters occupied half of the ground floor in the north wing. The east and west wings joined to form the house's southerly front façade. The windows on the uppermost stories were arched, reminding her of villas she'd seen in France. As she explored the perimeter, clutching her skirts as high as she dared, her admiration grew. Few homes outside the most prosperous Lowland counties were this elegant.

The house sat in a broad clearing above a river. The surrounding hills were lush and leafy, dotted by darker pines. The river formed a rocky, S-curved ribbon through sporadic clusters of alder, willow, and birch. In such a wild, remote setting, the house should look out of place. But surrounding slopes formed a pair of cupped hands with the house perched like a pearl in the center.

It was beautifully serene—and the very last place she would have pictured for Alexander MacPherson.

Several outbuildings sat a good distance from the house: a large barn, coop, and stables branched off the drive to the northwest with a beehive-shaped structure sitting above them on a northerly rise. Upstream along the riverbank was a mill, and beside that a wooden bridge. All the structures appeared to be in good repair if not newly built. However, the grounds were overgrown with grasses, unfenced, and unfinished. Every house should have a fenced kitchen garden with a well at the very least.

She picked her way toward the river, searching for a way down the bank. Was this how the other maids fetched water? There should be a path. Instead, the steep slope covered with rocks, reeds, and ferns was a muddy, precarious gauntlet.

But there was no well in sight, and a maid's tasks required water.

With a sigh, she found an opening between two boulders and started down toward the water's edge, holding her skirts high. Halfway there, her foot slipped on a mossy stone. She scrambled for balance, but the mud was slick and deep. She let go of her skirts, bending in half to brace against the slope. It didn't help. Jagged rocks ground into her palm. Her legs trembled as she tried climbing to regain control—and lost her footing. The bucket clattered down the rocks and splashed into the river. Her legs went out from underneath her, twisting painfully as she slid down and down.

A boulder broke her descent but at a bruising cost to her knee and shin. She sat panting for a full minute, assessing the damage. Ruined, muddy gown. Pain radiating from her knee, backside, and lower spine. A lost bucket that still had to be filled and hauled up to the house.

Her chest tightened into a knot. Tears stung. She stared at the swirling water and wondered why she was doing this. There was so little point, really. What was she clinging to?

No more pain. Simple. Just like falling asleep.

Nearby, a raven landed on a boulder and cawed. Another joined the first. Together, they created a racket loud enough to be heard above the river's whoosh.

She watched them for a while and, slowly, the dark thoughts dissipated. New thoughts formed: She'd endured much worse pain than this. Her skirts would wash. Her hands would heal. Sleep would come eventually, but that hour hadn't yet arrived.

Not today.

Pushing to her feet, she descended the last few yards to retrieve the bucket. Luckily, it hadn't floated too far away. After rinsing her hands, she gathered the water and found a shallower slope downstream for her return to the house. Climbing up was vastly easier than climbing down, she discovered, and within minutes, she reentered the kitchen feeling a wee bit better for having accomplished her task.

"Where in bluidy hell have ye been?"

His booming roar startled her so badly that she lost her grip on the bucket. *Thud!* River water poured out over the stone floors as the bucket tipped and rolled. The loss stung worse than her hands.

"Answer me." Behind the kitchen table, Alexander's snarling glower reminded her of a wolf. He was pouring steaming water from the kettle into a teapot.

Sabella's entire being slumped. Where had he found the water? "I went down to the river." Uselessly, as it turned out.

"That where ye tussled with a drove of pigs?"

She glanced down. Mud caked her skirt from her left hip to her hems. Likely her backside was worse. It certainly hurt more. "I fell."

"Christ on the cross, woman." He slammed the kettle down, making her flinch. Rounding the table, he reached her too swiftly for her to retreat. "Are ye injured?"

She shook her head. "It's fine. I'll be fine."

He seized her elbow and turned her this way and that like a cook inspecting a lamb shank. "Fell on yer arse. Could have broken yer damned neck. What were ye thinkin'?"

"I—I was fetching water."

He turned her to face the wall adjacent to the scullery. "Why didnae ye use the tap?"

She blinked. "Tap?"

Muttering another curse, he pulled her into the scullery, where a long bench with two large basins sat beneath a bronze pipe protruding from the wall. He turned a lever fitted to the top of the pipe, and water poured into the basin as if summoned by magic.

"How does it …? There's no pump."

He flipped the lever again, and the water stopped. "'Tis supplied from the pumphouse to cisterns in the attic. Ye'll find taps like this on every floor."

She reached out to test the lever—open, closed; open, closed—marveling at how it delivered water with so little effort. "I've never seen such a thing."

He grunted.

She turned the lever again, laughing in surprise as it sputtered a bit. "Why doesn't every house have this?"

"Most houses arenae near a river."

"The river drives the pump?"

"A water wheel, aye. Same as a mill, but with more pipes. And a lot more diggin'."

"This is why you don't have a well."

"I have a well, lass. 'Tis near the stable yard for use during the dry months. The cistern on the brae supplies the animals well enough outside summer."

She was about to question him further when blood pinkened the water in the basin. Her palm was dripping red. He seized her wrist, jolting her heart dreadfully hard. Kenneth had often punished her by squeezing and twisting her wrists until her bones and tendons ground together. Instinctively, she tried to withdraw.

Alexander's hold didn't hurt, but neither did it yield. He examined her palm with a frightful scowl. "Ye've gouged yerself."

"The rocks were sharp."

"Bluidy foolishness," he growled. He pulled her palm beneath the tap and flipped on the water.

She hissed in a breath at the throbbing sting, but within seconds, the cold water began to numb the pain.

"Keep this clean while ye work. Wrap it with linen. I've some strips in my washstand."

She tugged again to free her hand, and he finally released her. Fearing his nearness, she stumbled back a step or two. "Thank you for yer concern, Mr. MacPherson. I'll be fine." Once he stopped touching her and looking at her and standing so close, she would be fine.

He glared with strange intensity for a long moment then barked, "Follow me." For the next hour, he outlined her duties while leading her through the house, starting with the larders, storerooms, passages, cellar, and servants' quarters surrounding the kitchen.

She was to tend the kitchen hearth continuously, serving tea by daybreak and breakfast by an hour past each morning. Dinner must be served by six each evening. She would keep the larders, cellar, and stores in good order, delivering him a list of needed supplies every Wednesday. Rotationally throughout the week, all floors must be swept and scrubbed, all fireplaces cleaned, all surfaces and furnishings dusted, and all bedding changed. Linens and clothing must be washed and dried weekly.

Several times, she started to ask a question, but his long strides had her scrambling to keep up, and his terse bark brooked no interruption. He was the most intimidating man she'd ever encountered, and Sabella's sapling courage wilted with every word.

He led her through the formal rooms on the ground floor—the dining room, library, drawing room, parlor, morning room, and what appeared to be a small study—while describing how the carpets must be swept and beaten, upholstered furnishings must be carefully cleaned, wood surfaces must be waxed, and every room must be aired on a rigorous schedule. For the last point, he demonstrated how to open the windows with clever wrought-iron latches along the sill.

Her mind was whirling by the time they reached the upper floors—and his bedchamber. Her nape burned when she saw the size of his bed, eight feet at least. His mattress was so lofty and deep, she'd need a ladder to change the bedding.

She recalled the thin, lumpy mattress she'd collapsed onto the previous night. It certainly wasn't what she was accustomed to.

"At dawn, I'll expect hot water and fresh towels laid out in the dressin' room."

"Dressing room?"

He opened a door next to the fireplace, revealing a smaller room with built-in wardrobes, a washstand, and a high table beneath the window. A second door on the opposite wall connected to the corridor.

The sheer luxury of his house continued to astonish her. All of this for one man in the middle of nowhere?

Perhaps she shouldn't be surprised. Annie lived in a castle with her titled husband, and the laird's house was a small yet lovely manor set above Loch Carrich.

But Alexander MacPherson was no "wee tartan peacock" or titled gent. He was more akin to the ancient Highland warriors who'd slain Roman legions and English nobles than a gentleman who cared about how frequently his draperies were dusted. She certainly wouldn't have guessed he could afford a house like this. Which begged the question: Why didn't he have a household staff? Clearly, he didn't lack funds.

Once again, she started to inquire, but he continued barking, "Dinnae clean in here 'til after I've left each day. Lay a fire on cold nights before I'm home. If I'm in this chamber, dinnae disturb me. Ever."

She noted the immaculate tidiness of his domain, the fineness of the furnishings. The bed was weighty and golden—lightly stained mahogany, she thought. The tartan coverlet was a fine, soft wool in shades of bronze and green. She'd only seen its like in the finest Edinburgh drapers. Three arched windows let in southeasterly light, warming the square-paneled walls from nearly black to rich brown. Bronze sconces on each wall would add a golden glow at night, no doubt.

An oak secretary desk and matching bookcase flanked the center window, which doubled as a door to a small balcony. Between the bed and the fireplace sat a massive wing chair upholstered in caramel-hued leather, and above the mantel hung a lovely painting of the glen.

She wanted to linger here, to explore the intricate hawk carving perched on his bedside table, the numerous books on his bookshelf, and the cool, subtle scent that permeated his linens—rosemary or lavender, perhaps.

But whatever patience Alexander had shown until now evaporated as he strode into the dressing room and returned with a roll of linen and a round of soap. He thrust them into her arms and scowled at her neck. "Wrap yer hand. And wash the mud from yer skin, woman."

She ran her fingers over her throat and found a daub of grit. Embarrassment burned.

"Dinnae go wanderin' again," he snapped. "Yer work is here in the house."

She frowned. "Aye, about that—"

He brushed past her. "Dinner's at six," he said. "Best get started."

"I know nothing about cookery, Mr. MacPherson."

He turned on his heel, retrieved a slim volume from the bookcase, then added it to the pile in her hands. "Bluidy useless aristocrats."

Chasing him out into the corridor, she stammered, "I have one last question."

"Then ask it." He started down the stairs.

She clutched her bundle to her bosom and rushed to follow. "When might I expect to be paid?"

"A week from now, provided yer work isnae pure shite."

"Might we discuss an advance on my wages?"

"No."

"I'm without any belongings." Her cheeks stung as she followed him into the entrance hall. "Everything I own was in those three green trunks. I've no other garments, no … personal items of any sort."

He yanked open the front door and strode toward the stables. "This isnae a bluidy soiree. Make do."

She dashed to keep up with his pace. "If I had sufficient funds to return to Inverness—"

"Eager to fly back to yer sergeant, eh?"

"No, I … That's not why—"

"Let Munro come fetch ye. I'm nae givin' ye a bluidy farthing for work ye didnae do."

"But the thieves reside in Inverness. Perhaps I could persuade them to return my possessions." She might even be able to recover her money, and this dreadful interlude in Glenscannadoo would be over.

He stopped. Stiffened. Turned. "Ye ken who the thieves are?"

Stumbling to a halt, she answered, "Aye. A kindly couple I hired in Edinburgh to accompany me to Inverness. They needed passage home after a visit to the city, and I needed traveling companions. It was quite serendipitous that they answered my advertisement when nobody else responded. In truth, I don't think they meant to steal anything. This is all a dreadful misunderstanding; I'm certain of it."

Muttering something foul, he braced his hands loosely on his hips and shook his head. "Their names? Or didnae ye bother askin'?"

His implication about her intelligence—or lack thereof—stung. "McCabe. They're *old,* Mr. MacPherson." Old people couldn't be thieves, surely. "They said I remind them of their granddaughter. Mrs. McCabe helped me dress my hair. Mr. McCabe held my umbrella. They were both very … kind."

"Aye, right. Saintly. Mayhap they'll pray for ye while they're pawnin' yer jewels, eh?"

She went cold. "I'd like to speak with them before drawing any firm conclusions. The constable, Mr. Gillespie, has met the McCabes. I'm certain he'll assist me."

"Gillespie? That bairn's backside couldnae track the tin of lard he slathers on his head each morn."

"The mail coach returns in six days. If the McCabes return my belongings, including what's left of my inheritance, I could repay ye in full then depart for London as I planned. You'd never have to see me again. Nine shillings is all I require—"

He paced toward her, looming and thunderous. "After what yer kin did to me and mine, ye should be beggin' forgiveness, not favors."

The truth of his words struck her like a fist to the stomach. Nausea roiled. She retreated a step, dropping her gaze from the black fire in his. "Of course."

"No work, no wages. That's that. Do ye ken?"

She nodded.

Her new employer strode away without another word. Sabella returned to the kitchen, set her pile of items on the table, and read the rather lengthy title of the book he'd given her: *The Prudent Housekeeper's Guide to Modern Cookery and Domestic Economy on a Scheme Entirely New, With Useful Receipts and Instructions to Servants for Discharging the Duties of Their Station*. The author—named only as "a Lady"—began with a fiery warning about the dangers of slothful female staff. *Permissiveness is the enemy of an orderly household,* it read, *and eternal vigilance its staunchest ally.*

She closed the book. Eyeing the overturned bucket and puddled floor, she resisted the urge to crawl back into her narrow, lumpy bed.

Five weeks would earn her ten shillings. Nine would take her to Inverness. Inverness would regain her the remnants of her brother's fortune. Those remnants would purchase passage to London. London would take her to Paris. Paris would reconnect her to school friends who knew nothing of her brother's deeds. Those friends might invite her to house parties at which she might encounter noble gentlemen in need of a wife. If everything went well, she could be wed before spring.

Then this horrifying, never-ending nightmare could be buried alongside the brother she'd both loved and hated.

That singular hope made "not today" possible.

Five weeks. Ten shillings.

She righted the bucket and found a mop.

Five weeks. Ten shillings.

She donned an apron and bandaged her hand.

Five weeks. Ten shillings.

She ignored the pain and set to work.

Chapter Four

"McCabe? Cannae say I recall particulars." Gillespie smoothed the cowlick he fought with every ounce of lard at his disposal. "Is Miss Lockhart well?" His Adam's apple bobbed. "Has she mentioned me?"

Alexander longed for his dirk. He despised police of all sorts, but this eejit's fawning infatuation with Sabella Lockhart was grinding on his last nerve. "She said they accompanied her here from Edinburgh. Older couple. Would have seemed harmless."

"Oh, aye. Now I remember. They were at the burial yesterday."

Alexander frowned. Burial?

"Stood some distance from the grave, though. I dinnae remember much. Some time has passed."

"It's been a day," Alexander said dryly.

The lad snapped his fingers. "Mr. McCabe had a fine watch. Gold, I reckon."

Alexander resisted the urge to shake Gillespie by the Adam's apple.

"Kind of 'em to help a lady in her time of grievin'. Poor Miss Lockhart. An angel of mercy, she is. She brought him all the way from Edinburgh, ye ken."

"Brought who?" he snapped.

"Sergeant Munro, God rest his soul."

The world shrank down to one salient point. "Munro is dead?"

"Aye. Sad to say—"

"Was he murdered?" Alexander might have thought about it a few times. Or more than a few.

Gillespie's eyes rounded warily. The greased pup took a backward step. "No, sir. Natural causes. Somethin' to do with his heart, Miss Lockhart said. She promised to transport him back home for burial."

"Where is he buried?"

With another visible swallow, Gillespie named the cemetery.

Alexander left the sheriff's office with a second mission—he would find the thieves, and he would visit the man she'd allowed to … keep her.

Bloody hell. He'd promised himself he wouldn't obsess again. That way lay madness. But he had to see the bastard in the ground.

The cemetery was only a few minutes' ride. He found the grave near a yew tree. A wilted white rose lay near an etched stone marker. *Sergeant Neil Munro. Dutiful servant, beloved friend.*

Beloved.

He raked a hand through his hair. Crouching next to the mounded dirt, he glared at the headstone she'd obviously purchased for her lover. And she *had* loved him. A glance at the stones to either side revealed that much.

She'd returned him to his family. He hadn't realized Munro was widowed or that he had a daughter. Of course, the glorified watchman who'd waged an all-out war against the MacPherson Distillery wasn't his first choice for a friendly blether and a pint. Alexander had once accused him of getting hard every time he pictured jailing a MacPherson. Munro hadn't denied it.

Now, he had a new reason to hate the man. This wasn't mere dependence. She'd loved him.

Beloved friend.

He wanted to ram his fist through that stone until something cracked—his bones, the granite. Something.

But he had thieves to find. He'd expend his wrath on them.

Fortunately, he was a tracker, and their trail was fresh. He started at the inn from which the mail coach had departed. Two shillings bought him answers from the innkeeper. "Gold watch? An elderly couple, ye say? Aye, I do recall a man of such description. He was carryin' a mighty big umbrella."

A dram of whisky offered to one of the inn's customers purchased information about the likeliest pawn shop the McCabes might frequent. He recognized her emerald necklace straight away. "I'll take that one," he told the proprietor, laying out the coins. Casually, he added five pounds for a small indiscretion. "And direct me to the residence of the sellers if ye please."

Minutes later, he found their cottage near the river. Gleeful laughter rang out from inside—a man and a woman cackling over a jest. They sounded drunk. After searching the perimeter of the house, Alexander glimpsed three green trunks through a bedroom window. The smallest one was open with pink silk and white lace spilling out.

His gut hardened. Anticipation surged.

Alexander wasn't good at everything. He couldn't sing or play music like Broderick. He couldn't dance or charm the lasses like Rannoch. He had none of his mam's eerie visions like Campbell.

His gift was this.

The McCabes answered his second knock. Their rosy grins faded the moment they glimpsed his size. The old woman elbowed forward. "May we help ye, dearie?"

"I'm here for the trunks."

The husband frowned at his wife and shoved her back into the cottage. "Nae trunks here, sir." He tried to slam the door.

Alexander caught it easily and stepped inside, closing it behind him. The McCabes paled as if he was Death himself emerging from the gates of hell with their names on his list.

In fairness, he supposed he was. "Now, then," he said. "Let's try this again, shall we?"

On her first day as a maid, Sabella learned three important lessons: Dust *before* mopping, never after. Always have a towel in hand before reaching for anything hot. And season with restraint, as more salt may always be added, but oversalting cannot be undone.

She'd chosen the simplest receipt from the *Prudent Housekeeper's Guide to Modern Cookery*, a hotchpotch soup with mutton, though she only found beef in the larder. The initial instructions had been easy enough: add the diced meat, carrots, celery, turnips, and onions to a large pot, along with three quarts of water, a quart of beer, and "a little salt." The salt's precise measurement wasn't defined. In retrospect, Sabella considered this a grave oversight on the author's part.

However, burning the butter and flour mixture was entirely her mistake, as the author strenuously warned against it. How was one to distinguish between "browning" and blackening? The hue changed in less than a minute.

She'd thought returning the stewed liquid to the pot would diminish the essence of burnt failure. She was wrong. If it weren't for the salt, the whole lot would have tasted like charcoal soup with mushy vegetables and stringy meat. The salt rendered it inedible.

However, when Alexander returned home from wherever he'd been all day, his complaints weren't about dinner but about the floors.

"There's more dust now than when I left," he barked as she steadied herself against the banister and set her bucket on the floor. "How is that possible?"

Wiping her forehead with her wrist, she tried to focus on him, but he kept blurring, and the shadows in the stair hall were too deep to make out his expression. "Aye, sir. I shall do better tomorrow."

"Dinnae call me sir."

"Mr. MacPherson, then."

He rolled his shoulders and ran a hand over his beard. "What happened to yer hair?"

She patted the side where a lock had tumbled free while she was scalding the butter. "A wee bit singed. It's fine."

His looming posture grew more intimidating. "Both yer hands are wrapped, now. What happened to the other one?"

She glanced at her throbbing left hand. "Also singed. It's fine."

Jaw flickering, he growled, "Ye're a bluidy disaster, woman."

Her answer choked her. What did he expect? She'd certainly *seen* these things done before, but she hadn't ever attempted them, so most of it had been guesswork. Every lesson had come hard. She'd spent half the day sweeping and mopping the rooms on the ground floor, another several hours dusting, then the remainder cooking. Her arms were as mushy as her stewed turnips.

"Go wash yerself and find yer bed. Have ye eaten?"

She swallowed her sudden nausea at the thought of salty charcoal. "I'm not hungry."

Muttering something about stubborn lasses, he clasped her elbow and pulled her into the kitchen. The smoky stench was pungent, but he didn't remark upon it. He simply collected a chair, sat her down, and ordered, "Stay," before disappearing into the larder. Moments later, he returned with a round of cheese, a loaf of bread, butter, and ham.

"I—I made dinner," she said. "But it didn't go well."

He glanced over his shoulder at the pot sitting on a warming shelf between the ovens and the spit. His reply was to calmly slice bread, cheese, and ham, arrange them on a plate, and slide the makeshift meal in front of her. "Eat."

If the kitchen weren't blurring and tilting around her, she'd offer to serve his dinner in the dining room, as was proper. He didn't give her a chance. Instead, he plucked a bowl from the cupboard and filled it with her appalling soup. Then he buttered several slices of bread and sat across from her.

"Oh, Mr. MacPherson, ye needn't eat that."

Black eyes glittered as they roamed her face. "This is dinner, aye?"

"Aye, but it's too salty, and I burnt the flour, and—"

He took a bite. Chewed. Took another. And another. All the while, he held her gaze without wincing or gagging even once.

"Y-ye mustn't feel obliged … I ken it's dreadful."

Another bite. A bit of bread. Another bite and another. Soon, he was using his bread to soak up the last of the soup in his bowl. He popped the final bite into his mouth. Then he smiled. A slow, wicked half-curve. "Ye look hungry, lass. Eat."

She dropped her gaze to her plate, shaking with the ache he stoked in her. As always, she found her body's reaction to him mystifying. All he'd done was eat her food. Her atrociously bad food.

"Try the bread," he suggested. "It isnae Annie's, but it's decent."

Bread did sound like a lovely distraction. She dragged the butter dish closer.

He filled two cups from the cider cask near the windows and slid one in front of her. "Drink."

She drank. The bread went down easier once her thirst was quenched. Before long, she'd finished two buttered slices and half the ham on her plate. He sat across from her, long arm hooked over the back of the chair, casually sipping his cider. And watching her. His expression was both intense and unreadable, but his eyes painted her from her hair to her waist, lingering on her bodice. She smoothed her mud-stiffened gown and straightened her posture. Shame burned with a tingling flush.

"I intend to wash my clothing tomorrow morning so it may dry overnight," she explained. "Would it be acceptable if I continue borrowing your shirt?"

When he lifted his gaze, his eyes sparked like coal embers. "Aye."

"Once wetted, *gros de Naples* takes forever."

His eyes fell to her flat, sullied bosom and flared. "Grow the what?"

Flushing harder, she clarified, "*Gros de Naples.* The silk. It's thick and stiff."

The chair squeaked as he shifted in his seat.

"Wringing would quicken the process, but one shouldn't apply too much force. Better to handle it gently."

Even as he took a long drink of cider, his eyes didn't budge from her bodice. Presumably, he was appalled by her filthy state and perhaps resentful that she must borrow his clothing. But there was no help for it. She had nothing else to wear.

"By necessity, I shall be in a state of undress for much of the day," she warned. "If ye have no objection, I'll make use of one of your plaids." The soft, fine wool tartan she'd found in his dressing room could be draped and belted to fashion a traditional *arasaid*. The covering wouldn't be quite as modest as her carriage dress, but it would do.

His hawkish nose flared as he turned his empty cup round and round. "Dress as ye will. I dinnae get many visitors here."

She broke off a bite of cheese and took a nibble. Glancing around at the efficient, well-designed kitchen, she remarked, "I confess, I'm a wee bit curious."

"About?"

"This is a grand house. Yet, you haven't even a footman or a lad to light the fires." She frowned at the puzzle of it. "Why build such a splendid home for you alone? Why not—"

"Why, indeed," he snapped. "Mayhap all the distractions of the past two years caused a delay, ye reckon? Aye. Mayhap it was havin' my brother falsely accused of murder, imprisoned for months, and beaten until he's naught but a broken shell."

Sickened, she dropped the cheese back on her plate.

"Mayhap it was havin' my wee sister-in-law stuffed into a whisky barrel and left to suffocate for the pure torment of it." He tilted his head. His gaze sharpened. Hardened. "Or mayhap it was bein' shot while ye mewled for that pile of demon's shite ye call a brother."

Nausea heaved everything she'd just eaten against the back of her throat. She covered her mouth to keep it down. Whenever she closed her eyes, she saw his blood. The tablecloth she'd frantically wadded against his wound had soaked through within seconds.

"I'm sorry," she whispered. She'd repeated those words so many times to Kenneth's victims, she'd lost count.

He shoved to his feet and refilled his cup from the cask. "Sorry doesnae change what was done, lass. Broderick's eye can never be restored. Kate's nightmares may never let her sleep soundly again." He tapped a fist against his upper chest. "And this hole took its sweet bluidy time to close. So, forgive me if my household staff isnae up to yer standards. I was busy diggin' myself out of my own grave."

She wanted to weep. More than that, she wanted to die. Every time she thought about what Kenneth had done, every time she remembered his ghoulish, battered face gloating over Alexander's bleeding body, she wanted to die.

"When times are good," he continued hoarsely, "a man dreams of grand things. A home. A family. Buildin' somethin' that'll outlast him by centuries." A bitter smile twisted his lips. "All it takes is one bluidy pile of demon's shite to show ye how foolish ye've been."

Sabella couldn't bear to look at him any longer. All the exhaustion and pain of the past two days caught up to her at once. "Perhaps I—I should retire for the evening," she said. "Leave ye in peace." Shoving her plate away, she started to stand. The room tilted. Her knees buckled.

Between one blink and the next, he was by her side. He caught her arm in a powerful grip then pulled her against an unforgivingly hard body. Her cheek pressed against his chest. Every breath filled her with the cool evergreen scent of his shirt. She blinked. Clung. The pain in her hands would have made her gasp if she weren't already breathless.

"Steady, lass." He cradled her head against him, his heart thundering beneath her ear. In a fluid motion, he bent and scooped her legs from beneath her. Then she was floating. Her hands still hurt because she couldn't quite let him go. His beard caught in the hair at her temple. "Ye need sleep." He carried her into her plain, small bedchamber. "I'm going to set ye down then help ye undress. Dinnae panic, now."

She *should* panic. She should be alarmed and appalled. But his arms felt heavenly, and hers were so very heavy. "Ye should give me the nine shillings, Mr. MacPherson. Ye don't want me here," she breathed against his shoulder. "I don't blame you. I wouldn't want me, either."

He sat on her bed, holding her in his lap while unfastening her gown.

"If I had my funds," she assured him, "I'd be gone already."

A long pause. "Where would ye go?"

She closed her eyes as his ticklish fingers stripped away her silk. "London first. There's an old friend from school who hasn't heard anything about … Kenneth. She offered to introduce me to her husband's cousin. He's a duke."

His shoulder flexed against her cheek as he lifted her to strip away her skirts. "If London is first, what's second?"

"Paris. More friends from school."

"And more dukes, eh?"

"Perhaps," she murmured. "Regardless, I must marry someone. It seems best to begin with titled suitors."

His arms tightened, plastering her against him for a split second before loosening again. Cupping her head, he ran his thumb across her temple. "Why does rank matter?" he asked casually while plucking pins from her hair.

She liked how his voice sounded when his mouth was this close—low and ocean-deep, yet calm. A wry smile curved her lips. "In case ye haven't guessed yet, I've very few talents to offer the world. Certainly not cookery. Or cleaning."

He hummed a neutral response and unlaced her stays.

She sighed. "I'm a wife in waiting, Mr. MacPherson. A blue-blooded breeder of heirs. Born for it. Schooled for it. It's all I'm good for."

She had the vague thought that she might be the teensiest, wee bit tipsy. Her arms ached, and her head was positively swimming, despite being firmly anchored between his neck and shoulder. That usually only happened with champagne. "How strong is that cider, anyway?" she asked.

"If ye're not accustomed to it? Strong."

She frowned. "Are my eyes open?"

A deep chuckle. "No."

"Ye're very warm."

"And ye're very sleepy, Duchess."

"I'm not a duchess. Not yet."

His arms tightened again. His fingertips pressed into her nape, gently kneading the sore muscles there.

Soon, the aches receded into a soft, gray mist. As she drifted off, she heard him whisper something strange, something she must have imagined: "Wrong, lass. Not ever."

Chapter Five

On her second day as a maid, Sabella discovered her most despised duty—laundry. It was worse than mopping or sweeping, worse than cleaning ash from the fireplace, worse than washing up after breakfast. Cookery was a pleasure by comparison.

Glaring at the small book advising maids to "scrub vigorously any stain prior to washing" and neglecting to specify that one should *not* use scalding water to do so, she yanked her shift from the washtub with a curse. It was now a sickly shade of yellow along the top and dingy brown at the hem. She'd washed it four times with the same result.

"Drat, blast, and devil take it," she fumed, wringing the linen with all her might. The author had spent seven pages on a diatribe about female maidservants' susceptibility to the "importunities" of male employers. Seven. Yet only one page was devoted to washing and ironing.

Her carriage dress was permanently ruined. She'd hung it to dry in the sun, but the lovely lavender *gros de Naples* was now a blotchy brown rag. She'd missed a series of tears along the seam at the back of the skirt, and her vigorous scrubbing with soap and a brush, along with dousing in boiling water, had turned them into knuckle-sized holes.

Sabella's hands and forearms resembled boiled lobsters. With summer's heat finally paying a visit to the glen, she imagined her face was similarly flushed. Heaven knew the hearth fire she'd kept raging to supply sufficient hot water for laundry day wasn't helping.

She hung her head and braced against the table. Her arms, shoulders, and back were pure agony after hours spent hauling, heating, scrubbing, wringing, bending, crouching, lifting, and hanging the blasted laundry.

Her palms throbbed from the previous day's wounds, though she'd awakened with them freshly bandaged. Alexander's doing, she assumed. He'd left her to sleep in her shift, so he hadn't engaged in any "importunities" that she could discern.

Not that he would want to. He clearly despised her—which made his kindnesses a bit perplexing.

She tossed her shift into the line basket with a splat. There was no sense in mulling the contradictions of the man. She would only be here for five weeks. *Five weeks, ten shillings.* Thereafter, she'd never see him again.

Wiping her face and nape with a damp cloth, she hauled the basket of wet garments—both his and hers—out into the drying yard behind the house. One by one, she draped his shirts and breeches on the line beside her shift, stockings, and petticoats. The difference in their sizes was stark. Why that should send a queer pang through her middle, she didn't know.

Everything about him affected her strangely.

When she heard hoofbeats approach, she assumed Alexander had come home early. He'd certainly left early—before sunrise, in fact. But when she glanced toward the stable drive, she saw a woman riding a donkey.

"Och, lass, ye're wearin' his plaid!" the woman called, her voice jostling along with the donkey's gait.

Sabella glanced down at the soft russet plaid she'd belted and draped into a gown-like garment. The hem brushed her ankles, and his shirt fell to her shins. She was covered well enough for morning dress, she supposed, but not for company.

"I kenned he'd move fast, but I didnae think 'twould be *this* fast," the woman shouted. "Well done, laddie. Mayhap I didnae need the caterpillar fungus after all."

Frowning, Sabella shaded her eyes and squinted. The woman looked familiar, but she couldn't quite place her. That wiry shrub of hair and milky left eye were distinctive. "I'm sorry, have we met?"

The woman bent to mumble something into the donkey's long ears. Moments later, the donkey jostled to a halt at the far end of the drying line. The woman patted her mount's neck and slid awkwardly from its back, catching her ankle in the stirrup on the way down. The woman croaked while the donkey brayed.

Sabella rushed to help her, bracing her back and unsnagging her skirt from the saddle.

"My thanks, lass." She patted Sabella's elbow. "The last time I stretched my legs that wide, Mr. Brodie proposed marriage."

While Sabella puzzled over what one thing had to do with the other, the woman began digging through the donkey's saddlebags.

"Dreadfully sorry, but I fear I've forgotten your name," Sabella prompted.

"That's because ye never kenned it. Now, where did I put that—*argh!*" The old woman jerked her hand free and stuck her finger in her mouth. "Bluidy thorns."

Sabella glanced around for signs of additional visitors—perhaps someone to explain what in blazes was going on. But there was no one apart from a slow-blinking donkey munching the grass and a frazzled old woman pulling a burlap-wrapped clump of dirt from the saddlebag.

She shoved the clump toward Sabella. "Go on. Take it."

Blinking, Sabella accepted the … gift? "Er, thank you."

The woman nodded then shook her head. "Ye have far more patience than I, ye ken. Nae bloom is worth all that bother."

Bloom? She peered inside the burlap. A thorny stem poked out of the soil. "Is this a rosebush?"

"Aye. If ye plant her now, she'll blossom for ye next June."

"Oh, but I shan't be here that long." *Five weeks, ten shillings.* "Perhaps you should give this to—"

"Water it well. We're in for a blazin' summer." The woman dug through the small leather purse tied around her waist. "I've a few more items for ye." She clicked her tongue. "Hush, Bill. Of course I remembered the liniment."

Sabella glanced around. "Who is Bill?"

"Bill the Donkey. He's a wee bit crabbit with the heat, so dinnae take any sharp words to heart." She leaned close to whisper, "A bit lazy, that one. Dinnae tell him I said so."

The donkey brayed.

"Now, now, mind yer language. Miss Lockhart is a *lady*."

Another series of honk-and-squeak brays was followed by a huff.

"Aye, I told him as much, Bill. But ye ken as well as I do MacPhersons are a stubborn lot. Some lessons come easy, some hard." She glanced up with a twinkle in her good eye. "Same as men, aye, lassie?"

"I … I suppose …"

"Och, he hasnae built the garden yet, I see." She shook her head at the donkey. "Months ago, I warned him. 'Yer bride's comin,' I said. 'Take this time to build yer strength,' I said. Think he'd listen? Nae."

Bill snorted.

"Too busy nursin' his wounds and testin' my patience. Hard-headed MacPhersons." She produced a limp, silvery sprig from inside her pouch. "Dinnae fash, lassie. Plant this near yer roses. Deer dinnae care for the smell. Ye'll want a wall ere winter, though. Hungry beasties are determined creatures."

Sabella sniffed the small sprig. Lavender. She frowned. In France, lavender and roses were often paired together to control pests and attract bees. Perhaps the old woman wasn't as daft as she seemed. "I'm afraid I still don't ken your name."

"Mary MacBean, maker of potions and cures for ailments of every sort."

"A pleasure to meet you, Mrs. MacBean. I'm—"

"Sabella Lockhart. Aye, we've met. Last year at the Games."

"Oh!" Recognition dawned. Indeed, the half-blind woman had bumped into her during the weight-over-bar event. Alexander had won handily, and Sabella had been … distracted. She'd forgotten everything about that moment other than how he'd looked covered in sweat and victory. "I remember now."

Mrs. MacBean had said something bizarre about seeds sprouting in a tulip field and moles needing to be hunted before they destroyed the garden. Tulips sprang from bulbs, not seeds, and moles were typically trapped, not hunted. Clearly, the old woman's senility was an ongoing condition.

Searching her pouch, Mrs. MacBean withdrew a brown bottle and a round tin then stacked them on the burlap pile. "Liniment's his. Salve's for ye. But ye may need both." She eyed Sabella up and down then added a second bottle labeled *Everlast Unguent*. "Forgive him, lass." She patted Sabella's wrist. "He's a mite famished. Hard-headed MacPhersons dinnae ken what's good for 'em."

"Famished?" The man's larder would put the grandest houses to shame.

Next on the growing pile, Mrs. MacBean added a queer-shaped wooden object on a leather string. "He burned all the others. That's what took so long."

Sabella thought the carving might be a flower. It also might be a seashell. Or a part of the female anatomy. She couldn't quite decide whether the ruffled petals were intentionally or accidentally obscene.

"Wear it when he starts yer wall. Wear it again when ye forgive him."

Sabella gave the senile old woman a bland smile and stooped to place her pile of gifts into the empty laundry basket. "Well, your generosity is very much appreciated. It's a warm day. Perhaps we should let Bill have a drink whilst we visit for a spell, hmm?"

After leading the donkey to the stables, Mrs. MacBean followed Sabella into the kitchen while describing what a woman should feed a man who'd been starving for a year.

"*Meat,* lassie. Beef, lamb, venison. *Lots* of bacon. He likes that."

Sabella smiled. "No potatoes, then?"

"Bah! Use the tatties for cleanin' rust, nae for eatin'. Butter is good, but save the honey for yer bed. Cook *meat* and feed him 'til he's strong and braw again. Feed yerself, too. Ye'll need it for the wee rosebud. Oh, and cider is better than whisky. He's had his fill of that."

Sabella let the nonsense wash over her. Once she realized the woman was harmless, she stopped trying to understand and started playing along. As entertainment went, it was reasonably diverting. "He does seem to hold his liquor well. I watched him drink an entire bottle of whisky, and he was none the worse for it."

"Aye. MacPhersons are giants. Takes a flood to bring 'em down."

Sabella poured them each a cup of cider. "You've known them a long time, I take it?"

"Oh, aye. Longer than long, though they didnae ken me. Their mam became a friend after she died. Asked me to look after her laddies. Truth be told, they've done some lookin' after me, too. I've a fine cottage, all the bread I can eat, and a good business in fertility preventatives and liniment."

Nodding as if her ramblings made perfect sense, Sabella added a log to the fire and stirred the coals beneath the grate. "I had someone to look after me for a time. 'Twas a dear comfort."

"He thanks ye, lass. Eudora thanks ye, too. She promised to wait for him."

A quivery chill winnowed down Sabella's spine. Slowly, she turned. The old woman's milky eye caught a stray beam, turning it pure white. A moment later, a bird flew past the window, breaking the beam's cast. The woman's daft expression returned as she gulped down her cider.

Sabella wondered if the heat was causing her to imagine things.

Hours after Mrs. MacBean rode away on Bill the Donkey, Sabella stood in the larder, still puzzling over the woman's words. Eudora wasn't a particularly common name. How had she known?

She collected flour and butter for a paste, then took down a leg of beef. A beefsteak pie had sounded simple enough in the receipt. This time, she would go easy on the salt.

Could Mrs. MacBean have met Munro previously? Aye, that must be it, she thought as she laid her ingredients on the table and checked the fire. Perhaps Annie had told her about Sergeant Munro coming to Sabella's aid, and the old woman's muddled mind had put together the pieces.

Relieved to have solved the mystery, Sabella finished slicing the beefsteaks and squinted at the receipt. "'Season the fillets with spices.' Which ones?" she muttered. "'Add a mutchkin of gravy.' How does one make gravy?" She thumbed through the book searching for instructions but found only vague references in unrelated dishes. "Drat and blast, who authored this rubbish?"

Thankfully, the paste instructions were more straightforward. Though her hands were sore and swollen from the laundry, she found kneading the dough pleasantly mindless and spent a long while finding the right rhythm. The paste was hard to roll flat after she was finished, but she didn't see how that would make any difference.

Dicing the onions stung her eyes, and the spices could best be termed "experimental." But coiling the fillets into small rosettes was easy enough, and she found the idea of cutting leaves from the paste to decorate the top of the pie a delightful notion.

After assembling the seasoned meat inside the deep dish, she added water in place of the gravy. She thought it best to avoid the salt altogether, opting for more pepper instead. Once she secured the paste to the dish's rim, she used a knife to cut the leaves. The meat underneath caused the paste to stretch and shift while she cut, so the decorations looked more like fish escaping from an onion-strewn pond than bonnie leaves.

Perhaps he wouldn't notice.

She set the dish on the grate and used the towel to wipe her forehead. An unpleasant odor struck her nose. She sniffed the towel. Not the towel. She sniffed beneath her arm—and recoiled. Good heavens, she'd never needed a bath this badly. After the tortures of laundry day, she had no desire to lug more water. But a river lay nearby. A lovely, cool river.

The receipt didn't say how long the pie should cook, but she could take a few minutes for a quick wash, surely. Another sniff confirmed it. She *must* wash.

Quickly, she removed her apron and retrieved the almond soap he'd given her. Then she rushed outside, eyeing the stable drive to ensure he hadn't returned yet. She didn't expect him for another hour or so.

This time, she found a shallower bank downstream near a bend in the river, which made climbing down easier. Here, the water pooled and the current calmed into a swirl. Additionally, a cluster of alder trees screened the view from the house. Not perfect privacy, but better than nothing.

Another glance confirmed she was alone, so she unbelted the plaid and removed his shirt, leaving her completely naked apart from her half-boots. She'd gone without her stays, as any pressure on her bruises was painful.

Her breath caught as she waded in past her thighs. The water was positively frigid. The deeper she went, however, the better it felt. Soaping her skin and hair surpassed every luxurious indulgence she'd ever experienced. Who needed rose oil soaks in a copper tub? Who needed a lady's maid rinsing her hair with French tonics?

This was heaven. Cold water numbed her bruised backside while the swirling current eased her aching muscles. The pleasure was so acute that her eyes drifted closed on a sigh.

She didn't know how much time passed before the interruption. Ten minutes? A quarter hour? Regardless, the moment she heard his voice, her entire body sparked like metal striking stone.

"Try not to drown, Duchess. It'd be a fair bother to hire a new maid."

Chapter Six

Yelping like a plucked goose, Sabella frantically covered her bosom, even though he probably couldn't see anything beneath the water, and if he could, it was too late. The soap slipped from her fingers. *Plop.* She bent to retrieve it and nearly drowned herself.

"Drat and blast," she sputtered, twisting to glance toward the bank. "If ye'll grant me privacy, sir, I shall dress and return to my duties. Dinner should be ready soon."

He stood beneath the alders, arms folded, one broad shoulder propped against the trunk. "I told ye before, dinnae call me sir."

She released an exasperated sigh. "Mr. MacPherson, then."

"Alexander will do."

It most certainly would not. She was his maid. Maids did *not* address their employers by their given names. "That would be highly improper, Mr. MacPherson."

He chuckled. "Is swimmin' bare-arsed also highly improper?"

"I assumed I was alone."

"Ye were." A sardonic smile. "Then ye werenae. A lass should be wary of her surroundings, particularly when she's naked."

She swallowed, wondering why her nipples suddenly tingled against her palms. "I'm not naked."

"Ye look naked, lass."

"I'm still wearing my boots."

His smile vanished. A long, tense silence fell. Leaves rustled. The river sighed. Alexander stared at her for the longest time then ran a hand over his beard and shook his head. When he shoved away from the tree and started down the bank, those steel-on-stone sparks lit her up from her boots to her scalp. She scrambled deeper into the water, dipping past her shoulders.

He held up a staying hand. "Dinnae panic, Duchess." He crouched to place a bundle on the boulder beside her discarded garments then held each folded item up one by one. First came a new plaid of cream tartan crisscrossed with muted brown and green. The second item was another of his shirts. Last came a towel, which she'd forgotten in her rush to bathe.

"You … I … Thank you."

He nodded, climbed the bank, then disappeared toward the house. She waited a minute or two before wading back to the boulder. Shivering and dripping, she dried and dressed then returned to the kitchen.

There, she found her beefsteak pie more blackened than browned. Scrambling to remove it before it got any worse, she dropped it onto a trivet and threw the kitchen towel onto the table.

Pressure gathered in her chest. Great, heaving breaths didn't relieve it. She buried her face in her hands. The pressure ratcheted tighter.

Five weeks, ten shillings. Five weeks, ten shillings.

The chant didn't help this time. She was a failure. A hopelessly incompetent failure.

Distant bootfalls sounded from the stair hall. The sounds moved closer. Closer. She lowered her hands and drew a shuddering breath. By the time he entered the kitchen, she'd donned her apron and composed her expression. "If you'd care to wait in the dining room, I'd be glad to—"

"I'll eat in here." He moved into her periphery, but she kept her eyes on her task of cutting away the crust's burnt edges and sweeping them into the rubbish bin.

She brushed away the tingle in her nape as she sensed him looking at her. Recalling how he'd stared earlier when he'd caught her swimming, she reached for a distraction. "I had a visit from Mrs. MacBean today."

He grunted. "What did she want?"

Sabella gestured toward the sideboard where she'd placed the old woman's gifts. "To deliver your liniment."

He moved to examine the assortment of oddities. "Daft auld crone. I told her to stop makin' these for me."

She glanced up to find him dangling the wooden charm. "She intended it for me, actually. I'm not certain why. We weren't really acquainted until today."

That glowering black gaze shifted to her. The intensity of his regard sent hot shivers across her skin. That was when she noticed it—something was different about him. What was it? He looked handsomer, somehow.

Wiping her hands on her apron, she crossed to the cider cask and filled a cup for each of them. "Are you hungry?" she asked. "I can slice up a bit of the smoked brisket from the larder if ye like."

"What's wrong with the pie ye made?"

Her face heated. "I ruined it. Even cutting away the burnt parts, it's probably dreadful."

"Ye havenae tried it yet."

Sliding his cup across the table, she examined him again from beneath her lashes. Handsomer, aye. How that was possible, she didn't know. He was the most compelling man she'd ever seen. Thick, black hair. Piercingly dark eyes beneath low, straight brows. A hard, square jaw, hawkish nose, and thin-yet-defined lips. Every feature made him seem both lethally dangerous and wickedly sensual. On further examination of his mouth, the change in his appearance became clear.

"You trimmed your beard," she murmured.

He ran a hand over said beard. "Aye. The midges were threatenin' to take up residence. Somethin' had to be done."

A bubble of laughter took her by surprise. Covering her giggle with her fingers, she grinned up at him and teased, "Bold midges to brave such a forbidding visage."

His mouth quirked. "Those wee bloodsuckers are a darin' lot." His gaze warmed until her skin did likewise. "Are ye goin' to have some of that pie, or will I be eatin' it by myself?"

Resigning herself to her fate, she retrieved two wooden bowls from the cupboard then scooped a serving for each of them. If he had to suffer through it, then she would, too.

Her first bite confirmed her worst fears. The crust was gummy on the underside, faintly acrid on the top, and tough as shoe leather all the way through. The thin, oniony broth wouldn't be terrible if it weren't for the spices, which she now realized had been entirely wrong. Cloves did not belong with beefsteak. And much like salt, there was such a thing as too much pepper.

Perhaps the only redeeming aspect of the dish was the meat, which was tender and flavorful if a bit overcooked.

She managed to swallow her singular bite eventually, albeit with a long drink of cider afterward. Meanwhile, Alexander calmly added a pinch of salt to his bowl then finished the entire lot.

She could only conclude that the man's senses had been damaged. "Are you hard of tasting, by chance?" she inquired.

He arched a brow and served himself a second helping. "I dinnae take yer meaning."

"I mean that your mouth is clearly malfunctioning. It's the only rational explanation."

His grin melted her insides like butter in a hot skillet. "My mouth works just fine, Duchess."

He'd flustered her. Damn. He hadn't meant to. But that white skin blushed the most delicate pink, and those eyes, soft as spring grass, glowed with bashful curiosity. How was a man meant to resist such innocent beauty—even if it was a lie?

She excused herself to fetch a loaf of bread. After offering him several slices, she added salt to her bowl and proceeded to eat the only truly edible part of her dinner: the beef.

Each dainty bite between those petal-soft lips made him harder. It was bloody distracting. As always, he couldn't look away. He drank cider to rinse the flavor of onions and cloves from his mouth and relished the sight of her.

When he'd arrived home earlier and found dinner cooking but Sabella missing, he'd wanted to tear apart his own house piece by piece. A frantic minute later, he'd glimpsed her wading naked into the river.

Relief and desire had weakened his knees.

Then he'd noticed the bruises. Black and blue mottling stained her body from her knees to the middle of her back. Never again.

Even now, his instincts roared their outrage. *Never again.*

He calmed himself by drinking more cider and focusing on how bonnie she looked wearing his shirt and plaid. She'd plaited her hair after her dip in the river. It fell down her back in a golden rope to her waist while wispy curls dried around her lovely face. Dressed like a Highland wife, glowing from the kitchen's heat, she invoked a painfully vivid fantasy involving this table, her thighs, and his tongue.

Was it any wonder she obsessed him?

Her perfect nose crinkled as she washed down another bite with a swig of cider. Her eyes began to water, and she coughed delicately into her napkin. More cider and an apologetic wince. "Remind me never to use pepper again. Or cloves." She sighed and nudged an onion around her bowl of broth. "Or fire."

He tapped the singed bits on top of the remaining crust. "The moons are a clever touch."

"Those are leaves." Another sigh. "I'm better with gardening. Mrs. MacBean gave me a rosebush and some lavender. Would you mind very much if I plant them somewhere in the garden? I'd hate to see them wilt."

"Plant what ye like, lass."

Seeming more cheerful, she plucked a tuft of bread and popped it between her lips. "Roses require a bit of care, but they're not as difficult as some people imagine. Give them ample sunshine and the right companions, and they'll bloom 'til you're drenched in their nectar."

He stilled. Bloody hell. His fingers itched to make *her* bloom until *her* nectar drenched his tongue. Instead, he busied his hands turning his cup round and round. This was almost worse than hearing her deny she was naked because she was wearing boots.

Boots. He'd never wanted to laugh and spontaneously come at the same time. At four-and-thirty, he'd thought himself well past the age of new experiences. He'd thought wrong.

"I shan't be here to see them bloom next summer, of course," she said. "But it pleases me to ken that ye'll have a start on a proper garden."

He kept his expression neutral. The cider relaxed her considerably. Even her speech became more Scottish rather than starchy English aristocrat. It made him wonder how whisky might affect her inhibitions.

She drank more cider, propped her chin on her hand, and gazed out the window. "Five weeks, ten shillings," she murmured. "Then it's off to Inverness."

"What's waitin' for ye in Inverness? Yer sergeant?"

Her eyes glossed and her chin quivered just before she lowered her gaze.

Bloody hell, why had he prodded her? *Because, ye eejit, ye wanted to see if she grieves him, if she loves him still. Now ye ken.*

"Sergeant Munro is dead," she whispered as a tear spilled onto her cheek. She swiped it away with impatient fingertips. "If he were here, he'd tell me how foolish I was to try to reconcile with the MacPhersons. Then he'd bark at me to dry my womanly tears and get on with things." With a bittersweet smile, she lowered her voice to mimic her former lover's deeper brogue. "'There's nae time for grievin', lassie. Not when there's work to be done.'" Her chuckle was fond and sad.

Alexander held his body still while a black storm raged within. He'd brought this on himself. It was nobody's fault but his.

"Once I speak to Mr. and Mrs. McCabe, everything will return to normal," she said, blotting her cheeks and reddened nose with her napkin. "Five weeks, ten shillings. Ye'll be free of me by summer's end."

He'd never be free of her. Worse, since the moment she'd entered MacDonnell & Sons Tavern, freeing himself had been the last thing on his mind.

"They robbed ye blind," he reminded her. "What magical words do ye suppose will cause a pair of thieves to repent of their ways, hmm?"

She gave him a stymied frown. "I … I shall tell them how much I'm relying on my belongings to carry me forward. All my clothing, my funds, my slippers. Important letters and documents from the estate. Those trunks hold everything I have left in the world."

"Did they ken that before they robbed ye?"

Her frown deepened. "Some of it, aye."

"Yet, they still stole everythin' ye have left in the world."

"I don't think they meant to."

"Nah. Ye dinnae *want* to believe they're thievin' piles of shite, but ye ken better."

She shook her head. Solemn green eyes lifted to meet his. Turmoil furrowed her bonnie brow as she struggled with the only conclusion that made sense. Slowly, acceptance dulled her hopeful light. "Perhaps ye're right."

"I am."

"I suppose the coins I gave those two MacDonnell laddies are gone forever, too."

"MacDonnell." He held his hand four feet above the floor. "This tall? Both freckled?"

She nodded.

"Dougal MacDonnell's sons are two of the laziest lads in the glen. What did ye pay them for?"

Her cheeks pinkened. "To help haul my trunks."

"Ye gave them money *before* they'd done the task?"

She tucked her chin and dropped her gaze to her cider cup. That was answer enough.

Previously, he'd thought no one could be this credulous, that her naiveté must be a trick to dupe men into offering their protection. Yet, here was proof that he'd been wrong. Again.

He ran a hand over his beard. "Bluidy hell, woman. A newborn bairn is less gullible than you."

She stiffened. "I'll grant you that I should have withheld the coins until the lads finished their duties. But how was I to know the McCabes would make off with my trunks?"

"How much did ye pay the McCabes?"

"Five shillings each, along with passage to Inverness."

"That's how."

"But they were traveling home after a visit with their grandchildren. They said they were grateful for the companionship." She looked genuinely perplexed. "You didn't meet them. They're *old,* Mr. MacPherson."

"Auld thieves are the best thieves, lass. They're the ones who didnae get caught."

A mulish frown creased her brow. "So, I should trust no one. Is that it?"

"Aye. That's it, Duchess. This world isnae a bonnie garden with caretakers behind every rosebush. 'Tis a wild land filled with cunning beasts and vicious traps. Blindfolding yerself doesnae make ye safe. It makes ye easy prey."

"Nonsense. Not everyone is kind, perhaps, but some people are." She raised her chin to a challenging angle. "You are."

He snorted at the sheer absurdity of that statement. "That proves ye ken naught about the world. And less about me."

She stood and began clearing away the dishes. All her earlier relaxation had been replaced with tension. "Mrs. MacBean said you and yer kin have looked after her for years. That's a kindness."

The sway of her hips was too distracting for a reply. Instead, he finished his cider and enjoyed the pure pleasure of watching her potter about his kitchen.

She refilled his cup without him having to ask. "Ye continue to employ a maid who burns yer dinner and borrows yer shirts. That's certainly a kindness."

This woman had no sense of self-preservation. If she understood anything about him, she'd tell him to go to the devil then walk all the way to Inverness, risks be damned.

"The mere fact that ye've let me stay here when I remind ye of …" She focused on his chest, her hands wringing the kitchen towel repeatedly. "That's a kindness."

It wasn't anything like kindness. Not even close.

"Annie calls ye the most blackhearted of all her brothers. She says ye're ruthless when ye want something and that ye're more dangerous than the others because yer temper runs cold, not hot." She shook her head. "But that's not what I see, Mr. MacPherson."

Then she was blind. "What do ye see, lass?"

A blush bloomed. A sweet pink tongue flickered along that petal-soft lower lip. That long, lovely throat rippled on a swallow. "A man."

"True enough. I am a man."

"A strong one." She drew a shaky breath and pressed her towel to her bosom. "So very strong, Mr. MacPherson. I didn't think anybody could survive such a wound. All that blood." Her blush faded to pure white. "If Rannoch and Miss Cuthbert hadn't arrived when they did, ye'd be …"

The reminder was timely. He'd nearly let himself forget. "Dead." He smiled coldly. "Aye. And if ye hadnae thrown yerself in front of my blade, yer brother would have died first."

Now, even her lips lost color. "I had to do something. I couldn't let him shoot ye."

"Dead men dinnae fire shots."

She didn't seem to hear him. Glazed green eyes riveted to the spot where the bullet had torn through flesh and bone. "He raised the pistol. Ye were lyin' there unconscious, then …" Her breathing grew jagged. "Ye move so very fast, Mr. MacPherson. I didn't see until it was too late." Leaf-green eyes shimmered. A dainty brow crashed into a pained furrow as the rest of her color leached to gray. "I—I had to do something. I couldn't let him kill you."

Alexander had spent the last seven months fighting. First, he'd fought death. Then fever. Then hell's own agony. But the hardest battle had been with his instincts. They wanted her like air and whisky. The only weapon he'd had in that battle—the only reason he hadn't hunted her down and claimed her like a war prize—was his belief that she'd been protecting her brother.

Annie had railed at him that he was wrong about her. Magdalene had told him in her gentle way that forgiving Sabella Lockhart would "bring healing to the parts of ye only God can touch." Rannoch had warned him that he'd misjudged the lass before declaring him "too bluidy stubborn to bother with." In fairness, Alexander had threatened to cut his brother's ballocks off if he mentioned her again.

Now, here he was, staring at the lovely, ashen face of the woman who claimed she'd tried to save his life. Part of him wanted to doubt her. The world was full of cunning creatures. Perhaps she was simply cleverer than the rest.

This had been his hardest battle, and he didn't want to believe he'd fought it for nothing. But could she feign the trembling, the pallor, the haunted eyes? Could anyone? The odds said no. But his memory argued that she'd collapsed against him rather than her brother, that her gasping, distressed cries of pain had been a deliberate distraction.

Meanwhile, his instincts roared that it bloody well didn't matter. Munro didn't matter. Any other protectors she'd lured into her web didn't matter. He should have claimed her months ago, and he was wasting time ruminating when he could be making her his.

His instincts were winning the day.

"Dinnae punish yerself, lass," he said, turning his cup round and round. "I survived. He didnae. It all came right in the end."

"Right?" She laughed while she wrung the towel until her arms shook from the strain. Finally, she turned away to collect the dishes from the sideboard. "Nothing is right about what happened to you, Mr. MacPherson. And I don't have to punish myself. The memories do that well enough."

Chapter Seven

On Sabella's seventh morning as a maid, she thought she might be improving. Not a lot, mind. But bit by bit.

Preparing tea and delivering hot water to Alexander's dressing room was simple enough. She'd fully mastered those tasks on her second day.

But the eggs and bacon she cooked for breakfast were a different matter. On day three, she'd burnt the bacon and crumbled half a shell into the eggs. With a sheepish apology, she'd served it to Alexander, who'd eaten it without complaint.

By day five, the bacon was less burnt, and the eggs were runny but intact. This morning, both had turned out rather well, the bacon crisp and the eggs deliciously tender without a single stray shell.

She'd watched Alexander take actual pleasure in her food for the first time. Her body had effervesced like a glass of champagne.

Her reactions to him were growing worrisome.

In part, it was his handsomeness, but she mostly blamed his considerate nature. The man was a true gentleman at heart, eating her wretched food, tolerating the scorch marks she'd left on his shirts, and ignoring the dulled shine on his floors after her scrubbing failures. Even more endearing was the way he alerted her to his return each evening by immediately hunting her down in whatever room she happened to be dusting.

Three days ago, it was the drawing room. He'd found her on a ladder dusting the painting of a stag on a hill above Loch Carrich. He'd grumbled about the risk of falling and admonished her to "keep yer wee feet on the ground when I'm not here, woman." Then he'd threatened to hire a lad to assist her with outdoor tasks and heavier lifting.

She'd protested that it wasn't necessary—the last thing she wanted was to lose her position to a lad—but he'd barked about not wanting to come home and find her "lyin' with yer heid cracked open and all yer foolishness fallin' out."

Yesterday, he'd found her humming in his bedchamber as she changed his sheets. She'd grinned and welcomed him home, telling him he had just enough time to wash before dinner. He'd grunted, silently watched her fluffing his pillows, then stalked into his dressing room without a word.

She believed their conversation about Kenneth had improved their rapport. No, he wasn't any chattier, and yes, he still growled and glared a great deal. But for the first time, she thought it was possible he might forgive her. She doubted she'd ever forgive herself, but she was relieved that her presence didn't pain him too much.

Having him point out the futility of returning to Inverness and the truth about the McCabes had been hard. But she was, rather strangely, happier now. She'd begun to formulate a new, more realistic plan for her future, and as she improved at her daily tasks, she awakened each day looking forward to preparing tea and improving her cooking so she could feed Alexander properly.

It had been nearly a week since she'd had to answer, "Not today."

Her duties kept her too busy to despair. Rather than saving the laundry for one overwhelming weekly task, she'd begun washing a few garments each day to dilute the drudgery and take advantage of the hot, breezy weather. Because of this, she'd noticed Alexander's shirts smelled different from day to day—sometimes like peat smoke, sometimes like sawn oak, sometimes like his liniment. Underneath, his unique scent remained constant: evergreen, Highland air, and male skin.

This was yet another cause of her worrisome obsession. That intoxicating Alexander scent provoked wicked thoughts, which led to powerful aches in secretive places, which necessitated bathing with greater frequency.

Between when he left the house after breakfast each morning and returned for dinner each evening, she made the most of her time alone to bathe in the river. It had become a daily ritual—purely for cleansing purposes, of course.

Today, she was cleansing *quite* thoroughly. It was his fault. She couldn't stop picturing his mouth closing around his fork as he enjoyed the breakfast she'd prepared for him. Eyes glowing with appreciation, he'd licked his lower lip and murmured, "Delicious. Well done, lass."

Heavens, she'd wanted to stretch out on the kitchen table and offer herself as his dessert. The forbidden thought had fired her skin, turning it sensitive and hot. Now, as currents pulsed and pushed around her naked body, she stroked a palm down over her nipple, picturing *his* hands there instead. His mouth. His tongue.

With a sigh, she stroked and plucked and imagined how he'd touch her—the same way he touched his cider cup when he turned it round and round. Lightly, deftly. The way he did everything. The man moved like water.

Her hand slid lower, down over her aching belly to her slick, swollen folds. Last night, she'd dreamed of his hands there, those long fingers sliding and pleasuring. Would he fill her with them? Would he quench this infernal hunger coiling and squeezing around emptiness that longed to be stretched and filled?

Her head fell back on a gasp as the bud at the center of her folds swelled against her fingertip.

He'd lay her on the table. Aye, he'd strip her naked, those coal-ember eyes glowing with anticipation. First, she'd kiss him, demanding he let her have a taste of his tongue.

She stroked and swirled, picturing his black hair falling over his forehead, his hands between her thighs, his fingers sliding and caressing, opening and spreading.

He'd rise like a dark god with firelight behind him. He'd come over her like the blackest night. He'd put himself deep inside her and—

The explosion crashed over her in pulsating waves, rocking her with its force. For long minutes, she drew it out, imagining pleasuring *him* this way, welcoming his mouth with hers as she eased his tension and reveled in his scent.

She sighed at the blissful daydream and finished bathing. He'd provided more of his lovely almond soap without so much as a question.

Such a gentleman.

Before he'd left earlier, she'd mentioned needing to purchase a needle and thread to repair one of his shirts. He'd told her to purchase whatever she needed in the village and have the proprietors add it to his monthly billing.

A *true* gentleman.

Taking care with her favorite cream plaid, she dressed in her shift, petticoats, and stays then arranged the lengthy swath of wool over the top. She plaited and pinned her hair then donned her straw bonnet, using a strip of bronze tartan to tie it in place. As she turned this way and that in front of his dressing room mirror, she concluded she was as decently covered as any Edinburgh lady and twice as clean.

Before she left, she carried a pitcher of water out to her makeshift garden—a four-foot square of ground she'd cleared on the south-facing side of the house between the east wing and the river. There, she was happy to see the lavender perking up and the rose bush beginning to show signs of leafing. Another week or two, and they'd be putting on growth. The thought made her smile.

Walking into the village took her less than a half-hour, since it was all downhill. The skies were boundless blue above the loch. Shimmering light and a cooling breeze turned the glen into a verdant summer paradise. She smiled again as a playful pair of sparrows swooped past, appearing to dance in midair.

When she entered the square, she braced for the customary resentful gawking to begin. But it didn't. Nobody noticed the Lowlander in their midst. Well, perhaps a lady or two exiting the dressmaker's shop glanced her way. But their regard wasn't hostile or intrusive, merely curious. She nodded politely to the pair of women then entered the haberdashery.

"Be right with ye, miss!" called Mr. Cleghorn. "Ronnie, ye wee dafty. Take that pup out of my storeroom if ye aim to keep 'im."

A childish voice said something about a strawberry.

"Aye, ye can have some. But dinnae put that rope in yer—Ronnie!"

She wandered toward the tartan display near the front window. Amid the rusty browns, cloud grays, buff tans, and wooded greens, a singular bolt drew her eye. It was the gentle blue of a starling's egg crisscrossed with white, sandy gold, and dusky pink. She fingered the corner—light and feathery soft.

Once again, she smiled without meaning to. She'd been doing that a lot lately. Ordinarily, she smiled out of politeness or to please someone. Sometimes, she'd done it to appease Kenneth's temper or disguise pain. To smile purely because something delighted her felt foreign.

She stroked the blue tartan, imagining the gown she would create—long sleeves, a scooped neckline, perhaps a sash. The price wasn't too outrageous. She'd have to save for perhaps another two or three weeks, but it could be done.

She crossed to the other side of the shop where the linen and ribbons were displayed. Mr. Cleghorn didn't carry much silk, but three bolts sat on the far side of the thread shelf. She gazed longingly at the petal-pink satin.

Drat and blast. Too expensive. She had the two shillings Alexander had paid her that morning, no more.

The bell above the shop door chimed. A woman entered—plain-faced, modestly dressed, bone-thin—and halted as she caught sight of Sabella. Gray eyes blinked in recognition. "Miss Lockhart?"

Blood soaking her hands and skirts. Gray eyes, narrow features. Reddened, bony hands taking possession of the tablecloth. A soft voice telling her she'd done well, but she must let him go if she wanted him to live.

Aye, Sabella remembered this woman all too vividly. "Miss Cuthbert," she murmured, steadying herself against the shelf. "It's been a long while."

"I didn't ken ye'd come to the glen." Magdalene Cuthbert had the air of an ascetic nun—pious, pale, and tidy. She kept her mouse-brown hair scraped back from her narrow face and her full lips carefully closed to conceal her teeth, which were a bit large for her mouth. The young woman approached with gentleness, as if Sabella was still the frantic, sobbing mess Magdalene and Rannoch had found cradling Alexander's head on the floor of her Edinburgh parlor. "Ye look well."

Sabella summoned a smile. "As do you. Lady Huxley tells me you've been studying midwifery."

"And medicine, aye." She nodded toward Sabella's abdomen. "Did yer injuries heal properly? No pain or difficulty breathing, I hope."

Sabella shook her head. "I'm fine now. Thank you for your advice. It helped."

"Of course." Magdalene discreetly swept a glance over Sabella's clothing and tilted her head inquiringly. "Are ye in Glenscannadoo for a visit? Lady Huxley is away, I'm afraid."

"In England. I know. Foolish of me to arrive unannounced, but I was in Inverness for Sergeant Munro's burial—"

Gray eyes shone with sympathy. "Oh, no. Sergeant Munro died?"

Sabella's throat tightened. She swallowed to loosen it. When would this get easier? "Heart failure. He'd complained of chest pains for weeks. We kenned something was amiss, but the physicians couldn't help him."

"I'm very sorry, Miss Lockhart. I remember how fond he was of you."

Sabella nodded. "And I of him. I don't know what I would have done after …"

Magdalene's eyes warmed—her version of a smile. "Are ye returning to Edinburgh soon? Perhaps we could meet for tea before ye depart."

Cheeks heating, Sabella explained that she'd been robbed and left stranded. At the other woman's concerned frown, she reassured her, "Mr.

MacPherson—Alexander, that is—offered me a position in his home. I've been there for a week, now."

Magdalene's concern didn't dissipate. If anything, it deepened. "Alexander hired *you?* To do what, precisely?"

Sabella raised her chin. "I'm his maid."

Gray eyes widened with alarm. She muttered something about "dear God in heaven" then composed her expression and inched closer. "Broderick and Kate are away right now, but I'm certain they wouldn't mind if ye came to stay with us at Rowan House."

"Oh, you misunderstand. He's been very kind."

"Kind. Alexander."

"Indeed. I've no skills as a maid, Miss Cuthbert. His patience would make the saints weep."

Magdalene frowned. "Patience. Alexander?"

"Aye." Why did she keep asking? "He's given me food and a bed, a chance to earn back a bit of what the thieves took. He even lets me wear his shirts and plaids."

Gray eyes touched on Sabella's *arasaid*. Concern now carved a steep glen between her brows. "His shirts," she breathed. "*Alexander's.*"

"After I ruined my carriage dress, I had nothing else to wear."

A giant shadow passed by the shop windows. The shadow halted, peered inside, then stalked through the jingling door with intimidating strides. It took a moment for Sabella to realize he wasn't Alexander. Rannoch shared his brother's height and dark coloring, his broad shoulders, lean torso, and long, muscular arms. But even wearing a scowl, he was much less intimidating.

Noticing the direction of her gaze, Magdalene glanced behind her then spun to face him with her shoulders squared. "I haven't changed my mind, Mr. MacPherson."

"Send the bluidy physician to tend to her." He lifted his hat and raked a hand through black hair.

"I'm *his* apprentice, not the other way round."

"Fine. *I'll* go tell that tedious sod—"

"No, you will not. He's the only physician in Inverness-shire willing to train a female. I shan't let ye risk my position—"

"Ye're riskin' yer *health*. Mayhap yer life. For what? Nothin'!"

Calmly, Magdalene replied, "It's my duty to tend the sick."

"She's ninety. That's practically dead, anyway. Only a matter of time."

"Then I shall do my best to ease her suffering until the Lord comes for her."

"And make yerself ill like last time, eh? Christ on the cross, how ye try my patience, Mouse."

"I'll thank you to refrain from such blasphemies."

"Ye're lucky blasphemin' is all I'm doin'."

Wearing a glower instead of his usual grin, he reminded Sabella keenly of Alexander, though, strictly speaking, Rannoch was the handsomer of the two. His features were less hawkish, his nose more refined, his eyes less intense, and his grin devilishly flirtatious. Also, he was clean-shaven and kept his hair neatly trimmed above his collar, which put him closer to the gentlemanly ideal she'd been accustomed to during her seasons.

And *everyone* agreed Rannoch was the most charming MacPherson brother. According to Annie, he had all the lasses in three counties convinced "his trews are heaven's door" and that "every last one of 'em should crank that latch 'til it squeals from the friction." Sabella hadn't fully understood her metaphor, but she'd met the man, so she had the general idea.

She *should* be more drawn to him than Alexander. Why wasn't she? He had less reason to hate her and a much easier temperament—present vexation with Miss Cuthbert notwithstanding.

Sabella cleared her throat, but neither of them paid her any mind.

"Dinnae expect me to haul ye to Inverness for treatment this time," he snapped. "If ye take ill, it's yer own bluidy fault."

"I'd be a fool to expect anything from ye, Rannoch MacPherson." Magdalene sniffed. "And if there's one thing I intend to be cured of, it's foolishness."

His jaw flickered. He muttered a curse and shook his head in exasperation. "Do ye need a ride to the MacDonnell farm? I have the wagon."

"A ride would be lovely. Thank you."

"Fine."

"Good."

"What is Sabella Lockhart doin' here?" His gaze hadn't moved an inch from Magdalene, so the mention of her name took Sabella by surprise, as did Magdalene's matter-of-fact answer.

"She came to see Lady Huxley, but her trunks were stolen, along with all her money. She's been working for your brother this past week."

When his eyes finally shifted to Sabella, his expression eased. He arched a brow and quirked an admiring grin. "I didnae think anything could suit ye better than silk, lass, but that tartan comes close. 'Tis good to see ye lookin' so well after Edinburgh."

She blinked. *Heaven's door, indeed.* "I … thank you."

"Are ye workin' for Broderick or Campbell?"

"Oh, neither."

Magdalene stiffened. "Alexander hired her as his maid."

Rannoch's grin faded back into a scowl. *"Alexander?"*

"Aye," Magdalene sighed. "I know."

"Bluidy hell."

"Mr. MacPherson, the blaspheming."

"Right. Sorry, Mouse."

"I think it would be best if we pay Alexander a wee visit tomorrow." She cast Sabella a pitying glance. "If it's not too much trouble."

Naturally, Sabella assured them of their welcome, and minutes later, they left the haberdashery with Magdalene chiding the towering giant by her side, "How many times am I supposed to repair the same hole in the same shirt before ye take more care loading yer deliveries?"

Sabella gathered up her purchases—needles and thread, a thimble, and, on impulse, a lovely set of toilette brushes carved from deer antler. She was surprised when Mr. Cleghorn added her purchases to Alexander's account before she could offer her shillings. She protested, but the paunchy proprietor said he had his instructions and meant to follow them. Presumably, the instructions had come from Alexander—yet another demonstration of his generosity.

Such a gentleman.

As she exited the shop, her stomach rumbled its emptiness, so she headed for the most popular tavern in Glenscannadoo. The interior was dark and cool at midday, offering relief from the burgeoning summer heat.

"Is that you, lamb?" Joan MacDonnell called from the far end of the bar. "Didnae expect to see ye in here again."

Sabella smiled and fished one of her coins from her makeshift pocket. "I've come to repay your kindness." She laid the coin on the bar. "And to beg for your receipts."

Two hours later, Joan wiped down her bar as she explained why her eldest son was named after a Frenchman. "Étienne mayn't have had but one leg and six fingers, and a bald man with nae eyebrows is an eerie spectacle to find huntin' mushrooms in yer front garden after midnight. But, by God, that wee, fancy man could cook." She flopped the towel over her shoulder and poured Sabella a fourth cup of MacPherson cider—or was it a fifth? "Ye ken what he told me ere he returned to France?"

Sabella drank and shook her head.

"Butter and better are only one letter apart. That cannae be a coincidence."

The cider's pleasant glow made the simple observation sound like wisdom.

"He also taught me a wee secret—start by masterin' the meat. All else is decorative."

Sabella blinked. Hadn't Mrs. MacBean said something similar? "Is it true that one can use potatoes for cleaning rust?"

Joan seemed unfazed by the change of subject. "Aye. Good for tarnished silver, too. Takes a bit of scrubbin', but tatties can work wonders if ye use 'em right."

During the tavern's afternoon lull, Joan generously shared her tips for improved cookery. "Ye needn't learn all the receipts, lamb. Start with ten."

"Ten?"

"Aye. Practice those ten 'til everybody's beggin' for a second helping." She nodded to Sabella's empty bowl. "When ye get complaints about the repetition, then ye can fash about learnin' more. By that time, ye'll be ready to write yer own."

She even granted Sabella a tour of her reconstructed kitchen. Envious of the clever enclosed range with its built-in boiler, Sabella asked who'd constructed it. "My husband," Joan replied. "But the design is Alexander MacPherson's."

She explained that her husband worked at the MacPherson Distillery helping build and maintain the pipes, cisterns, mash tuns, stills, and other equipment. "Adam's a fine craftsman, no doubt. But all that machinery starts as a notion in Alexander's head. Some complain his designs cost men their jobs. Too efficient, they say. Too modern. All I ken is that the MacPherson Distillery wouldnae do half as well without him. Half a distillery employs half the men. That simple."

Hearing Joan's account only deepened Sabella's fascination with the man. She wanted to quiz him about how he devised his schemes. She wanted to ask whether a similar range could be installed in his kitchen and how soon that might occur. Why hadn't he already done so?

The list of Alexander's unfinished projects—the garden, the grounds, household staffing, even furnishing the empty bedchambers—puzzled her. He'd built his home with extraordinary thought and care. Then he'd stopped. The upheaval of Kenneth's horrifying crimes against the MacPhersons over the past two years explained much of the pause. But not all.

Sabella's curiosity got the better of her. She asked Joan, "Does Mr. MacPherson work at the distillery every day?"

"Most days, aye." Joan greeted a pair of young women entering the tavern then resumed cleaning whisky glasses. "He's also helpin' build Campbell's house." Joan described the dreadful fire that had consumed his older brother's farm last spring. The MacPhersons had broken ground on a large new house for Campbell and his wife less than a month later. "He aims to have it finished by winter. I doubt even Alexander can manage that."

Sabella didn't know anything about constructing a house, but she wouldn't wager her last two shillings against him.

After refilling Sabella's cup for a fifth—sixth?—time, Joan served ale to the two young women who'd entered earlier. The lasses were rhapsodizing about Rannoch MacPherson. "Did ye see him haulin' that cask?" sighed the dark-haired one.

"Aye. My Jamie couldnae lift it without three other lads to help," answered the ginger-haired one. "That's a MacPherson for ye. Giants, all."

"Do ye suppose Rannoch will compete in the Games, this year?"

A scoff. "Best save yer fancies for a man who wants to be caught. Only way ye'll get near Rannoch MacPherson's bed is if he's hirin' an upstairs maid."

"I'd take that position." The dark-haired lass swigged her ale and fanned herself dramatically. "I'd take any position he asked me tae."

The pair laughed.

As more customers began filing in, Sabella switched to a table nearer the lasses. "I do beg yer pardon, but are you ladies employed as maids, perchance?"

They peered at her curiously. The ginger-haired one answered first. "I was until I married. Now, I've a house of my own to clean." She nodded to her companion. "I keep tellin' her unpaid cleanin' is better than paid when a husband comes with the job, but she willnae believe me."

The dark-haired lass chuckled. "Give me a MacPherson, and I'll surrender my dust cloth gladly."

"They're braw men, true enough. But some'd be easier to live with than others."

"One in particular, ye mean. A rabid badger would be pleasant company by comparison." The dark-haired lass propped her chin on her wrist and sighed. "Still might be worth the trouble."

Mrs. Ginger, as Sabella had begun to think of her, raised her cup in hearty agreement. "I'll drink to that." They both laughed and downed their ale.

Were they talking about Angus? Annie had mentioned her father's blustering a few times, though her affectionate tone always made it sound endearing.

Miss Darkhair's eyes lit upon Sabella curiously. "Are ye lookin' to hire a maid, then?"

"No, I recently began a new position in Alexander MacPherson's household. I could use a bit of advice."

The two women shared a glance before shooting her twin looks of pity. "So, now ye're seekin' new employment," said Mrs. Ginger. "Aye. Understandable."

Sabella started to correct her assumption, but Miss Darkhair added, "One maid for a house that size, and every inch scrubbed to his standards." She shook her head. "Do ye ken he cut my wages the second week for putting a wee dent in a copper pot? It's true."

"He wanted his bedsheets washed and pressed every other day," said Mrs. Ginger, emphasizing her points by tapping her fingertip on the bar. "Every. Other. Day. Nae weekly, like all the sane, proper households in Scotland. And he refused to send the washin' out to Mrs. Cockburn or hire lads to haul water. Said that's what the taps were for."

"Aye. Then there's all the bellowin'," complained Miss Darkhair.

Mrs. Ginger hummed her agreement.

"Sunrise to midnight, like a bear roarin' for blood: 'Where are my bandages, Miss MacDonnell? Why isnae the soup warm, Miss MacDonnell? What use is it havin' a maid if she cannae carry a tray without spillin' it down the staircase, Miss MacDonnell?'" Miss Darkhair—or, rather, Miss MacDonnell—cast Sabella a commiserating glance. "Has he tested yer folds yet, lass?"

Sabella blinked. "M-my what?"

"The towels. He likes 'em precisely square and stacked in three piles of six." She smirked and mimicked his deep voice, "'Standards arenae optional, Miss MacDonnell.'"

Sabella swallowed. "He hasn't mentioned the folds yet."

Mrs. Ginger patted her hand and suggested seeking out new positions in Dingwall. "The pay is lower, but the employers are reasonable. The same cannae be said for Alexander MacPherson."

She might have queried the women further, but just then, the door swung open, and the subject of their discussion stalked in like a thunderstorm ready to rain hell upon the earth.

Chapter Eight

Chairs scraped as the two lasses scurried to the opposite end of the bar. Alexander's black gaze locked on Sabella. He headed straight for her, forcing anyone in his path to cede ground.

"Oh, my," she breathed.

When he reached her, he braced his hand on the table and lowered his head near hers. "It's past seven."

She glanced outside. It was? In summer, the sun didn't set until nine or ten.

"Why havenae ye headed home yet?"

He smelled like pine resin and sunshine. She inhaled deeply, and a wee smile curved her lips. "I spent the day with Joan. She's been such a help, Mr. MacPherson. I only have to learn ten receipts! Ten isn't too many."

His jaw flexed. He dragged a chair close to her and straddled it. "How much cider have ye had?"

She propped her chin on her hand. "*Several* cups. I lost count."

"Bluidy hell, lass."

"I might be a wee bit tipsy."

"Aye. Ye might."

"Were you working on Campbell's house today?"

"How do ye ken about that?"

"Joan mentioned it. She doubts ye'll finish by winter, but I think she's wrong."

His mouth quirked. "Why do ye think so?"

She eyed his shoulders, his powerful jaw, his dark, calculating eyes. "I just do. I don't care what the other maids say. Your voice sounds nothing like a bear's growl. Of course, I've never heard a bear growl, but your growl is more like an ocean, and you're not a rabid badger. You're just a bit out of sorts sometimes." She leaned closer to whisper, "They told me about the folds. I shall try to remember."

He glared toward the bar. Joan held up a whisky bottle. He shook his head then stood and helped Sabella to her feet. "I'm takin' ye home, Duchess. Dinnae cast up yer accounts. My maid just finished laundering these trews."

Outside, he lifted her onto his horse with the effortless strength that made her thighs tingle and her knees sweat. When he mounted behind her, flattened his palm across her belly, and murmured, "Steady, now," her breath hitched at the sudden ache below her navel.

Perhaps she could bathe in the river after he went to sleep. What if he saw her from his bedchamber window? Drat and blast. Why did the thought quicken her pulse?

As the horse carried them south along the loch, warm sunlight and his strong, hard frame at her back softened Sabella into butter. She relaxed against him, resting her hand lightly on his forearm. His shirtsleeves were rolled up to his elbows, and the crisp black hair covering his muscles fascinated her fingertips.

Noting how yellowed his sleeve was, she winced. "I'll wash this again tomorrow." She traced the seam between his skin and the linen. "Though, it mightn't come out any whiter. I can't seem to find the trick of it."

He grunted.

"Sadly, *The Prudent Housekeeper's Guide* is of little help. I'm not even certain it's written by a lady, let alone a housekeeper."

Another grunt. His arm flexed as she petted the muscles near his wrist.

"The receipts are too vague to be useful. And laundering?" She snorted. "One page of instructions. One. Apart from the chapters about budgets and being fleeced at the market, the author offers very little that one couldn't discover on one's own. All she does is complain about maids seducing their male employers. I daresay, she's either a scorned wife or a spurned man. Nothing else explains the vitriol."

His forearm flexed in a captivating fashion.

"If I'd had more time with your former maids, perhaps they would have shared some tips. Joan's were so very helpful."

Silently, he guided the horse onto the road branching toward the east hills.

"And her *range*, Mr. MacPherson! It's a marvelous design. The boiler. The efficiency. The ovens and steam apparatus. Have you considered installing something similar in your kitchen?"

"Aye."

She frowned. "Why haven't you?"

"Campbell's farm burned to the ground, lass. His wife and the bairn she's carryin' will need a roof ere winter. That's the priority."

The ache in her middle expanded to squeeze her heart. Goodness, the selflessness of this man. He'd been abducted and shot trying to aid Broderick in Edinburgh.

According to Annie's letters, he'd then risked his recovery defending Campbell and his wife from a dangerous attacker. And now, he'd delayed finishing his own house to build one for his brother.

She sighed, her eyelids growing heavy as the horse rocked her against him. "The MacPhersons make splendid cider."

An ocean-deep chuckle. "Ye should taste our whisky, Duchess."

Grinning, she replied, "I probably shouldn't."

Her assessment was confirmed when they arrived home and he lifted her down. The world spun so wildly, she teetered into his arms. Rosemary, pine, and pleasantly earthy male skin filled her senses. Some kind of long, hard tool prodded her belly and ribs. It had prodded her hip earlier, too. Did he routinely carry a hammer home in his trousers?

"Oh, dear," she mumbled against his chest. "I think I'm a wee bit more than tipsy. Sergeant Munro would be scandalized. He didn't approve of drunkards."

He braced her elbows and set her firmly away. "Go inside," he ordered, his voice rough and threadbare. "Dinnae do aught but sit or lie down."

She managed to weave her way into the kitchen. Then she remembered he likely hadn't had dinner yet, because that was her job. But he'd told her to sit or lie down. Could she prepare dinner lying down? No. But she could slice a bit of ham, cheese, and bread while *sitting* down.

A perfect solution.

Lurching into the larder, she gathered her supplies and tried to recall where the ham had gone. In its place, she piled the last of the smoked brisket. Back in the kitchen, she selected her knife and began slicing. The bread was easy enough, though it came out dreadfully uneven. The brisket was harder and sliced too thick.

The cheese was her downfall.

Halfway through the sticky block, the knife ground to a halt. She needed to stand in order to apply proper pressure, she thought. Clumsily pushing to her feet, she braced her hips against the table and grasped the knife's handle. Using both hands, she steadied the block and pressed down.

A sudden give. Flashing pain. Blood.

She shook her head, staring at the deep gash near her thumb's knuckle. Between the cider, the heat, and the sight of blood dripping onto the table, Sabella's vision began to waver like a wheatfield in a windstorm. The knife clattered. She reached for the table's edge.

Somebody was shouting at a duchess. An enormous shadow sprinted across her vision. From behind her, a hand reached for her wrist.

And Sabella's mind misfired.

Pain. Blood. A hard grip on her wrist. A furious male.

She scrambled backward, yanking hard and jerking from his hold. Cold, slithering fear coiled inside her chest. It squeezed and pressured. It made her shake.

Smaller, Sabella. Ye must stay quiet and small. Wait for his temper to pass.

He froze. So much bigger than she remembered. Darker, too. But he was blurry and wavering. She couldn't see him clearly.

"Easy, lass."

Sobs gathered, expanding her breastbone. "Ye promised, Kenneth. Ye promised not to leave any more bruises." She stumbled and collided with the sideboard, cradling her wrist and remembering the pain. Vicious, throbbing pain. "I've been good. I did everything ye asked, didn't I? I didn't betray ye. Ye don't have to hurt him."

He was saying something, but she couldn't hear him. The gasping sobs were too loud. Like wailing gusts, they were.

She held her breath and shut her eyes, but a wheezing keen escaped, high-pitched and pathetic. She rasped. She begged. "Pl-please." She slid. "I'll wear the long sleeves. I won't tell anyone." She huddled on the stone floor and folded her arms tightly against her body. Rocking. Rocking. "Ye don't have to do it again. I'll be good."

His voice, low and calm, was as deep as oceans. "Sabella. Listen to me, lass."

Her knees drew up to protect her body. She lowered her head and tucked in tight. "I'll be good."

"I'm Alexander."

"I'll be good."

"Say my name, love. Alexander."

Hard, grinding breaths. God, her hand hurt and her head was spinning. "A-Alexander."

"Aye, that's it, Duchess." His voice softened to a hypnotic cadence. "All is well. Ye've had a bit too much cider. But all is well. Easy."

She lifted her head. The world was still blurry and tilting like a skiff at sea, but he hadn't lied. "Alexander?"

He crouched in front of her, his elbows propped loosely on his knees, his expression unreadable. "I need to lift ye up and bandage that hand."

She glanced down. Blood had seeped into the cream tartan. Her throat swelled with nausea. "Oh, God."

"Shh, lass. Look at me."

She did. Dark eyes, not green. Calmness, not vicious rage. "Alexander."

"Aye. Will ye let me touch ye?"

She nodded.

With motions that reminded her of smoke rising, he scooped her up and carried her into the scullery. There, he sat her on the washing bench and gently moved her injured hand beneath the tap. Cold water stung, but it also soothed.

"I—I stained yer plaid," she whispered.

"It'll come clean. Dinnae fash yerself."

"I ruined yer supper."

"I'll manage, lass. Havenae starved yet."

"I'm sorry. I don't usually fall apart like this."

His mouth twisted as he stared at her hand. A muscle near his eye twitched. "'Tis the drink. There's a weaker cider in storage at the distillery. I'll bring a cask home tomorrow." He switched off the tap and collected a towel from a lower shelf. After binding up her wounded thumb, he scooped her into his arms again and carried her to her bed. Then he helped her undress down to her shift.

It felt as comforting as a ritual.

If she weren't so weary, she'd thank him for taking care of her again. But she was already drifting off into a velvety gray mist and only managed to whisper, "Ye're such a gentleman, Alexander MacPherson."

Firm lips pressed against her forehead, and a voice as deep as an ocean murmured, "Not for much longer, Sabella Lockhart."

Chapter Nine

Alexander didn't have favorites among his brothers. But right now, his least favorite was Rannoch.

All MacPhersons were cut from the same mold, their roughest edges broken early by Angus and smoothed by Annie's sisterly fire. They'd all inherited a share of Angus's black temper. They all remembered his relentless lessons about controlling it. And they all would sooner swing an ax at their own ballocks than hurt a woman.

Rannoch didn't know about the previous night or what Sabella Lockhart had revealed when she was blootered on hard cider. But he was a MacPherson, so he should have known better than to come at Alexander with his shite accusations.

"What happened to yer hand?" asked his least favorite brother after Sabella and Magdalene left the yard to prepare dinner. "Tangle with the quarry stone again? Or is it somethin' to do with Miss Lockhart's injury?"

Alexander glanced at his split, swollen knuckles. "I mistook the arse end of a donkey for yer face. Donkey took exception to the comparison."

He hefted one of the cider casks from the wagon and carried it into the kitchen. Though the lasses glanced in his direction, Sabella continued to avoid his gaze. She hadn't looked him in the eye since last night. Not over breakfast. Not when he'd arrived home to find her hanging laundry. Not when he'd asked her how her hand was feeling. She'd assured him she was fine then carried his dried shirts inside without another word.

He'd begun the day in a black mood. Now, when he returned to the wagon, his patience for Rannoch's inquisition was down to bone on bone.

"She saved Annie's life, ye ken," Rannoch said. "She helped save yers, too. If ye'd seen her after ye were shot—"

"I was busy bleeding."

"I remember, brother. When we arrived, she was holdin' that tablecloth against yer chest like it was her own blood soakin' the floors."

He hated thinking about that day, about the memories he might have gotten wrong. "Do ye have a point, or are ye just here to foul the air like Bill the Donkey after too many turnips?"

"Whatever yer plan is for her, ye must reconsider."

"What makes ye think I have a plan?"

"Only every day I've kenned ye. Which is all of 'em."

Alexander glared at his youngest brother and hefted another cask onto his shoulder. "Mayhap I needed a maid and she needed a job. Did ye think about that?"

A snort. "And mayhap Bill the Donkey will cure his turnip affliction with purple mushrooms and unicorn shite."

"I wouldnae put it past Mrs. MacBean to try it."

Rannoch grunted his agreement.

They carried the two remaining casks down to the cellar. When they returned to the yard, Rannoch continued pressing his point. "Ye cannae keep her here, Alexander. Send her to live at Rowan House until Annie returns."

"This is Magdalene's idea, aye? The little nun thinks I need savin'."

"She thinks ye have Miss Lockhart in yer sights and that there's no better hunter in all of Scotland."

She wasn't wrong.

"But I ken she's wrong."

Alexander arched a brow.

"Ye dinnae have her in yer sights. Ye have her livin' in yer house. Ye have her wearin' yer plaid. Ye have her cookin' yer meals and washin' yer sheets. The hunt is long over." Rannoch leaned against the wagon, arms crossed, expression grim. "What was it ye told Campbell? Somethin' about what ye'd do to keep the woman ye want more than air and whisky under yer roof?"

Bloody Campbell and his big bloody mouth. "Ye dinnae ken what ye're talkin' about." Campbell might. Broderick might. Rannoch didn't. Not yet.

"I ken ye're willin' to do things the rest of us would balk at. Hell, brother. I've watched ye do them. Unsettles my stomach if I think too long about it."

"Ye always had the stomach of a wee, sickly lass. Those putrid piles of shite took Broderick's eye. They deserved everything they got."

"Aye. But if ye do this, if ye ruin her, ye'll regret it."

Alexander tilted his head. "Ruin? Who said aught about that?"

Rannoch's head jerked back. "Ye cannae be plannin' to wed a Lockhart."

He was planning a good deal more than that. But Rannoch wouldn't understand. He still believed life was a long road, and the more often he changed mounts, the more pleasurable the ride would be. He'd learn better one day. But until then, he couldn't possibly fathom how the truth focused a man.

For now, Alexander patted his shoulder and said calmly, "I'm pleased ye feel protective of her, brother. That's a good instinct and one that'll serve us well in the future. But if ye ever try to come between me and Sabella Lockhart again, ye willnae have to worry about purchasing fertility preventatives. I'll take yer ballocks for free."

"Have ye tried bluing?"

Sabella glanced up from her chopping board and frowned at Magdalene Cuthbert. "Bluing?"

Gray eyes took on the soft, patient cast that made Sabella feel like a precious simpleton—and a churl for resenting the feeling. Magdalene disappeared into the scullery for a moment. When she returned, she placed a bottle of blue powder on the kitchen table. "This is smalt. Add a wee bit to yer rinse water to whiten yer linens."

"Rinse water?"

Another patient glance. "Aye. Have ye been using only one tub for everything?"

Shoulders slumping, Sabella nodded.

"Even the starching?"

"Starching?"

This time, the other woman couldn't disguise her amusement, though it was tinged with compassion. "Not to worry, Miss Lockhart. Ye're doing well for never having performed such tasks. If ye like, I can pay another visit Monday next and teach ye the proper techniques."

With a nod, she thanked her and focused on something she could manage: chopping carrots. Sabella was determined to serve her guests a proper venison stew. As long as she followed Joan's instructions, the meal should come out reasonably palatable. She'd been deep into the cider's glow by the time Joan had dictated the receipt, so it was possible she'd missed a step or two. But stew couldn't be that complicated, surely.

Magdalene slid her pile of onions toward Sabella and started peeling potatoes. "For now, ye may use potato water for starching. Rice water is superior for some items, but I didn't see any in the storeroom. That's my fault, I expect. I fed Mr. MacPherson so much rice during his recuperation, he now loathes the stuff."

Sabella resisted the urge to query Magdalene about Alexander's recovery … for approximately ten seconds. "How bad was it?"

"His wound? Quite serious, I'm afraid. The bullet glanced off bone and lodged deep into the muscle. Along the way, it opened arteries. The surgeon removed it and repaired what he could, but the damage was extensive. He still suffers pain and swelling now and then. I suspect his bone didn't heal smoothly and continues to trouble him."

Sabella stilled her knife, forcing herself to breathe. How she hated the thought of him in such agony. "Is that why his recovery took so long?"

Magdalene's lips quirked wryly. "He can thank his MacPherson stubbornness for that. Weakened though he was, he refused to rest, particularly when his brothers needed help." She shook her head with exasperated affection. "He pushed himself to the point of collapse and reopened his wound twice. The last time it happened, I threatened to summon Lady Huxley for a thorough reprimand. He followed my instructions more diligently after that."

Sabella smiled. "Annie has her ways; that much is certain." She finished her carrots and stirred the coals beneath her stew pot. The venison was sizzling away in the tallow, just as Joan had said it would. She turned the pieces over, pleased to see they were nicely browned rather than charred black. Keeping her tone casual, she asked, "Is he fully healed now?"

"Aye. He has some strength to recover yet, but he looks much healthier now than when I visited last month." Magdalene paused. "When I fetched the wine from the cellar, I didn't see any whisky, nor was there any in the delivery wagon."

"He hasn't been drinking it of late," Sabella said absently. "He prefers cider."

"Cider. Alexander?"

Wiping her hands on her apron, Sabella turned to examine Joan's instructions again. She'd soaked the venison in milk to remove some of the stronger flavors, but she wondered if she should add bacon, as well. "Does bacon belong in a stew, do you suppose?"

"Miss Lockhart."

Sabella glanced up to see a concerned Magdalene staring at her bandaged thumb.

"Ye must ken by now how he feels about …"

Sabella blinked. "Aye?"

"Alexander can be quite ruthless."

"Perhaps he appears so to some, but I find him an admirable gentleman." Particularly after last night. She didn't recall anything after arriving home, not even how she'd cut her hand. But she'd awakened in her shift with her thumb bandaged and the kitchen cleaned. It had happened twice, now.

"A gentleman," Magdalene repeated incredulously. "*Alexander?*"

The scent of charring meat struck her nose. Sabella turned back to the stew pot. "Drat and blast!" She reached for the pitcher and poured far too much water into the pot, sloshing it onto the coals and drenching her hems. Slumping, she stared at what her panic had wrought—charred venison broth and a dampened fire.

Two hours later, after a great deal of sweat and suffering, Sabella carried a tureen of beef stew into the dining room while Magdalene followed with wine and bread.

Magdalene knew even less about cookery than she did, as it turned out, so she hadn't been much help after the great venison disaster. "Miss Lockhart, I wish I kenned more. I worked as a companion, lady's maid, and laundress."

"Never a kitchen maid?"

Magdalene shook her head. "I always hated kitchen work. If it's boiled rice or broth for an invalid, I could probably manage." The last part sounded as if it ended with a question mark.

They had no choice but to carry on. The venison had been ruined, and there wasn't any more, so Sabella followed Joan's instructions using beef instead. She and Magdalene struggled through the process together, laughing at their mistakes and groaning at the results by turns. Sabella felt a wee bit better for having a fellow failure by her side.

The potatoes and carrots turned out mushy, the bacon rubbery, and she'd added far too much rosemary. But Rannoch only winced after his first and third bites, and Alexander didn't wince at all. She and Magdalene had agreed the extra bread and wine would balance the scales.

They were wrong, upon further reflection, but the meal was technically edible, and Alexander, at least, ate every morsel.

After Rannoch and Magdalene departed, he even helped her wash up. As they stood together in the scullery, he handed her a bowl to dry and quirked a smile. "Fond of rosemary, are ye?"

She sighed. "Not that fond. I was compensating for the lack of sage. I should have been more restrained. Apologies."

"Dinnae fash." Another bowl went into the basin. His sleeves were rolled up to his elbows again, his muscles rippling with every small movement. "How's yer hand?"

She stacked the dried bowl on the bench and accepted the next one. "Better. Mrs. MacBean's salve helped."

"She's a mite daft and tryin' at times, but her formulations cannae be matched."

"Perhaps you could use it on your knuckles." She'd noticed his injuries when he'd arrived home with the wagon. Right now, his hands were veiled by soapy water, but the right one was swollen and scabbed. When she'd asked what had caused his injuries, he'd replied, "Fellin' trees is rough work, Duchess."

Now, he simply grunted and handed her another bowl.

"If I didn't say so last night, thank you for taking care of me again. My memory is a bit … well, missing." She chuckled. "The same thing happened with champagne once. I was in Paris for my fittings, and a friend invited me to attend her brother's house party."

"Was he a duke, too?" he asked dryly.

She laughed. "Aye, in a sense. He was a *comte* at the time, but he may be a *duc* by now." She turned away to shift the stack of bowls and fetch another towel. "It was an enchanted evening, silky and warm. We danced for hours beneath the stars. Whenever my glass emptied, he delivered a new one. A charming gentleman." Lost in her reverie, she murmured, "I suspect he might have kissed me in the hedge maze, though I can't recall."

Alexander ceased washing.

"Champagne is a sly saboteur of a lady's dignity, I discovered. The following morning, I awakened in my brother's villa with the worst megrim I'd ever suffered. This morning's headache was dreadful, but that one was much worse." She'd also had to wear long sleeves and gloves in the hottest part of a Paris summer, but she didn't discuss those matters with anyone. Not her lady's maid, not her friends, not anyone.

Noting Alexander's sudden tension, she wondered if it had been wise to mention Kenneth. She cast him a sideways glance. He stood rigid, his hands fisting so tightly beneath the water that his forearms bulged. Perhaps he wasn't angry but in pain. And perhaps she shouldn't have allowed him to do the washing.

Sabella frowned and stacked her final bowl. "Are your knuckles bothering you? Let me fetch the salve." She carried the bowls into the kitchen, tucked them away in the cupboard, then retrieved the small tin.

When she turned, Alexander filled the kitchen doorway. "Ye've mentioned Paris before, Duchess," he said. "Is that still where ye intend to go when ye leave Scotland?" His relaxed posture—arms crossed, one shoulder carelessly propped against the jamb—shouldn't have sent warning prickles down her spine. But his nonchalance didn't match his eyes. Those burned like coals.

Her heart gave the tiniest flutter. This was how he'd looked at her that first night in the tavern. Focused and purposeful, heated and dark. She didn't understand why that intense gaze enlivened her skin, why it stirred this strange ache in her blood.

She rested her hands on the edge of the sideboard beside her hips and answered, "Assuming all goes well, aye. But many things must fall into place first."

"Such as?"

"My gowns. I'm a fair hand with a needle, and Cleghorn's tartans are reasonably priced. But making enough frocks for a season will take time."

"How long?"

After some quick calculations, she answered, "At my current wage? Three weeks per gown. I shall require at least five for evening and seven for day dress, but with diligence, I'll have them fashioned before spring."

"Then ye'll travel to Paris, eh?"

"London first, Paris if necessary. Assuming I have sufficient funds, of course. When Annie returns in autumn, she'll doubtless insist on helping me." She smiled. "And I shall insist on repaying her once I ..."

His gaze settled on her throat. "Once ye're wed."

"Aye." She fingered the spot he'd fixated upon, a notch at the base of her throat. This shivery, sensitized feeling resembled fear, but it was different. She'd feared Kenneth—his anger, his satisfaction in her pain. Fear was ice-cold, shriveling her into nothing.

This was heat. Expansive, thrilling. It might be tinged with feminine alarm, but it was undeniably heat. Even now, she yearned for a wee dip in the river.

Furthermore, her alarm was nonsensical. He'd done nothing but take care of her and patiently tolerate her failures. Even on that horrid day in Edinburgh when he'd unwittingly caused her pain, he'd released her the moment she'd cried out. That single moment of concern for a woman he should hate had given Kenneth an opening to take his life.

Alexander was a good man, a true gentleman. If anything, she'd harmed him far more than he'd harmed her. The least she could do was tend his wounds.

"Why don't you let me put some salve on yer hand, Mr. MacPherson? Those injuries must pain you."

His biceps flexed, but his gaze didn't move. "I've been hurting a long time, lass. Nothin' new about that."

She nudged away from the sideboard and pulled out a chair. "Come," she ordered softly. "Sit. Let me help."

After a long silence, he did as she'd asked, lowering his giant frame onto the creaky wooden chair. Having him seated in front of her should have made her less nervous, not more. But she had to work to disguise her quickened breaths.

Taking up the tin in trembling hands, she gathered a dab on her fingertip then held out her hand. After a pause, he granted her request. His palm slid across hers, callused and warm, sparking a shivery cascade from her hand to the tips of her breasts.

Drat and blast. She must focus.

Careful to keep the contact light, she gently applied the salve to the swollen, broken skin around his knuckles then smoothed it over the back of his hand to his wrist. His injuries were worse—and more puzzling—than she'd thought. "Remind me again how this happened," she murmured.

"Doesnae matter."

"The skin is torn. It's almost as if you tried to pummel something unyielding. A boulder or a log, perhaps."

"Most things I pummel yield eventually. The benefits of bein' a MacPherson."

Using her thumbs, she traced his veins from his wrist to the reddened swellings. "I ken ye're strong, but you must be more careful."

A deep grunt. "Is this how ye'll tend yer husband, Duchess? Will ye scold the *duke* while ye patch him up?"

She frowned at his mocking tone. "I doubt a duke would have occasion to require patching up. At most, he might suffer from ink stains. That's what a valet is for."

"Right. Dukes have better things to do than get their hands dirty."

When she glanced up, she found nothing but hard, icy blackness staring back at her. Something had made him angry.

"Now, plantin' his sons in yer belly, that's what a duchess is for."

Shivering, she released him and retreated a step. But he wasn't finished.

"If ye cannae land yer duke, mayhap ye could offer to let him tup ye. Ruttin' is what mistresses are for. Ye'd ken plenty about that."

She turned away to cap the tin and place it on the sideboard. Why was he saying these hateful things?

"Better a duke's whore than a peasant's bride, eh?"

Flinching, she removed her apron and hung it on the peg beside the door. His bitter insults sliced deeper than they would have a week ago, before she'd begun imagining he thought her worthy of kindness. But in the process, they sliced through an old barrier she'd put in place long ago. Anger seeped upward from the cut. It filled her, stretched her to the cracking point.

"Or mayhap any man will do," he snarled. "A humble sergeant, for example. So long as he has something to offer, ye'll have favors to give. Is that it?"

She bit down on an equally vulgar answer involving what he could offer a sheep and how disappointed the creature might be. But that was something Annie or Joan might say. Not Sabella.

Never Sabella.

Rather than lobbing the volley with full fire, she edged toward the door. "I should check the line. The sheets may have dried by now."

"Careful not to roughen yer skin too much, Duchess. A soft duke might have a need for soft hands come spring."

Fighting the sickening urge to rage at him in return, she swallowed her responses: that he might have sound reasons to hate her, but she was not a whore, nor anything like it, and she didn't deserve to be insulted; that even if she *were* a woman of loose morals, he had no reason to take such personal offense, as if he were her husband rather than her employer. He *wasn't* her husband. He wasn't even attracted to her, as far as she could tell.

But she didn't say any of that. Instead, she did what she'd always done in the face of male anger—retreat. "If you're still hungry, there's bread in the—"

For a split second, raw fury flashed across his features. He shoved to his feet, sending the chair clattering across stone and knocking into the cupboard. The sudden move kicked her heart into a panicked gallop.

He glanced at where she'd automatically wrapped her arms around her middle. Within two breaths, he calmed. His hands relaxed. He retrieved the chair and slid it back into place. "I didnae mean to startle ye," he said grudgingly.

She almost left without answering. But that reservoir he'd opened with his unwarranted cuts was raging now. Before leaving the kitchen, she faced him squarely, dropped her arms to her sides, and raised her chin. Then she opened her reservoir's tap and let the tiniest bit run free.

"How gallant of you, Mr. MacPherson. Nevertheless, if you ever wish to be compared favorably to rabid badgers, I'd suggest acquiring manners superior to theirs. An oversized rodent's charms carry him only so far before everyone agrees his demise is preferable to his stink."

Chapter Ten

By Sabella's fifteenth day as a maid, she learned that laundry wasn't as bad as she'd thought. It was much, much worse.

"If ye lay the shirts flat on a nice, green lawn to finish dryin' in the sun, they'll whiten even more," advised Magdalene during Monday's instructional torture session.

Sabella glanced around at the tall, unruly grass, rocks, and weeds where the gardens should be. "Grand. Afterward, we can play lawn bowls."

She'd been working on her sarcasm. Her progress was swift for a beginner, she thought. Bitterness helped.

Magdalene smiled at her quip, though she still avoided full-on grinning. Sabella wished she knew how to reassure her friend that nobody cared about her teeth or any of her other features. It was her heart that mattered. That feature shone brighter than the sky.

The plain-faced, generous-hearted woman pulled a bedsheet from the second washtub of the four and moved it to a larger rinse tub a few feet away. Most of them were copper or wood. Some of them were boiling hot. All of them turned Sabella's hands into painful, irritated lobsters.

And thanks to the bluing, her lobsters were looking more purplish by the second. That was likely her fault. She kept forgetting to use her paddle.

Clicking her tongue, she wrung out one of Alexander's shirts then carried it to the line.

Meanwhile, with aggressive whacks, Magdalene began thrashing a pair of trews against a board with her battledore, a smaller paddle used to help expel the water and reduce wringing. Sabella suspected Magdalene used it to expel her vexations toward a certain MacPherson male. Surprisingly, it wasn't Alexander.

"What did Rannoch say after you helped deliver the bairn?" Sabella asked, pulling another dripping shirt from the rinse tub and flopping it onto a board.

"That he was glad to have been born male." *Whack, whack, whack.* "And gladder that the bairn wasn't his." *Flop, whack, whack.* "Then he wondered how any man was meant to sleep with so much caterwauling going on." *Whack, whack, WHACK.*

"Wasn't he the one who insisted on accompanying you to Mrs. Stewart's cottage?"

"Aye." *Whack, flop, whack.* "He's never approved of my apprenticeship with Dr. Cameron. I've told him there's no need to cart me everywhere."

"Can't you refuse the ride?"

"He follows me anyway." *Whack.* "Dr. Cameron has been understanding thus far, but I worry he may decide a female apprentice isn't worth the bother."

Sabella thought protectiveness must run in the MacPhersons' bloodline along with gigantic proportions and sour tempers. Since their argument a week ago, she'd scarcely spoken to Alexander, but Alexander would not stop griping at her about proper knife use, the inadvisability of ladders, and the risks of river currents.

He also griped about her conversing too frequently with the new lad he'd hired to tend the animals and haul heavy things. But that wasn't protectiveness. That was more of his nonsense, and she'd had her fill.

The lad in question approached carrying two more pails of well water, which was less yellowing than river water. "Here ye are, Miss Lockhart. I brought a ladle in case ye get thirsty." Gavin MacDonnell was a robust, strapping young man of seventeen years. He had a ready grin, curly brown hair, and sparkling blue eyes that must drive the young lassies wild.

Sabella got along with him famously, which seemed to displease Alexander to no end. Not that he'd witnessed her conversing with the lad. Alexander had been leaving before sunrise and returning with a weary scowl at dusk every day, long after Gavin went home. She'd concluded Gavin must have told him about their interactions.

When she'd asked the young man about it, he'd revealed that Alexander questioned him at length every morning. "I havenae said a cross word about ye, Miss Lockhart," Gavin swore earnestly. "Even when he threatens to castrate me like a bull calf in springtime, I make sure he kens how hard ye work."

Naturally, Alexander assumed Sabella's lack of virtue and devastating wiles would lead Gavin astray. Why *wouldn't* she seduce a seventeen-year-old boy between scrubbing floors and wringing out bed linens?

The thought made her snort.

Yesterday, Alexander had warned that if she spoke to Gavin "about aught but haulin', ye might as well dismiss him yerself, because he'll be gone."

The absurdity galled her more every time she thought about it. And she still didn't know what had precipitated his fit of irrational temper. All she'd done was recount her misadventures after imbibing too much champagne. Tales of drunken regret were hardly rare, even among genteel ladies. And for a man who distilled whisky for a living to pass such judgments was breathtakingly obtuse.

"It could be worse," Sabella observed as Magdalene began beating another pair of breeches. "At least Rannoch doesn't accuse you of improprieties with the doctor."

"He wouldn't." *Dunk, plop, whack.* "To him, I'm scarcely a woman." *Whack, whack, WHACK.* "The idea of any man engaging in improprieties with me wouldn't cross his mind."

Sabella frowned and hung another shirt on the line. Magdalene wasn't wrong. Rannoch flirted reflexively with females of every variety. It was part of his charm. Notable exceptions included his sisters-in-law, Mrs. MacBean, and Magdalene Cuthbert, whom he treated like a nun.

Considering how the young woman's longing gaze followed Rannoch like a midge swarm when he wasn't looking, this was deeply unfortunate for Magdalene. Sabella hadn't asked her about it because she didn't have any solutions to offer. Indeed, her own unrequited longing problem seemed to be worsening by the day, despite reversing her opinions about his being a gentleman.

Later that evening, after Magdalene and Gavin departed, Sabella carried her soap, towel, and fresh clothing down to the river for her daily—now nightly—ritual. Stripping naked, she waded deep into the water, chiding her body for its stubborn arousal.

"He's a rude, beastly, presumptuous oaf," she muttered to her bosom. "Other men have muscles. Other men are tall and strong." Her nipples didn't care. Neither did her mind, which fed her visions of soap sluicing down his chest and firm lips closing around a bite of her food. Or a bit of her. "Other men have deep voices and strapping shoulders." She soaped her skin and hair, rinsed beneath the cold water, then tossed the soap onto the bank. "Other men wouldn't accuse you of indiscriminate harlotry."

The river swirled and danced between her thighs, both soothing and stimulating. A forbidden thought intruded. She'd had too many of those lately. Sensual, erotic, forbidden thoughts about whether kissing must be restricted to mouths, and whether his mouth would quench like pulsating water.

With a sigh, she conceded that she might be prone to *discriminate* harlotry. Highly discriminate. Exclusive, in fact, to a single beastly, presumptuous oaf.

Just as her hand was sliding down to alleviate her harlotry, movement downstream caught her eye. Two deer were dipping their heads for a drink. A third moved into view from beyond the east wing of the house.

She froze.

It was munching.

"No," she breathed. Quickly, she thrashed her way back to shore, pausing only to throw one of Alexander's shirts over her wet, naked body. "No, no, no!" All three animals raised their heads then bolted away. Sabella scrambled up through the alder grove and dashed to the small patch of tilled ground near the southeast corner of the house.

As she stared down at the uprooted, denuded corpse of her rosebush, despair clogged her throat. The lavender likewise had been uprooted and left lying like refuse a few yards away. But her rosebush had suffered the worst of it. All the tender young leaves that had emerged over the past week were stripped away. Thorns hadn't protected the new growth sprouting from half-broken stems. Roots that were just beginning to gain purchase had been torn asunder.

The longer she stared at the damage, the more anger gushed forth from her open reservoir. She stomped to snatch up the lavender lying on the ground like a pulled weed. Glaring toward the woodlands where the deer had disappeared, she screamed, "If I see ye again, I'll turn ye into stew meat, ye vile, ravenous creature!"

She stomped back to her cultivated patch and crouched to replant the struggling sprig. Squeezing water from her dripping hair, she wet the soil. Then she carefully examined the remains of her rosebush. Helpless fury choked her. She straightened to shout toward the tree line, "Drat, blast, and devil take it! I hate you, ye infernal beastie! I hope ye get yerself shot!"

"That's a hell of a thing to say to a man, Duchess."

She spun to find a huge, looming, sweaty MacPherson male standing feet away and staring at her like she'd lost her mind. Black eyes swept from her hair to her toes then resettled below her collarbone, reminding her that she wore nothing but his shirt. And she was wet underneath. And the shirt gaped obscenely. Yet, apart from an initial bloom of tingling heat, she couldn't bring herself to be embarrassed.

She was too infuriated.

"Why haven't you enclosed the garden?" she snapped, pointing toward the drying yard. "It's nothing but weeds! Grass and weeds as far as the eye can see!"

He blinked, though he didn't lift his eyes past her chin. "Aye."

She plucked up her sad, mutilated rosebush, and held it aloft. "*This* is what happens when ye don't bother with fencing, Mr. MacPherson. Look at it!"

"I'm lookin', lass."

"I can't grow so much as a lettuce leaf without those red pests thinkin' I prepared them a feast." She turned her back and bent forward to replant her sad, sad rose. Scooping out the soil, she gently rearranged the roots in the hole and squeezed more water from her hair. "I don't know why I'm bothering," she said, giving her hair a wee shake then patting the soil back into place. "It shan't survive further incursions by the horned menace."

His voice was hoarse when he corrected, "They have antlers, nae horns."

"Ye have no kitchen garden," she snapped, spinning to confront him. "Your well is a dratted mile from anyplace convenient. The drying yard is mud when it rains and dust when ye're lucky. And I can't dry your shirts properly because I don't have a lawn." She pointed once again at the expanse of weeds behind the house. "A lawn! Ye haven't even bothered to scythe!"

Eyes flickering strangely, he rasped, "I'll tell Gavin to start scythin' tomorrow."

Her fury boiled over. "He could have started a week ago if ye hadn't barred me from speaking—"

"Ye're not to go near him. Neither of ye need the distraction."

"Aye, right." She snorted and folded her arms across her bosom. "Between scrubbing the coppers and starching your collars, I like to take a wee pause for seduction, especially with a lad six years my junior. Harlotry is very relaxing. Loosens the joints."

His nostrils flared. His jaw flexed. "When did he depart?"

"Oh, after we dallied. I thought I'd have a wee dip to recover from all the exertion."

"Ye're flyin' close to the sun, lass."

Shouldering past the infuriating giant, she stomped down the bank to collect her plaid, soap, and clothing. "Is it too much to ask for a dratted warning before you sneak home in the middle of the day?"

"'Tis past six."

Propelled by rage, she climbed up the slope in four strides and halted beside him. "Every day, you come home at nine, sometimes later. Sometimes after dark!"

"Miss me?"

He leaned against a tree with one long arm extended and the other propped on his hip. Despite his relaxed posture, she sensed volatile energy radiating underneath. Perhaps this was him in a temper. And perhaps she didn't care.

"It's about scheduling, Mr. MacPherson," she snapped. "To plan properly, I must know what your days are like. Are ye working at the distillery or your brother's house?"

"Both."

"What hours will ye be keeping?"

"Dinnae ken. Feels like all of 'em."

"How am I to know when to have dinner prepared?" She waved at the river. "Or when to have my bath?"

Swiping a hand over his beard, he closed his eyes and muttered something about Christ and crosses.

"Or perhaps I should bathe while you're at home," she said sarcastically. "It's not as if ye'll be tempted by my nakedness. That's only a risk for *other* men, aye? Gavin MacDonnell and Sergeant Munro."

His eyes flashed hot enough to burn. His jaw hardened to granite. He looked ready to kill something with his bare hands. This was Alexander MacPherson at his most intimidating.

She should fear him. She should cower and appease as she'd learned to do when facing Kenneth's temper. She should shrink into nothingness.

But Alexander wasn't Kenneth. And Sabella wasn't afraid.

She felt enlivened. Expanded. Her skin hummed and sizzled. Her fingertips pressed into the plaid, wishing it was his muscular neck. Her thighs squeezed together to quell the pulsebeat she hadn't quenched earlier.

He lowered his head, lowered his voice to an ocean-deep rumble. "I'll say this once fer yer sake, Duchess. Listen well. Dinnae. Fucking. Push me."

Radiant spirals bloomed across her body. Lightning arced across her nipples and her sex, her scalp and her nape, her thighs and her throat. She was steeped in his scent, swelling into a burn.

She didn't know what might push him. But everything inside her wanted to find out what would happen when she did.

"Perhaps I should bathe again now, hmm?" she taunted softly, holding up her hand to show him the soil beneath her fingernails. "A dirty lass needs washing."

The shift happened in his eyes first. They'd always burned when they lit upon her—hatred, she'd assumed. Resentment for who she was, what she was. The burning made her nervous but not fearful because he controlled it. He controlled *himself* to an eerie degree.

She'd assumed he wouldn't bother restraining himself if he wanted her. Why would he bother?

Now, she saw what he'd been hiding. The black was a forge. A velvety abyss designed not for burning but for binding. Claiming.

The abyss looked upon her with unveiled possession, and a wicked smile curved his wicked mouth. That mouth swooped down to claim hers as powerful arms pulled her in tight against impossible hardness.

She dropped everything—the plaid, the soap. She needed her hands free for this. To grasp and hold his hair, to bring him closer and hold him still for her kiss. Because she *was* kissing him. And he was kissing her. His tongue took her mouth while hers welcomed him home.

The forge fired hotter. Their breath pumped faster. Need spiked higher.

He pivoted and the world spun. He braced her back against bark and her head spun. He cupped her throat and slid his palm down over yearning flesh and needy bones. He nudged his gaping shirt aside and traced her nipple with a callused fingertip. The friction made her writhe.

Winding her hair around his fist, he arched her neck against his open mouth. Her hands left his cool, black hair to go exploring, but her urgency didn't leave time for delicacy. She needed his shirt gone *now*. She needed her nipples touching him *now*.

She tore at the linen, clawing it away from his muscled belly and yanking until he grunted and tore it off over his head. Another kiss, deep and grinding and not nearly enough to quench her. She arched her back to force her breasts harder against him, but he kept that hand bound up in her hair, holding her tightly to brace her for his mouth. Then his mouth moved to where she needed him.

Oh, God, yes. There. On her breasts. She'd dreamed of this, imagined it so many times, but the reality was better. This Alexander was infinitely better.

Hot, engulfing pleasure devoured the sensitized tips whole. He intensified his suckling as she pleaded with him to answer the aching, gnawing need for more pressure, a sharper bite. His teeth offered pressuring nibbles and pleasurable, peaking stings. As he shifted back and forth between her nipples, his beard chafed the delicate areolas. By the time he lifted his head, she was consumed. Wet. Agonizingly empty.

And distracted by his mouth returning to suckle her throat while his fingers tickled her nape.

That explained how she missed the part where he'd torn her shirt down the middle, leaving her wearing an open scrap, the summer heat, and nothing more. But when he pulled back briefly, she glimpsed the results of his attentions—her skin flushed scarlet where his mouth, teeth, and beard had been. Heat pulsed everywhere. Her bones loosened and liquified.

She groaned his name, a plea for easing.

"Too fast, but ye need it." He absently strummed her nipple and held her gaze with that black forge until she felt the binding—binding, melting, and merging. "Aye, ye need it badly, lass. How long have ye gone, eh?" His nostrils flared as he breathed her in. "No matter. I need it, too. Ye can take me."

His hand worked between their bodies. Then he was shoving down his breeches and releasing a huge, darkly flushed stalk with a rounded head and fascinating veins. Her eyelids fluttered at the enormity. Surely, he wouldn't be putting that inside—

His mouth swooped down to claim hers again as his hand hooked beneath her knee. He hitched her higher, bent his knees, and opened her legs wide.

One gasping breath later, a hot, impossibly wide *something* intruded against her opening, stroking and swirling for a moment.

His gaze hinted at the feverish need driving him. He gripped her legs harder, yanking them apart to settle his hips deeper. Then his hips angled against her differently, and he shifted her higher against the tree.

The pressure separating her folds grew.

"Ye're runnin' like a river, love. Swollen tight. Let me in. Let me ease ye."

She dug her fingernails into his neck, focusing on his eyes rather than the painful pressure. It was so much that she had to hold her breath and grit her teeth.

"Tight," he repeated in a growl. "How long, Sabella? How long?"

She shook her head and clawed deeper. Stretching. The beginnings of pain. She whimpered her distress. "Alexander," she panted.

Upon hearing his name, his feverish light turned explosive. Veins in his forehead pulsed. His brow crashed into a pained glower.

In the next moment, he clutched her tightly, withdrew slightly, and thrust hard and deep. Pain tore her open. She whimpered and gritted her teeth, trying to breathe through the dreadfully stinging, relentless pressure.

He went still, his muscles rigid as stone. "Sweet, bluidy Christ, woman," he panted. "Ye're a *virgin?*"

Chapter Eleven

Entering heaven had put Alexander in hell. His cock had never been so agonizingly engorged, which made him even bigger than normal. It would be a tight fit with an experienced lass. Manageable, but tight.

With a virgin? Sweet, bloody Christ. Her gasping whimpers and sharp-biting nails left no doubt about whether it was heaven or hell for her.

Yet, with half his length buried inside her fist-tight sheath and his instincts roaring loudly enough to drown out an ocean, he wasn't sure he could stop. "Dinnae move," he ordered. If she didn't move, he could fight this. He could withdraw.

Probably.

He almost managed it. But she moved, rubbing those wee, ruby nipples against his chest. The muscles of her slick sheath fluttered around his cock like a butterfly fighting a net. She tilted her hips, forcing him an inch deeper.

His vision darkened. His head lifted from his body. And the need to claim her filled him until nothing else existed.

He surged into her, driving a gasping cry from her long, beautiful throat. Aye, she was his. *Thrust.* His. *Thrust.* His alone.

"Al-Alexander."

She was his. Not Munro's. Not young Gavin's. Not the French duke's. No other man had felt this silken heat flexing around him. *Thrust.* Alexander's cock was the first. *Thrust.* He was the first. *Thrust.*

She'd fooled him with her taunts about dirty lasses and seduction pauses. *Thrust.* She'd tempted him with her wet, white skin beneath nothing but his thin shirt. *Thrust.* Her nipples had been begging. Begging. *Thrust.* Her mons had been a shimmering, golden shadow teasing. Teasing. *Thrust.*

His cock had readied to fill her in seconds. Then she'd bent over in front of him, presenting those sweet, firm buttocks and long, bonnie thighs for his consideration.

He'd nearly come watching her water her plants with her hair.

God, this woman. *Thrust.* His woman. *Thrust.* This sweet, lustful woman. *Thrust.*

He'd mistaken her blistering arousal for that of an experienced mistress slaking her needs after a drought. Naturally, she'd be drenched and desperate, he'd told himself. She'd tear at his shirt and grip his neck like a lifeline and shove her breasts into his mouth. An experienced woman would boldly demand his hands and his cock. She'd swell so tight, she'd feel like a virgin.

A virgin.

"Too much, Alexander." Her voice now was a frayed plea. Tremulous. Distressed. "Hurts."

He halted. Focused on how she panted against his shoulder. Felt how she clawed his neck.

She was his. And she was delicate. Those dainty breasts he'd devoured like a hungry beast were bright, ruby red from the pressure of his teeth and mouth. That fluttering sheath he'd breached with headlong urgency quaked as she flinched with every thrust.

She was his to take, aye. But she was also his to care for as delicate creatures demanded.

Just now, she was demanding, "Need more."

More?

"Let me slide my hand between us," she panted. "I want … There's a wee spot I can touch that will …"

Was she giving him tupping instructions? Bloody hell.

He lifted her and pivoted, taking her to the ground. With quick motions, he dragged the plaid she'd dropped earlier over the grass and laid her down. Propping on his elbow above her, he watched those leaf-green eyes as he shifted his to penetrate her at an easier angle.

A surprised blink instead of a wince. Good.

He drew her knees up and wrapped those long legs around his waist.

A wee, dainty moan as she licked her lips. Very good.

He kissed her. Better.

He thumbed her nipple. Hotter.

He trailed his fingers down to the top of her slick, swollen folds—and nudged.

"Oh, God." She arched. "Again."

He did it again, swirling this time.

She squeezed his cock until he thought his head might explode. Or perhaps his ballocks, which ached to flood her with seed.

He chased her hitching breaths and feminine groans like prey in a hunt—steadily, relentlessly.

Her pleas became a chant. "Aye, Alexander. Aye, there. Round and round. God, it's so good."

He sank as far inside as her sheath would allow, inching forward little by little as her spiraling arousal warmed her, wetted her, deepened the home she made for him.

"Alexander! It's so goooood."

He smiled, watching his woman flush and bloom. She shivered as she neared her peak, eyes glowing earthly green and locking on his mouth.

"Kiss me. Move. Please."

He kissed her softly. Then he moved. A small nudge for his needy woman. *Thrust.* A tiny pluck of her tender bud. *Thrust.* Drenched and slick. *Thrust.* Tight as a fist. *Thrust.* Hotter than summer's peak. *Thrust.* A sobbing affirmation of pleasure from his woman. *Thrust.* His. *Thrust.* Exquisite. *Thrust.* Woman. *Thrust.*

She seized upon him, clawed into him, milked and goaded him. Her screams of ecstasy sent the birds in the trees skyward. And while he took his woman with a final, frenzied pounding, she enfolded him in light and launched him from hell into heaven. Pure, radiant bliss exploded outward from everywhere they were joined—their mouths, their sex, their skin.

A long while later, sound returned. First the leaves. Then the birds. The rushing river and the rustling grass.

Sensation came next—the wetness between them and her fingers stroking his beard. Then her hand settled onto his scar, tracing the puckered patch of skin with trembling hesitation.

"Does it hurt?" she murmured.

"I should be askin' you that question, Duchess." He rasped. "But the answer's no."

As gently as he could, he withdrew. After stripping them both, he gathered her up and carried her down into the river. As the cool water swirled around them, she shivered in his arms and buried her face against his neck.

When they were deep enough, he lowered her to her feet and gently washed between her thighs. She hissed in a breath. Slowly, however, she relaxed against his hand and let the water soothe her soreness.

"Ye should have told me ye were untried," he rasped.

"Why should I need to say something so obvious?"

"It wasnae obvious to me."

She shoved his hand away then shoved *him* away with a simmering frown. "Only because you drew preposterous conclusions about Sergeant Munro."

"He was a stranger to ye before he showed up in Edinburgh searchin' for yer brother."

Her hands moved beneath the water in the mysterious, alluring motions of a lass having a wash. "Aye. And your point is?" she said tartly.

Alexander glanced down. He was chest-deep in cold water after coming so hard he'd gone blind. How in bloody blazes had she managed to arouse him this quickly? She was vexed and snappish. Her nakedness was nothing but a shifting pink swirl beneath the water. The only visible part of her was her face, and that was glaring daggers. His cock not only didn't care, the damned thing was standing at attention and giving her a salute.

Shaking his head, he attempted to focus. "Munro was an ambitious sod prone to thinkin' of his policing duties in grand terms. He spent a decade chasin' dubious glory in the Inverness constabulary. The thought of shuttin' down the MacPherson Distillery gave him nocturnal emissions."

The sergeant had been forced to change targets temporarily after Broderick, with help from Campbell and Alexander, had broken Kenneth Lockhart out of the Inverness jail. Knowing that the well-connected lord was close to escaping justice for his crimes, Broderick had hauled him to a remote corner of the glen, beaten the man to within an inch of his life, then lost track of him after the future Mrs. Broderick MacPherson stumbled upon them in the dark and distracted him from finishing the job. Lockhart had escaped back to Edinburgh—aided by his sister—where he'd managed to target the MacPhersons again.

Sergeant Munro, eager to return Lockhart to the Inverness jail, had surveilled the house Lockhart shared with his sister for signs of the escapee. Alexander had done the same thing. He understood how watching Sabella Lockhart affected a man. So, when he'd discovered that she and Munro were meeting in secret, he'd concluded she was either working against her brother in secret or she was leading Munro away from Lockhart. Considering how she'd helped her brother leave Inverness, Alexander had thought the latter far more likely.

After the putrid pile of demon's shite had been sent to hell by Broderick's blade, Munro hadn't returned to Inverness to continue his war against unlicensed whisky production. Instead, he'd resigned his position—the one he'd spent decades pursuing—to help a bonnie aristocrat he scarcely knew mop up the mess. As far as Alexander was concerned, that was proof of Sabella Lockhart's power. He'd felt it himself.

Hell, he felt it now.

"Once yer brother was dead, Munro had nae earthly reason to stay in Edinburgh," he argued. "Yet, he resigned his post for you. What in bluidy hell was I supposed to think?"

Leaf-green eyes snapped at him like the tip of a whip. "Perhaps that he was an honorable man who'd devoted his life to serving the causes of order and justice."

He scoffed. "Servin' the cause of bloated honorifics, ye mean."

"And perhaps there are men in this world more interested in *helping* a lady in distress than in bedding her."

"With other lasses, mayhap. With you? Nah."

She threw up her hands. The exasperated gesture splashed water across his shoulders and face. She either didn't notice or didn't care. "Now, I'm a veritable succubus, feeding on the lusts of unwitting males. Is that it?"

It wasn't the worst explanation he'd heard. "Makes more sense than ye bein' a virgin."

This time, she splashed him on purpose. "Ye big, oafish beast! What have I ever done to warrant such aspersions on my virtue?"

He raked a hand through his hair and swiped away the dripping water from his beard. "'Tis not about what ye've done, lass. 'Tis about what ye are."

"What, pray tell, is that?"

He took in her fury-flushed skin and long, elegant neck, her delicate bones and willowy frame, her verdant eyes lashing him for his presumptions and summoning his most barbaric instincts like a lodestone. She was an unearthly pleasure garden locked behind walls and gates. If a man had a key, he could unlock the wonders of heaven. How to tell her?

"To a man, ye're temptation itself."

She threw up her hands again and thrashed angrily toward the riverbank. "And you are infuriating!" she yelled over her shoulder.

He thought she might have continued ranting about his hard head being a good substitute for a battledore, but he was a mite distracted by her dripping-wet nakedness as she emerged like a water nymph from the swirling depths.

By God, she was a bonnie sight. Long, slender legs curved into firm, heart-shaped buttocks. Wet, golden hair brushed the base of her elegant spine. When she bent forward to snatch up the plaid, his breath stopped. Then she gave it a shake, and his heart stopped.

"My brother's crimes against ye don't give you license to accuse me of harlotry!" She wrapped herself in the plaid. "Or to accuse a good man like Sergeant Munro of lascivious intentions!"

Though he wasn't a particularly good man, Alexander's intentions were deeply lascivious. He could scarcely think past the resonant pounding in his cock.

"For your information, Mr. MacPherson, the sergeant's attachment to me was fatherly. I happened to resemble his beloved daughter, Isobel." She collected the discarded soap but left the towel and his clothing on the ground. "He was a dear man. A friend." Her voice quavered on the last two words, either from anger or grief. "Even if he had desired a different sort of arrangement—"

"Havin' ye as his mistress, ye mean."

"—I would never stoop to trading my virtue for coin and comforts."

Dark instincts, deep and cold, seeped up from the well he preferred to keep safely sealed. Lately, it had sprung a few leaks. He blamed her. "Isnae that precisely what ye plan to do, Duchess? Sell yerself and yer womb to a duke? Mayhap his coin is better, but I reckon he'd be purchasing the same goods."

Her eyes narrowed. "You are swine. No! Ye're a vile insult to swine."

"Cannae blame any man for buyin' a ticket, costly or no." That pleasure garden was sinful beyond imagining. If other men knew what he'd discovered inside, he'd spend the rest of his life defending the gates.

"Now, I'm a whore for wanting a husband!"

"If the grass stains fit, Duchess."

"Ye rude, enormous …" She sputtered, reaching for another insult. "Highlander!"

Slowly, he grinned. "Too bad for ye that ye'll be marryin' this rude, enormous Highlander, eh?"

"Marry?" Outrage lit her ablaze. "I'd sooner wed Bill the Donkey and feed him from the turnip bin!"

His grin faded. He started toward her. When the water reached his waist, he stopped, glanced down, and cursed. He wished the river was colder. With a shrug, he continued toward the bank.

Leaf-green eyes drank him in then locked on his groin and went alarmingly wide. She stumbled back a step, tripping on a tree root and catching herself against an alder.

Calmly, he plucked up the towel and dried himself. "Ye didnae give yer virginity to Bill the Donkey," he said. "Ye gave it to me. So, ye'll wed me."

Blushing bright ruby, she turned sideways to peer with tremendous interest at a patch of weeds. "I most certainly will not."

He donned his trews, wincing as he tucked his cock away. Bloody hell, the thing loved her temper. But there would be no relief until they were wed, and that would take at least a day or two. "I might have put a bairn in ye," he pointed out. "Now, I'm nae duke or French count, but my seed plants in fertile ground same as any man's."

"I refuse to wed a man who thinks me a whore."

No. She refused to wed a man who was beneath her. As always, the thought provoked his blackest instincts.

Controlling his movements through long practice, he shrugged on his shirt then raked his hair out of his face. "I ken ye're not a whore. Whores are cheap. A pedigree like yers commands a higher price, Duchess."

She sucked in a breath at the insult.

"Dinnae fash," he said. "I'm keen to pay it. Mayhap ye'll add a bit of bluing to the MacPherson bloodline, eh?"

Shaking with tension, she spun to bellow at him, "I shall never, *ever* marry you, Alexander MacPherson! Do you hear me?"

"Hard not to hear ye, lass."

"Ye're a rude, insufferable beast—"

"Aye, ye mentioned that before."

"—and nothing on this earth could convince me to bind myself to such an odious, bad-tempered, blackhearted—"

"What happens if yer belly swells before spring? Think a duke will pay if he kens he's buyin' used—"

She lobbed her soap at his head with a gritted scream. He ducked, and the missile plunked into the river. *Bloop*. By the time he straightened, she was halfway to the house.

He climbed the slope in two strides. "Where ye headin', lass?"

"The kitchen. There are knives there. I'd suggest ye don't follow me if ye wish to keep yer appendages attached!" She detoured to the drying yard and yanked one of his shirts off the line, followed by her shift and stockings. "Tomorrow, I shall take Magdalene's invitation to stay at Rowan House." She wadded a pair of his breeches and threw them at his chest. He noted they were cleaner than usual. "Ye can do yer own dratted laundry from now on!"

Her declaration focused him, shoving his instincts aside long enough for the more reasoned part of his mind to take over. He'd pushed her too far. Bloody hell, he'd let his instincts rule, and now she was leaving.

He ran a hand over his beard as she stomped toward the kitchen, slamming the door behind her. God, he'd made a hash of this. There was nothing for it. He'd have to take a different tack.

Everything he knew about Sabella indicated she should have taken his offer, or at least reacted more favorably. But much of what he thought about her had been wrong. All the cool delicacy he'd seen before was another piece of her cage—the innermost layer she'd worn to protect herself. As she grew more comfortable with him, she'd revealed the woman beneath—persistent, resilient, domestic. Then she revealed more—fiery, sarcastic, sensual. While he didn't quite know what to do with this Sabella, he did know how much he wanted her.

More than air and whisky.

So, he would persuade her to wed him. And he would keep her under his roof until she wanted him the same way. It was just a matter of applying the right pressure in the right places.

Alexander wasn't skilled at everything. Apparently, wooing was a weak point. Controlling his jealousy? Not his finest talent. And soothing his woman's temper might be the skill most in need of honing. He suspected the first two would improve the third.

He'd work on it. Meanwhile, marriage wouldn't wait.

Flanking and driving were old hunter's tactics. He was an excellent hunter. He was also adept at designing systems that took advantage of natural forces rather than working against them. The flow of the river drove the pump, which fed the cisterns in the attic, which piped water down to the kitchen via gravity.

Sabella Lockhart had a nature, and she wanted a husband. He just had to convince her that he was her best option. So, he would apply a bit of pressure, redirect her toward the right conclusions, and let her flow into his hands like water from a tap.

How hard could it be?

CHAPTER TWELVE

"Well, ye've done it this time, son." Angus MacPherson cuffed Alexander's neck as he'd done since he and his brothers were wee lads. "Damned shame. She'd have made a bonnie bride."

Alexander scowled at the door leading from the dining room to the kitchen. It still reverberated from her slam. "All I said was that she could leave after the bairn is born, so long as she leaves it with me."

"Aye. Probably sounded better in yer head, eh?"

"I wasnae serious, Da." He raked a hand through his hair and drank his tea. Sabella made the best damned tea he'd ever tasted. Her bacon was also excellent. "I need more time with her. If I can persuade her to stay for short while, I can use the momentum to carry us into a long while. Then gravity takes over."

Angus patted his shoulder and took a bite of his eggs. "Let Nora talk to her. She's been practicing puttin' up with my nonsense of late. Ladies like to commiserate over how daft their men are. Gives 'em a wee sense of accomplishment to boast about how they've managed not to kill us."

Nora was Eleanora Baird, a dressmaker from Inverness with whom Angus had been carrying on a torrid courtship over the past year. Angus hadn't yet convinced Nora to marry him, which meant he had little to offer in terms of bride wooing strategies. But Alexander had hoped inviting them to breakfast might apply pressure to Sabella.

It had, but things hadn't gone as well as he'd planned.

"Mayhap ye shouldnae have said aught about takin' her virginity," said Da.

"How else were ye meant to find out?"

"And mayhap ye could inform the lass that ye *want* to marry her whether there's a bairn or no."

Alexander shook his head. "Because that's worked so well for you."

Angus glowered and downed his tea. "Could use some whisky."

Munching his crisp, salty bacon, Alexander brooded on what had gone wrong. He'd applied pressure in the right places, he thought. Sabella was from a genteel background. She wouldn't want to be seen as having broken society's rules. Therefore, he'd brought in two people whose good opinion she might value, Angus and Nora. He'd added pressure by revealing the reason Sabella must marry him. Then he'd offered a vent, as one must do in a piping system, by telling her a wee fib. There was no way in holy hell he'd let her birth their bairn then leave. But she liked having her goals defined by a schedule, and he thought it would help her justify the commitment.

It hadn't. She'd dumped his eggs in his lap and stormed off to the kitchen.

"Look, son," said Da as he pushed his plate away. "I ken how it pains ye not to have her."

Alexander gritted his teeth and nodded. It did pain him. Angus knew better than anyone. Better than Campbell or Broderick, even. Alexander was the brother most like their da. A bit quieter with his bluster, perhaps, and his temper burned cold instead of hot. But they were similarly calculating, similarly ruthless, similarly made.

Angus cuffed his nape again and gave him a shake. "She's yers. Of course ye wanted to claim her as soon as ye recognized her. But if we go about turnin' lasses into wives the first day we clap eyes on 'em, everyone'll think we're as mad as Mrs. MacBean."

Alexander grunted his agreement. "Like ye did with Lillias, eh?" Angus had offered marriage to Annie's mother within an hour of meeting her. As a widow with a wee daughter to feed, she'd agreed to wed the giant with four sons who "needed civilizin'."

Angus nodded. "MacPherson males ken sooner than the lasses do. It's how we're built."

"Except Rannoch."

"Aye." A father's sigh. "Except Rannoch. It'll hit him harder for the delay. No help for that. Lad's goin' to suffer. But our problem isnae blindness. It's seein' too clearly and too soon. Ye cannae just take a lass and keep her under yer roof, son, even if she belongs to ye. She has to be won."

"Fine. But how?" He gestured to the eggy mess on the carpet after her fit of pique.

"She liked ye well enough to let ye bed her once. That's encouragin'."

He shrugged.

"Ye could try askin' her what she wants."

"She wants to gut me like a trout."

"Aye. What I meant was, ask her what she wants in exchange for weddin' ye. That's how I persuaded yer mam to wed me after I broke Ewan Wylie's jaw. She was also in a guttin' mood."

Alexander quirked a smile. Ewan Wylie had been a rival for Mam's affections, and Angus had nearly killed the man twice. "What did ye promise her?"

"That I wouldnae kill him. Said he'd be important someday. Yer mam had her visions, ye ken. I also promised that each of our bairns would have land. And that she wouldnae have to tend the laundry."

Come to think of it, he didn't recall Muriel MacPherson ever washing laundry. Angus had always hired a laundress. Perhaps Alexander could offer a similar arrangement to Sabella.

"What have ye offered Nora?" asked Alexander.

Angus's glower deepened. "I bought her a shop here in Glenscannadoo, but she's reluctant. Says she doesnae want to split her attention away from her shop in Inverness."

"Understandable."

"Nae, it bluidy isnae!" he growled. "Stubborn woman willnae listen. She willnae wed me. She says she likes her life and doesnae wish to upend everythin' she's worked for. Truth is she doesnae wish to be beholden to me because she fears I'll use the new shop to force her hand."

"Which ye would."

"Of course I would! I'm nae daft."

Alexander nodded. "Female nonsense drives a man straight to the whisky bottle."

"Aye." Angus shoved his plate away. "Speakin' of which, I'm thirsty."

"Sorry, Da. I've none here."

Da peered at him like he'd suddenly sprouted a pig's nose. "No whisky. In *your* house. None, Alexander?"

"There's cider. It's the weaker stuff, though."

Wiping a big, gnarled hand down his face, Angus muttered, "Weak cider. Bluidy hell. 'Tis worse than I thought."

Alexander poured himself more tea.

Da leaned forward and braced his elbows on the table. "Listen to me, son. Ye must wed the lass."

"That's what I've been sayin'."

"Offer her whatever she wants. Anythin'. Give her a horse."

"I dinnae ken if she wants one."

"Doesnae matter. A lass needs a horse. Or a donkey if she prefers. I noticed she's wearin' naught but yer shirt and plaid. Offer her gowns."

Part of him hated that idea. If she had gowns, she'd stop wearing his shirts next to her skin. She'd stop wrapping herself in his plaid and pottering about like a Highland wife.

"I ken what ye're thinkin'," said Da. "She'll stop wearin' yer plaid, and that twists yer ballocks. Dinnae fash. Once she's past the guttin'-ye-like-a-trout phase, she might surprise ye."

Sabella's cleaver sailed through the tenderloin with heaving force and buried itself in the carving board. She yanked it free and took another swing. "He thinks I'll wed him?" *Thunk.* "Think again, ye blackhearted, oversized clodpate." *Thunk.*

"A smaller blade might work better for that cut, dear." Eleanora Baird was a lovely, elegant woman with white-threaded blonde hair, a gentle mien, gracious manners, and a soft Lowland inflection that reminded Sabella of her former home. "The cow is dead and won't ken the difference. But yer meat will be tough if ye don't trim off that whitish skin on the top, there. Also, ye can portion twelve steaks rather than four if ye're a bit more precise."

Sabella paused to wipe her forehead with her wrist. Breath heaving, she laid the cleaver down and nodded. "My thanks. I'm not very good at cookery."

"Oh, I think ye're doin' well," said Nora with a bright smile. "Ye've been here, what? A fortnight?"

"A wee bit longer, but aye."

"Yer eggs and bacon are as good as any I've had. And yer tea is superb." Nora raised her cup and took a savoring sip.

Some of Sabella's tension eased into a small smile. "You're too kind." She selected a smaller, thinner knife and started removing the whitish layer from the tenderloin. She'd never bothered before, which might explain why her meat kept coming out tough.

As Nora sat sipping, she carried on discussing the best fabrics for a "fine evening dress" one could wear for a wedding. "I've an exquisite silk crepe in precisely the green of yer eyes. A bit of lace would make it perfect."

"I can't marry him. He's insufferable."

Nora nodded. "I ken. Alexander is very much like his father—uncivilized."

"Barbaric and rude."

"Bellowing and unreasonable."

"He accused me of being another man's mistress. Me!" Sabella sliced beneath the skin then ripped the tough membrane free with a furious yank. "He implied I would sell myself for gowns and jewels." Slice. Yank. "Not cheap ones, mind. Only the finest for this harlot!"

"'Tis a wonder ye haven't killed him in his sleep, dear."

"Oh, it was tempting, believe me."

Nora hummed her agreement and sipped her tea.

"He presumed my rampant harlotry based on a single drunken interlude with a Frenchman. I should never have told him."

"Frenchman?"

"I don't even know if Henri is a *duc* now. He might still be a *comte*. He might already have a wife. Yet, Alexander will not stop griping about me traveling to Paris and marrying a duke."

"Do ye intend to travel to Paris?"

Sabella set down her knife and calmed her breathing. "I did."

Nora's voice softened. "Did ye intend to wed a duke?"

"What else was I meant to do?" She gestured to the roughly hacked tenderloin. "Earn my way with my butchery skills? I come from a noble bloodline, Mrs. Baird. My worth lies in that inheritance and the value it brings to my husband." These words were etched in her bones after so many years of repetition. The first time

Kenneth said them to her, she'd sat shivering beneath his coat, trying to understand why a bloodline mattered to two starving orphans. She'd been seven at the time, and a fourteen-year-old Kenneth had nearly lost his fingers to frostbite so she could stay warm.

"Please, call me Nora," the older woman corrected gently. "And ye're more than a bloodline, lass. Yer worth is inherent, not inherited."

Sabella shook her head, her throat tight. "Alexander seems to think my worth lies in selling my womanly favors to the highest bidder. He assumed I'd already done so."

Nora smiled. "He kens better now, aye?"

Cheeks heating at the reference to his mortifying announcement about taking her virginity, Sabella busied herself with placing the meat scraps into a pot for making broth later. "Rude, uncivilized beast."

"I'm afraid I can't fashion a silk gown before tomorrow," said the kindly dressmaker, "but I can work with yer plaid and petticoats to make something lovely for yer wedding."

Sabella blinked. "Wedding? Perhaps I haven't been clear. I'm not marrying that oversized oaf."

Nora glanced pointedly at Sabella's abdomen. "A bairn might have something to say about that."

"It's only happened once."

"If he's anything like his father, then it won't be once for long." She took a wry sip of tea.

Sabella raised her chin. "Perhaps you should be forced to wed Angus, then."

An amused, maternal smile. "I'm a grandmother, dear." She didn't look like a grandmother. Eleanora Baird had two grown daughters, so she must be above forty, but her face was free of telltale creases, making her appear closer to thirty. "My days of birthing bairns are over."

"Nothing is certain," Sabella said. "I shall go to live at Rowan House."

"And Alexander will find ye there."

Why did her belly swoop at the thought? "He infuriates me. I can resist him."

"That's what we all say."

"I shall wait and see. I don't have to marry him yet."

The older woman set down her teacup with a dainty clink. "Alexander invited me and his father to breakfast a day after you refused his offer of marriage."

Sabella frowned. "Aye."

"He then declared ye ruined and demanded marriage again."

A deeper frown. "Aye. He's maddening."

"He's desperate. If ye wed him now, *you* can set the conditions for the marriage. If ye wait until ye're certain there's a necessity, the advantage goes to him."

"You're saying I should surrender early in exchange for better terms."

"I'm saying ye should claim the victory he's handing ye and settle yer new territory more to yer liking."

When she put it that way, it didn't sound nearly so intolerable. A victory over Alexander MacPherson would be deeply satisfying.

An hour after Angus and Nora departed, Sabella was washing up in the scullery when she heard swishing. *Swick-shh. Swick-shh.* She dried her hands and glanced out the window to find Gavin MacDonnell in the drying yard.

He was scything.

Her nape prickled. A tiny shiver chased across her skin.

Alexander had followed through on his promise. Perhaps he *could* be reasoned with; perhaps she *could* gain more concessions simply by asking.

But victory would come with a cost. She'd have to marry him.

"Enjoyin' the view, Duchess?"

She turned to find him leaning in the doorway, black eyes flashing with volatile heat. She threw her towel at him.

He caught it against his chest then arched a brow. "I see yer temper is nae better."

"You're not making this easy, ye boorish lout."

"Making what easy?"

She shoved past him and charged into the kitchen. After stabbing the fire with an iron, she started to check her broth and realized she needed a towel. She glared over her shoulder. Alexander held it out. Snatching the dangling cloth, she lifted the cover of the Dutch oven to see the liquid boiling nicely.

Straightening, she raised her chin and faced him squarely. "I want a range."

His gaze, previously locked on her hips, flew up to meet her eyes. "Done." No hesitation. No negotiation. Just *done*.

Triumph flickered in her breast. "It must be the equal of Joan MacDonnell's."

"Is superior acceptable, Duchess?"

She swallowed against a dry throat and nodded. "I also want a lawn in the drying yard."

"Might take a while to clear it properly and have the grass take root. Will autumn work?"

Triumph now tingled in her nipples. "Aye. Autumn is … fine."

"Anythin' else?"

"A fenced garden for the kitchen. A walled garden for flowers. And more rosebushes. I want leave to acquire as many as I please."

"Done."

Triumph surged harder. She pressed her advantage. "I want a wash-house with an attached laundry of your design."

He frowned. "Where?"

"Near the well. It should have a boiler if possible. Basins, taps, and drying rooms, too."

For a long minute, he appeared to be performing complex calculations in his mind. Then he swiped a hand over his beard and nodded. "Ye'll have it by winter."

Triumph soared into a blaze. It danced over her skin, sank between her thighs, and thrust with all its might. "I want a bathing tub."

"Done."

"A new carriage dress."

"Done."

"New gowns generally. As many as I please."

He bit down until his jaw flickered. "Very well. But ye must agree to wear what I ask once per week."

She squeezed her thighs together and nearly moaned. "Agreed."

His gaze burned over her before settling on her mouth. "Now, here are my demands. Ye'll wed me tomorrow."

Her breath caught. She'd thought the triumph was potent. This was more. "Fine."

"Ye'll sleep in my bed."

"I'd prefer a chamber of my own."

"Not negotiable, Duchess. My wife, my bed."

She wasn't certain she'd ever been this … triumphant. "Very well. Your bed will be our bed."

He grunted. His nose flared as his eyes burned a hole in her plaid.

"I want a dressing table," she breathed. "And a chair beside the fire."

"Done."

"If you ever imply that I'm a whore again, I shall make good use of my cleaver. It's a bit messy for tenderloin, but it gets the job done. Do ye ken?"

"I ken, lass." His throat rippled on a swallow, though with his lustful smolder, it struck her as more of an excited response than a nervous one. Her threats aroused him. How strange.

Stranger still was *her* response. She wanted to devour him—one part of him in particular. She licked her lips, squeezed the towel, and braced herself against the kitchen table. Her bath was going to be lengthy this evening. When she had command of herself again, she straightened. "Then we shall wed tomorrow, Mr. MacPherson."

"Aye. Tomorrow." He moved so smoothly that she didn't realize he'd shifted closer until he was inches away. He lowered his head near hers and murmured a promise before he departed for his day's work. "Tomorrow, ye'll be mine."

Chapter Thirteen

On Sabella's first morning as a bride, summer attempted to stew them all into broth. The parlor, positioned on the northwest side of the house, offered some refuge from the sticky heat. The newly scythed grounds weren't so pleasant.

Fortunately, the alders offered shade, and the river cooled the air around the grove where they planned to have the ceremony. Unfortunately, midges had decided to take refuge nearby. Sabella hoped for rain but would settle for a breeze.

"Last time I sweated this much, Mr. Brodie nearly expired from exhaustion." Mrs. MacBean fanned herself with a handful of chicken feathers. "Have ye ever tried to clean four pounds of melted butter from a man's trews? 'Tis a thankless task. I dinnae recommend it."

"Mary, don't be silly," mumbled Nora around a mouthful of pins. The dressmaker secured a pleat in Sabella's plaid then set the remaining pins on the carved oak table. "The heatstroke-and-butter incident was Mr. Dubois, remember? I believe mushrooms were involved."

"Och, right ye are. I think ye ken my stories better than I do, Nora."

"Étienne Dubois?" Joan MacDonnell frowned and poured more weak cider. Soon, only the strong cider would remain. Sabella hoped it wouldn't come to that, but this was thirsty weather, and it was a Scottish wedding.

Mrs. MacBean blinked. "Aye. Bald. Nae eyebrows. Ye ken him?"

"Fifteen years ago, mayhap. After he returned to France, I didnae hear much."

"Hmm. Could be His Majesty finally did away with him. Poor, wee Étienne. Couldnae hide forever, I suppose. Not too many one-legged Frenchmen runnin' about with nae eyebrows."

Nora frowned. "Why would His Majesty want him dead?"

"Why does he want me dead? Kings are a moody lot."

"You? Mary, what did you do?"

Mrs. MacBean shrugged. "Ye bribe one wee Frenchman into dressin' like the prince's mistress, and suddenly, ye're an 'enemy of the Crown.'" She scoffed. "His Highness wasnae wearin' a crown at the time. Wasnae wearin' much at all. The sheep was wearin' an ermine cape, though. Clover liked the finer things."

Nora hummed and lifted Sabella's arm to adjust a seam as if this was all perfectly normal. "Ermine and wool are splendid for muffs."

Joan had stopped pouring to stare at Mrs. MacBean. Finally, she closed her mouth and left the room, presumably to finish the wedding cake. It was a French receipt she'd learned from Étienne.

Magdalene entered a moment later carrying a stack of washcloths and a basin of cool water.

"Oh, bless you," Sabella sighed, wiping her face and neck. "I feel like a sheep in an ermine cape right now."

Magdalene shot Mrs. MacBean an amused glance. "Have you been telling the Clover story again?"

Nora snipped a thread and stood back. "There. All finished."

Sabella smoothed the bonnie cream plaid Magdalene had managed to clean until not a drop of

Sabella's blood remained. Nora had sewn tiny pleats in place at the waist to help the fine, lightweight wool fall gracefully over layered cotton skirts fashioned from Sabella's petticoats. Cleverly constructed from the plaid's upper half, the bodice was refitted to form tiny cap sleeves and a wide, scooped neckline. Nora had finished the gown with a green silk sash around the waist and a thistle brooch pinning the pleats at the center of the bodice. One would be forgiven for thinking the ensemble had been purchased from a costly dressmaker in Edinburgh or London.

"It's lovely, Mrs. Baird."

Nora patted her arm. "Call me Nora, dear."

By the time the priest arrived, Sabella was ready for the strong cider. Joan finished preparing the white-iced cake, along with a feast of bread, cold ham, lamb pies, and several salads. Magdalene and Mrs. MacBean assembled a stunning bouquet of damask roses, lavender, and white heather. A red-headed young man named Stuart MacDonnell brought his fiddle and began playing for the men assembled in the grove near the river.

One of those men caused her to shake like an alder leaf.

The priest looked nervous, sweating profusely and casting baleful glances at Angus, Rannoch, and

Alexander. All three MacPhersons wore dark coats and russet-red kilts. All three were handsome. But Alexander was sin itself—the kind a lady wouldn't mind being condemned for.

Drat and blast, he made her ache. That trimmed black beard. Those long, powerful arms. The shoulders and chest that seemed to grow more muscular by the day. Even the man's legs were beautiful.

"Are ye ready, lass?" Nora asked.

Sabella watched as Magdalene and Mrs. MacBean followed Joan and her husband down to the grove. Stuart MacDonnell played a plaintive Scottish air to the accompaniment of birdsong. A light breeze riffled the trees.

And Sabella's heart pounded. Her sapling courage wavered.

Would he turn cruel, as Kenneth had? Would he deride her for allowing mud to spatter the gowns he'd purchased? Would he punish her for taking pleasure in low things—a bawdy jest, a braw Highlander's chest, a quenching river bath, a slow ride in a hard rain?

She held her breath, tightening her hand on her roses. The lush white blooms looked as if they'd been dipped in the pinkish red of a sunset. Leda was the variety, she thought. She squeezed the stems harder, finding the thorns, feeling the pain.

Would he keep his promises to her?

The wind strengthened, cooling her skin with the scents of lavender, heather, and damask blooms.

Would he rule her as a tyrant while claiming it was for her own good?

Angus pointed in their direction. Alexander turned and spotted her. A hawkish nose flared. Black eyes claimed every inch of her, from the curling wisps around her face to the battered half-boots on her feet. He didn't smile. He didn't move or glance away. He didn't cross the yard and grip her wrist.

He stood waiting for her. Watching her. Wanting her.

Not the Sabella she'd been, but the one who bathed in the river and burned his dinner. He wanted *her*.

She released a breath and eased her grip before the thorns broke her skin. Finally, she nodded to Nora. "I'm ready."

The air carried her to him—the music, the breeze. He offered his hand rather than taking hers. She slipped her fingers across his roughened palm. The priest wiped his high forehead with a handkerchief and began the ceremony.

Marrying her tall, braw, beastly Highlander took almost no time at all. First came a wee admonition or two about God and a man's promises and the importance of wifely obedience. Then came the vows—simplified and beautiful—and the call for the ring. Angus handed Alexander a glinting band, which her Highlander then slid onto her finger. Leaf-etched gold framed an oval cabochon emerald. The verdant stone glowed every time her hand caught a bit of sunlight.

Finally, the priest declared them wed. And just like that, she became Alexander MacPherson's wife.

Everyone cheered. The fiddler struck a joyful melody. Birds launched from the trees. Rannoch and Angus clapped Alexander's shoulder with hearty blows that would have knocked a lesser man on his backside. A strong gust plucked at her refashioned petticoats.

She accepted her bouquet from Magdalene then blinked down at the red-dipped white petals. Her ring winked and glowed.

She was married. A wife.

Her eyes flew up to find her husband's. Her. *Husband.* Hers.

Good heavens, why hadn't she focused on this before? She was his bride, aye. But *he* also now belonged to *her*.

This big, strong, clever Highlander was hers.

Nora and Magdalene congratulated her in their soft Lowland tones. Joan and Mrs. MacBean blessed her with mysterious Gaelic well wishes that all sounded like fervent throat-clearing to her.

Soon, they retreated to the part of the garden cooled by the house's shade, where Joan and her husband had assembled their feast. Whisky and strong cider began to flow. By the time Sabella took her first bite of cake, Nora was casting flirtatious glances at Angus, and Mrs. MacBean was casting flirtatious glances at a mossy stump.

Sabella was too distracted to flirt.

He was hers. She could touch him whenever she wanted. Squinting, she tried "accidentally" extending her pinkie finger to brush his wrist. He glanced down at her with an unreadable expression then casually drank his cider.

As the morning inched past noon, the wind blew harder. She and the other ladies helped clear the tables so that Alexander and Rannoch could carry them back inside. The sight of her husband lifting that much weight so effortlessly sent every inch of Sabella into a clench.

A short while later, after the washing up was done, the MacDonnells departed, followed by Rannoch and Magdalene with the priest in tow. Angus gruffly welcomed Sabella to his clan, assuring her that he held no grudges toward her for her brother's actions. "Pour good whisky in a bad barrel, and ye get bad whisky," he said. "Ye dinnae discard the whole batch over one tainted barrel." Then he cupped Alexander's nape, pounded his shoulder with two more hearty whacks, and muttered something in Gaelic. Finally, he swept a fully inebriated Nora into his arms and carried her out to her gig or, as he called it, "yer bluidy, useless trinket."

As Alexander saw his father off, Sabella's nerves began to hum. She made her way into the kitchen, hoping for a task to keep her hands busy. But Joan had left everything tidier than before. Drat and blast.

Spying her flowers on the sideboard, she sighed in relief. Something to do. She fetched a pitcher, filled it from the scullery taps, then returned to the kitchen. The heat was starting to wilt the petals—and her—so, she fetched another pitcher and another. As she carried her last pitcher of water from the scullery, she discovered a beast had invaded her kitchen.

He leaned against the table with his arms crossed and his brow furrowed. "If something's on fire, lass, ye should tell me now while the blaze is wee."

He'd dispensed with his coat and waistcoat, leaving only his shirt and kilt. His sleeves were rolled past muscular forearms and thick, hair-dusted wrists. She'd felt those wrists earlier. She had every right to them.

He was hers.

Squelching the urge to declare it aloud if only to see his response, she rounded the table and began disassembling her bouquet. "Did your father have any trouble with the gig?"

"Other than loathing it with every bone in his body, no." He tapped a fingertip against one of the pitchers. "What is this, Duchess?"

"It's water."

"I can see that."

"Then why did you ask?" She placed her Leda roses into the tallest pitcher then picked through the lavender sprigs.

"Ye have seven pitchers here."

"I'm pleased you can count." She fetched a pair of shears from the cupboard. With a few quick snips, she had the height she wanted.

"What's the purpose?"

"It's a stifling day, Mr. MacPherson."

"We're wed, lass. Mayhap ye could call me Alexander, now."

She blinked. Yet another benefit to this union she hadn't considered: She could call him whatever she pleased. He was hers. "It's a stifling day, Alexander."

"Aye, but drainin' my cisterns willnae change the weather."

Tucking a third sprig of heather between a rosebud and a leafy branch, she turned the pitcher to view her work from all angles. "Midges are abominable creatures."

"True."

"They're currently occupying my favorite bathing spot." She snipped away a leaf and examined the result. Better. After moving the arrangement to the sideboard, she swept the flower debris from the table into the rubbish bin.

"So, ye're havin' a bath one pitcher at a time, eh?" His voice had gone thready.

"I don't yet have a tub, so aye. Pitchers will have to do."

"Ye're wastin' yer time. Ye'll only get sweaty again before the day is done."

"One could say that about most things, husband." Oh, she liked calling him that. *Husband.* "Why bother washing one's shirt? It will only need washing again tomorrow."

His shoulders rippled in a fascinating fashion, as if he was clenching his fists. "Some of my lazier maids would agree with that sentiment."

"Well, they're clearly hard of smelling."

He chuckled and swiped a hand over his beard. "Hard of smellin'. Bluidy hell, lass."

Eyeing the length of the table, she began transferring the pitchers to the opposite end.

"Ye do ken there are more efficient ways to have a bath, aye?"

"Such as?"

"Ye could fill one of the basins in the scullery. Ye could use the taps upstairs and fill the basin on the washstand."

She fetched a shallow washtub from the scullery then a cloth from the shelves beneath the sideboard. "Not everything is about efficiency, husband." God, that word. She also liked "Alexander," but the wee hint of ownership in "husband" sent a pulsing thrill down her spine.

"'Tis a bath, Duchess. Ye're either clean or ye're not. Nae need to complicate it."

"Clean isn't always the point." She removed the thistle brooch. "Sometimes, a lady desires more from her daily rituals." She untied her sash.

His breath hitched. "Lass."

"Sometimes she wants to enjoy the sensation of water pouring over her skin." She unfastened the hidden buttons Nora had sewn into her bodice. It came off easily after that. "Or the flow of a current pressing in certain … ways."

His unblinking black stare locked on her. The only indication that he hadn't frozen solid was a wee muscle flickering next to his eye.

She unpinned her hair and let her skirts fall to the floor, leaving her shift and corset. She dispensed with the latter. "Sometimes a lady wants to be wet, husband, purely for the pleasure of it."

"Sweet, bluidy Christ."

She stepped into the washtub and poured her first pitcher down the front of her body, starting above her collarbone. Her shift instantly plastered to her nakedness, the damp linen cooling her skin. Her nipples were spiking and flushed red, but that was no surprise. They'd always bloomed for Alexander. She used a second pitcher on her front, making sure to fully saturate the linen over her breasts and hips.

One second, she was dripping in a washtub. The next, she was being crushed against an enormous, powerful male while he lifted, pivoted, and plopped her backside down on the kitchen table.

"If ye want me to control myself," he growled, "then dinnae bluidy *push me, woman!*"

She spread her knees to straddle his hips then snagged the nearest pitcher. Pouring it down his chest, she said, "Sometimes a lady wants to make sure her husband gets a proper washing, too."

Something flickered in his eyes. A blackened spark ignited into an inferno. He shoved her shift to her hips and yanked her forward until her thighs splayed and her folds lay open and exposed. After stripping his shirt off over his head, he poured half of another pitcher over his own chest and half over hers. Watching water sluice down through thick, black hair and hard, flexing muscles invoked a hard, agonizing ache from her breasts to her knees. She couldn't stop herself from moaning.

"Proper doesnae get ye wet," he seethed. "For that, ye need yer big, brutish Highlander, eh?"

Humming and nodding incoherently, she thrust out her bosoms to make sure he noticed how needy they were.

But his gaze focused lower, where she was wetter, where her folds glistened bright pink among her curls. He swirled a fingertip round and round. Round and round. "Ye need me here, dinnae ye, Duchess?"

"Aye," she groaned. "Need ye."

He slipped his longest finger inside, smooth and deep, while keeping his thumb circling round and round. Round and round. "Take off yer shift."

Her hands were braced behind her, so it took a bit of angling and fumbling, but she finally managed to wrench the garment over her head without dislodging his hand.

"Ye're so tight, love. Are ye still tender here?" He withdrew his finger a fraction and thrust it deeper.

She whimpered and shook her head. A wee fib. She was a bit sore, but she wanted him too much to care.

"Let's have a closer look, hmm?" He lifted her to scoot her toward the middle of the table then laid her down and lowered his head to kiss her bare belly.

"Alexander," she panted, clutching his hair in her fists.

"Aye, lass?"

"I—I've imagined …"

"What have ye imagined?"

"Yer mouth. There."

His finger pulsed deeper as his tongue flickered out to replace his swirling thumb. "Ye mean here?"

"Oh, God."

Grinning, he swirled his tongue round and round. Round and round. As if he wound a spring tighter and tighter. The flickering tease wound her tighter and tighter.

"Alexander!"

"Can ye take a second finger, love?"

"Aye!"

The tiniest pinch, then the relief of being filled. She arched her back and groaned her pleasure, though it only spiked the need to be further stretched.

Round and round, wet and warm and lapping. "Show me what ye like," he rasped, his breath steaming against her delicate flesh. "Show me how those sweet nipples prefer to be stroked."

Her hands went to her breasts, palming and twisting the sensitive nubs while her hips writhed for deeper penetration.

"Aye, that's it," he murmured. "Ye like a wee bit more pressure than I would have thought. Proper isnae hard enough, is it, Duchess?"

"No," she choked. "It's not."

Round and round. Round and round. "Clean isnae dirty enough, is it?"

"No. Not enough." She squeezed her nipples harder, wishing he would use his teeth on them, as he had the first time. "Please, husband. Please."

Cool water poured over her breasts, hands, and belly. The shocking sensation sent her hurtling over a precipice she hadn't realized was imminent. Light exploded. Her sheath seized while sharp, blistering pleasure pulsed outward from where his mouth and hand worked her body.

"That's it," he said. "Almost there."

Almost? She'd passed "there." She was in the blissful aftermath of "there."

But he wasn't finished. His tongue continued its flickering stimulation, but now his mouth closed over the centermost nub, adding heat and intense suction. Meanwhile, his fingers began to move inside her in a spiraling motion. Round and round. Round and round.

With her peak having come and gone, she found the additional stimulation uncomfortable at first. "Alexander." She gripped a handful of his hair and arched her back to ease the intensity.

But rather than retreat, he continued adding subtle pressure inside, particularly to the top of her sheath.

"Alexander!"

The tension returned. Round and round, tighter and tighter.

"Oh, God. It can't ... I can't ..."

Her nipples were on fire. Her sex was on fire. Her body was on fire.

He poured more water over her breasts. She screamed her ecstasy. The pitcher clattered to the floor. His hand replaced hers on her nipple, squeezing and pinching with highly improper pressure.

"Dear God, Alexander!"

He rose up, withdrew his fingers, lifted his kilt, and slicked the head of his enormous staff with her juices.

Licking his lips and then his fingers, he forced the stiff, engorged stalk down to stroke her folds. Finally, he snugged the broad head against her opening.

Bracing himself above her, he held her gaze with boundless, bone-melting fire and forged inside. As it had the first time, the invasion felt stunningly absolute. The stretch. The pressure against flesh that had been waiting far too long for him.

But this time, she had patience for the discomfort. She knew what was coming. Pleasure, aye. But more. Much more. His body inside hers eased a hunger that couldn't be satisfied by anything or anyone but him.

He lowered his head to kiss her lips for the first time that day, and he kissed her so gently and sweetly that she could scarcely believe he was the same man thrusting with hard, steady purpose between her thighs. Each thrust went deeper. Each thrust came a wee bit faster than the next. Soon, his hips drove against hers at a pounding pace while his tongue sensually stroked and played. With every thrust, her nipples zinged from chafing against his chest.

She would not have thought she could peak again. Her body felt too sensitized. She shook with the agonizing tension of an imminent release, yet every thrust seemed to drive her higher, shake her harder, wind her tighter. The sheer force of his pounding hips scraped the table across the floor. She could only wrap him in her arms, take his demands for deeper penetration and more intense pressure, and hold on for the ride.

But the moment she began to doubt he could draw any further sensation from her, he pulled back to growl, "Take it. Take yer pleasure. Come for me, woman."

As if her body only needed his command, it hovered for a moment like a feather in an updraft then burst skyward with explosive force. Light shattered behind her eyes. She screamed his name over and over as the shimmering, pulsating waves of pleasure rippled through her.

He cupped her arching throat and pounded harder, gritting his teeth with the force of a tortured man. Finally, as her peak eased enough for her to reach for him, he let her wrap him in her arms.

She kissed his tortured jaw and his reddened cheek. She stroked his sweat-dampened hair and his tension-furrowed brow. "Fill me," she whispered. "I want it. Yer pleasure *belongs* to me."

A deep groan. Three bone-rattling thrusts. A surge of heated seed inside her. His roars of anguished pleasure hummed against her neck and cheek. His sweat dripped onto her skin, blending with her own. More deep thrusts. More seed.

She stroked his neck and back, sifted her fingers through his hair, and took his pleasure as was her right. Easing him filled her gnawing emptiness as nothing else ever had. She reveled in his slowly relaxing muscles, the small, compulsive thrusts as she milked him for every drop of her due.

He was hers. Her husband, her man, her Highlander.

"I think ye might have killed me, Duchess," he rasped in her ear. "Seems to have been some kind of clerical error, though. A devil doesnae belong in heaven."

She grinned. "I think my devil is right where he belongs."

CHAPTER FOURTEEN

On Sabella's tenth day as a wife, she managed to cook dinner without burning a single thing. Not the venison. Not the potatoes. Not the gooseberries. In fact, when Alexander found her in the kitchen, she was grinning from ear to ear.

"Husband!"

"Aye." He wiped his face with a towel. He'd recently shaved his beard, and, while she adored his handsome, hawkish features regardless, she'd been vexed that he hadn't discussed it with her first. He was hers, after all. She should have a say.

He'd explained that beards itch in the heat, so he'd regrow one when it wasn't "hot enough to turn my ballocks into Scotch eggs." Then he'd demonstrated how lovely a man's bare face could feel against one's bosoms.

She'd forgiven him rather quickly after that.

"I made dinner." She beamed and wiped her hands on her apron before gesturing to the feast she'd prepared: venison stew seasoned lightly with salt, pepper, and thyme; bread from Glenscannadoo's finest (and only) bakery; a salad of lettuce, parsley, bacon, boiled eggs, and chives dressed in wine vinaigrette; and, finally, her rendition of Joan's gooseberry pie. The pie was her first attempt with paste since the Dreadful Meat Pie Incident during her first week as a maid.

Grunting, Alexander dipped his towel in the bucket of well water and wiped his nape. "I see ye have, lass. Looks good."

She poured him a cup of cider. "What was all that noise earlier? I thought I heard pounding."

"Fence posts dinnae set themselves."

She invited him to sit then fetched dishes from the cupboard. "Nora delivered three of my new gowns earlier. I left the bill for you in the study."

He grunted.

"Oh, and Magdalene wants me to ask whether ye plan to compete in the Glenscannadoo Games this year." Magdalene was helping to organize some of the

Gathering's events, such as the fair and picnic, during Annie's absence.

A dismissive snort. "'Tis Rannoch who really wants to ken. He doesnae wish to be the only MacPherson competin' in the heavy events."

She frowned as she filled their bowls. A waft of thyme and savory meat hit her nose. Her stomach growled—a good sign. "Why would he mind? He'll dominate every event he enters, as you did last year. MacPhersons are another breed, better in every way."

He smiled. "Every way, lass?"

She set his bowl in front of him. "*Every* way."

With a chuckle, he said, "That's why. Rannoch likes to forget that he's built the same as the rest of us. He prefers to be the likable one." He took a bite of the stew. His brows went up. He hummed appreciation. "This is good, Duchess."

Her eyes flew wide. "Really?"

"Very."

She beamed and bounced on her toes. "Oh, I'm so pleased you like it, husband."

He took another bite and raked her with a now-familiar look that said, "I have only one appetite, and ye're the fare I want on my table."

She scooted the salad toward him. "Try this one."

He wasn't as enthusiastic about eating leafy green things, but he gathered a forkful, popped the bite in his mouth, then nodded. "The bacon is perfect."

"Don't you think the chives are a good addition for summer? So light and refreshing."

He drank his cider and ate more venison.

She clicked her tongue. "Very well, I shall stop trying to 'feed you yer food's food.'" He'd only complained once about her cookery, and that had been over a spinach salad she'd tried to serve him with beefsteak. He'd suggested she put it to better use either fertilizing her rosebush—which had miraculously survived the horned menace—or "fattening up the deer for yer stew pot."

"Might ye give the pie a chance?" She twisted her towel between her hands. "I'm hoping to improve my paste."

He immediately reached for the gooseberry pie. A bite later, she couldn't tell whether she'd been successful because his expression didn't change.

"Is it … good?"

Holding her gaze steadily, he took another bite.

She blinked. After portioning out a piece for herself, she took a taste. Sour, sharp, and bitter vied for dominance in her mouth. The paste was tough, but that was the least of her problems. She wasn't certain she could swallow this. After a single bite, her eyes were watering.

Her husband, meanwhile, calmly finished his portion bite by bite.

She finally managed to swallow, guzzling cider to wash away the horridness. "How did you …?" She coughed. More cider. "Alexander."

"Aye, Duchess."

"You needn't eat my failures."

"I ken."

She set aside her towel and rounded the table to stand between his sprawled knees. Cupping his jaw, she bent down to kiss him. "I don't know why you do this. You're going to make yourself sick."

His hands closed around her waist, pulling her closer. "Whose hands made that paste?"

"Mine."

"Whose hands made the stew?"

She paused. "Mine."

"Stew's better than last time, aye?"

She nodded.

"There ye have it. These arenae failures, lass. They're wee stops on the road to mastery. Every inn has lessons to teach a weary traveler."

"Hmm. And horrid meals to offer an unsuspecting husband, apparently." His answer was sweet—and a great lot of nonsense. He ate her food because it pleased her. That was obvious. Still, she didn't want to make him sick, so she would work on improving her cookery. "I shall add more sugar to the gooseberries next time. I followed the receipt to the letter. I don't know where I went wrong."

"Is that Joan MacDonnell's gooseberry pie?"

She nodded.

"That's where." His smile turned sardonic. "Joan hates gooseberries, but her man, Adam, loves 'em. He kept after her to make him a gooseberry pie like his mam makes, so Joan made sure he stopped askin'."

"Why would she give me such a dreadful receipt?"

"Dinnae ken. Are ye certain ye read it right?"

"Well, I was in my cups when I wrote it down. Perhaps I missed something." She moved to the sideboard to examine the slip of paper again. Some of the instructions were muddled by drips of strong cider. There were no mentions of sugar, apart from the following admonition: *Gooseberries are vile; sweeten until tolerable.* She'd initially read this as *Gooseberries ate whilst seated still adorable*. The grammar had been puzzling, but she'd shrugged it off as the result of Joan's accent and her own intoxication.

She sighed. "Perhaps we should hire a cook."

His chair creaked. "I thought ye didnae want one."

She didn't. He'd offered to hire a full household staff—footmen or "lads," as he called them, maids, a housekeeper, a cook—but Sabella enjoyed having her husband all to herself. She liked being able to kiss him in the kitchen or seduce him in the stable or importune him in the drying yard whenever she pleased. She liked swimming naked with him in the river. She liked feeding him breakfast and mending his shirts and making their bed.

"I also don't want to poison you," she said, laying the receipt in the tray of useless items she kept on the sideboard because she couldn't bring herself to toss them in the rubbish bin.

"Mighty generous of ye, lass."

A little smile broke through her despondence. "It's selfish, really. I need you hale and vigorous for all the tupping."

He cursed under his breath. "Ye're beggin' to get tupped again right now."

Was she that obvious? She turned to lean back against the sideboard. "Oh, dear. I'm not much of a lady, am I?"

His chair creaked as he widened his legs—a sign she'd learned to watch for. An aroused Alexander needed more room.

Fortunately for her, an aroused Alexander was a frequent occurrence. She didn't know whether it happened as frequently as *her* arousal, of course. That was embarrassingly constant. Every time he ate her food, every time she glimpsed him from the kitchen window, every time she caught him watching her from a doorway, her body readied to be taken.

"Perhaps you were right about my harlotry," she murmured, "though my tastes are quite specific."

Another creak.

"I prefer Highlanders, ye see. Big ones."

His chair scraped as he pushed to his feet and came slowly toward her.

"Black hair and eyes." She licked her lips. "A beard is preferable but not required."

He bracketed her between long arms, hands braced near her hips.

She inhaled his scent—earthy skin and evergreen. "He must be able to set a post hard and deep—"

A hard hand gripped her nape, and a hard mouth slammed down on hers as a hard staff ground against her belly. On his tongue, she tasted hard cider and sweet lust. He hoisted her up onto the sideboard, yanking her skirts past her thighs with fevered motions. "Six times, woman," he growled against her. "Six bluidy times today. I promised I wouldnae take ye a seventh."

"A foolish promise," she panted against him. Clawing at his fall, she spread her thighs wide and licked his lower lip. "Why would ye limit yourself?"

"Because ye willnae be able to walk if I tup ye as often as I want."

"A novel idea. Let's try it."

She freed his hard, beautiful cock. A moment later, he slid inside with a rough, deep thrust. Two moments later, he was driving into her like a man setting a fence post. Every stroke rattled the sideboard harder, clanging crockery and slamming the wall. He ate at her mouth and drove into her body at a furious pace. Heat and triumph and desire filled her to the bursting point.

Her peak came with such stunning sharpness, she screamed his name and thrashed wildly as the concussive force broke through her in waves. Crockery crashed to the floor. A tray went flying. The loud clatter of falling things blended with her ecstatic cries, his peaking groans, and the rhythmic slam of a large, heavy object against the wall.

The cacophony sounded glorious to Sabella.

In the aftermath of the frenzied storm, she felt half drunk. He often had the same effect on her as strong cider or champagne—sweet euphoria, head-spinning pleasure, and blissful relaxation. He lifted her down, making sure to place her in an area free of debris.

"Heavens," she chuckled. "We made a mess, didn't we?"

He grunted and fetched a broom while she wandered over to pick up the wooden tray that had landed near the hearth. Her random assortment of useless items had scattered everywhere. She swiped up Joan's gooseberry pie receipt and a button she'd saved from one of Alexander's waistcoats. When she spotted the pendant Mrs. MacBean had given her smoldering among the coals, she reached for it without thinking.

White-hot pain seared her hand. She cried out and reared back. Her momentum sent her crashing into a hard, bellowing wall. The wall gripped her wrist and plunged her hand into a bucket of cold water.

"Bluidy hell, woman!" he roared. "What were ye thinkin'?"

"I—I wasn't."

"Obviously!"

Wincing at the throbbing burn, she shook her head. "Ye make me drunk, husband. After we tup, I can scarcely function."

Chest heaving, he lifted the bucket onto the table then dragged a chair closer with his foot and sat down with her in his lap, all while keeping her hand immersed. Then he gently cupped her head and kissed her temple. "How bad is it, lass?" Though his hands were steady, his voice was frayed thin.

"It's fine."

He pulled her hand from the water. She was still clutching the pendant. He tossed the thing on the table and examined her fingers. Red. Blistering. "Ye're nae fine," he growled, plunging her hand back into the bucket. "I cannae bear for ye to be injured. Ye must be more cautious, ye ken?"

Hating that she'd caused him distress with her carelessness, she reached up to stroke his jaw. "You mustn't worry. I'm well accustomed to pain. More so than most lasses."

The arms surrounding her went from warm muscle to rigid stone. "Accustomed?" The word thrummed with dark tension.

"Aye. Cold water helps. A comfrey poultice when it's bad. After a few days, the bruises don't even hurt, really."

"Bruises." He handed her his cup of cider to drink. "Where did ye acquire such knowledge about bruises?"

She drained the cup then let her head loll into the solid crook between his upper chest and neck. "Kenneth lost patience with me from time to time. If I planned to appear in public, I'd wear my gloves. Dreadful in summer, but it's important not to let them see."

His shoulder flexed against her head. "Who's 'them,' lass?"

"Anybody."

"Why mustn't ye let them see?"

"We're Lockharts. They'd think us quite low, wouldn't they?"

With his strong arms around her and the worst of the burning sting soothed by the water and the cider, she began to feel pleasantly sleepy.

"Annie saw us once," she murmured. "Kenneth and I were meeting friends at an inn near Parliament Square. His temper was sore that day."

He'd been unusually erratic, snapping at her over every wee thing. Kenneth rarely lost his temper in public, but that day, he'd done so in unprecedented fashion. Months later, after his crimes had come to light, she'd realized what had set him off: Broderick MacPherson's release from the Calton Hill Bridewell, where he'd arranged for Broderick to be first imprisoned then tortured and killed.

Above all things, Kenneth couldn't tolerate being thwarted. Little wonder he'd behaved so aggressively on a day when he felt powerless.

Sabella squeezed her eyes shut, remembering how he'd punished her as he sometimes did at home. While his friends stood mere feet away, he'd seized her wrist in a grinding, bruising hold. Sabella didn't even remember what she'd said to provoke him, only the shift from annoyance to fury. A flare in his eyes had signaled an imminent explosion. Then had come pain. And finally, the humiliation of having others witness what she could ordinarily hide.

"Annie recognized me," she said. The brash, fiery-haired lass had charged in to disrupt Sabella's argument with Kenneth as if she and Sabella were old friends. At the time, they'd scarcely qualified as acquaintances, having spoken for less than a minute the previous autumn.

"She told me to poison him like the rats in the larder." Sabella smiled now, but at the time, she'd been shocked down to her slippers to hear a young woman say such things. "I envied her boldness, her strength. Annie said if I ever had a need, I should take the mail coach to Glenscannadoo and ask for her. She offered to feed me venison with onion gravy." They'd become friends over the ensuing months, primarily through correspondence.

"Annie mentioned seein' ye there," said Alexander. "It's what made her suspect yer brother." His voice was deeply calming as he stroked her wrist with his thumb.

"Aye. She told me."

"She didnae think it was the first time he'd been cruel to ye."

Old, familiar embarrassment surfaced to heat her skin. She burrowed against him, wishing she could shrink down to nothing. But she wasn't nothing. She'd never been able to make herself small enough. Always, the answer had been *not today*.

He held her calmly, patiently. They breathed together while birds sang outside and water dripped from the table.

"I vexed him sometimes," she whispered.

His thumb moved in soothing circles on her wrist, round and round.

"He was careful not to crack bones. Just twisting." Just agonizing pain. "The physician always assured me I'd be fine."

"Physician." Alexander's thumb moved round and round.

"Aye. Dr. Phillips. He's English. Bit of a peculiar man. Kenneth seemed to think very little of him, yet he was the only doctor he'd summon."

"I'm surprised he bothered with a physician at all. Only twistin', and all that."

She hummed agreement. "Breaks take too long to heal. His aim was punishment, not damage. Dr. Phillips diagnosed my broken ribs during our last week in Edinburgh—"

"Yer ribs were broken?"

Sabella found it remarkable how still Alexander could hold his body. It gave her comfort to know he was calm. "Aye, but apart from that, Kenneth only ever left bruises, and even the sight of them would vex him all over again," she said. "I found it best to keep them covered. Long sleeves. That's the key. Gloves for when the sleeves are insufficient. Never red, of course. He disapproved of red for unwed lasses. He disapproved of many arbitrary things. Feathered hats. Syllabub. Frenchmen."

"Frenchmen can be vexin'."

She huffed out a dry chuckle. "So can Scots."

"How's yer hand, Duchess?"

She tugged and he released her wrist immediately. She examined the puffy red blisters forming. "I shan't be playing the pianoforte for a few days, but I expect I'll be fine."

When the burns started to sting again, she wetted a towel and wrapped it around her hand like a bandage. Alexander, staring from his chair with that calm, inscrutable expression, suggested, "Ye should eat. I've some work to do yet before the day is done. Might be late to bed."

She nodded and pasted on a smile.

When he left, she noticed the pendant lying discarded on the table. A shaft of light was hitting it just so, deepening the shadows along the queer ridges Mrs. MacBean had carved into the wood. Sabella peered closer, dangling it by the leather cord. No, it wasn't light or shadows. The highest points of the relief had been charred, and the roughness in the lower points had been smoothed by the fire. She ran her thumb over the surface of each whorl, each petal, each cupping leaf.

The pendant had transformed from a vulgar oddity into something quite extraordinary. It was a pair of blooms. Roses, to be precise. Like densely-petaled centifolias entwined in an embrace, the lushness drew the eye deeper. Fire, ash, and smoke had colored the interior as if every shade and line was painted by a Dutch master.

Later, after she'd managed to clean up and feed herself, she carried the pendant upstairs to the dressing room and looped it over her head. The roses settled neatly into place over her breastbone. She wondered how the pendant would look with her new gown. Quickly wiping it down to ensure none of the char would transfer, she gingerly donned the lovely confection of green silk crepe overlain by creamy French lace.

Pleasing, she thought, brushing a finger over the wee pendant. *Quite pleasing*. When she noticed the leather cord was leaving a line of ash on her skin, she removed the necklace and placed it on her new dressing table.

Just then, a flicker of movement caught her eye outside the window. Fury prickled through her very soul. "Red spawn of unholy pestilence! Get yer furry arse away from my roses!"

She flew down to the kitchen, fetched the broom, then ran outside pell-mell to rescue her beleaguered garden. Rounding the southeast corner, she startled the dratted beast by waving the broom and screaming insults. She wasn't sure which one worked, but the deer leapt away with her wee, uprooted rosebush dangling like a thorny thistle from its pestilent jaws.

Sabella chased the beastie past the house, along the drive toward the stables, then past the yard to the pumphouse. From the pumphouse, she crossed the footbridge arching over the river then veered into the thick woodlands beyond. She rarely came to this side of the river. There was nothing here but trees and pestilence.

"I ken ye're here!" she shouted, heaving to catch her breath. Her bandaged fingers stung where they gripped the broom handle, but nothing stung so keenly as the loss of that dratted rosebush. She couldn't even say why, precisely. She didn't know the breed. It wasn't as if roses were particularly rare. Alexander had agreed to let her purchase and cultivate as many as she wanted.

But it was hers—something she'd planted, something she'd nurtured, something she'd grown. It didn't deserve to be uprooted and unceremoniously stripped of every hopeful leaf.

She bent forward and rested her hands on her knees, trying to get her bearings and catch her breath. That's when she heard the sounds. Deeper into the wood, they sounded like a ram colliding with a wall, a resonant, thudding *crack*. Several blows later, the crack lengthened. Then came louder, windier crackling and an enormous *whump*.

She blinked as birds exploded into the sky. The day had suddenly brightened. Why had it brightened? Spinning around, she finally spotted what had changed. The trees. One of them was missing.

Frowning, she started toward where it stood before the *whump*. The cracking thuds started again. Through the underbrush, she glimpsed russet red tartan. It draped over the heavy, powerful muscles of an enormously tall, devilishly braw Highlander.

Who'd apparently lost his mind.

The man wore no shirt, only his russet plaid wrapped haphazardly around his waist. His right fist dripped blood. His veins stood in high relief. Heaving with exertion, he hauled back and struck a birch of middling size directly in the trunk. The thing shivered at the force. *Thud-shiver. Thud-crack. Thud-CRACK! Thud-crackle-crackle. Whump.*

What in dratted blazes was her madman of a husband doing felling trees … with his *fists?*

CHAPTER FIFTEEN

For Alexander, the world was white and red. White birch. Red blood. Repeat.

Her ribs had been broken. That was why she'd mewled and crumbled against him the day he was shot. She'd been in excruciating agony because the bastard had broken her ribs.

White birch. Red blood.

The bastard liked to twist and bruise her delicate wrists. Not to fracture, mind. Just for pain. To watch her writhe in pain.

White birch. Red blood.

She'd worn long sleeves and gloves. She'd kept her gaze low and sweetly bashful. She'd held her skirts high above the mud. She'd done everything to avoid perturbing the bastard because when he was vexed, she suffered.

White birch. Red blood.

Alexander had watched her in Charlotte Square. He'd seen her go several days without eating. He'd seen her speaking with Munro at her servants' entrance, risking herself to warn the MacPhersons about her brother's plans.

White birch. Red blood.

He'd ignored his instincts because nobody could be that damned *good*.

White birch. Red blood.

Another tree fell. The rage continued pounding inside him, so hot it burned cold. It wanted a dead man's blood, a dead man's pain.

"Alexander?"

He stilled.

"What in the name of all God's wee creatures are ye doing?"

Awareness of her charged through him like a lightning storm. His muscles seized and rippled with the force it took not to reach for her. Not to take. He commanded his body to calm. After several slow breaths, it complied—reluctantly. "Go back to the house, Duchess."

She wore silk. Leaf-green, the same color as her eyes. He hadn't seen her wear silk since her arrival in the glen. She was as bonnie as summer itself. And she carried a broom, for some reason, waving the thing at a swarm of midges as she picked her way toward him. "You're bleeding. What have ye done to your poor hand?"

He glanced down. "It isnae broken." It might be broken.

"How many trees have ye pummeled into falling?"

"One or two." It was definitely more.

"Alexander! This is madness."

It definitely was.

"Have ye tried using an ax, for God's sake?"

"Willnae work."

"Why not?"

"This isnae about the trees."

After eyeing his hand, her gaze went from perplexed to frustrated. She shook her head. "Why would ye punish yourself this way?"

He had many reasons, but he settled on two: "I need it. And I deserve it."

With a click of her tongue, she lifted her skirts and picked her way toward him. She took his uninjured hand and tugged him in the direction of the river. He allowed himself to be pulled because he was curious about what she planned to do. Only for that reason. Not because she bloody ruled him. She didn't. He was in command of himself.

When they reached the river, she unwrapped the cloth from around her hand, dipped it in the water, and very gently laid it across his knuckles. "You don't enjoy seeing me injured. Is that right?"

He frowned. "Bit of an understatement, that."

"Well, I don't want you to be injured, either. I especially don't want you injuring yourself on purpose." She took his hand in both of hers and raised it to her lips, carefully kissing the unbroken parts. "Please, please don't do this again," she whispered. "If ye must pummel things, find a way to do it without hurting yourself."

She didn't rule him. It wasn't as if he would fall to his knees every time she demanded something.

"Done." He didn't know where that answer came from. But her lips were soft, her breaths warm and sweet against his hand.

She rinsed the towel and dabbed gently. "Why did ye say you 'need' to pummel trees?"

Telling her the truth seemed like a very bad idea—the sort a man might pay for into old age. Yet, she'd likely learn the truth on her own. And she'd asked so sweetly, with a wee kiss on his forearm. "My nature isnae easy," he said. "Do ye ken I was in a Highland regiment as a young man?"

She nodded. "Annie told me. You and Campbell both, aye?"

"I followed him into the regiment, then into war on the Continent. Didnae think much about killin' before then. I've hunted since I was a wee lad, but that was always to feed us. We raised coos for the same reason. Da taught us to respect every beastie, to never take our survival for granted. Just because we *could* kill didnae mean we should."

Quietly, she rinsed and dabbed and dotted wee kisses above his wrist.

"But sometimes a man is good at things he shouldnae be."

Her tender ministrations paused.

"And sometimes a man doesnae discover that until he does them."

Leaf-green eyes lifted. "Are you good at killing, Alexander?"

"Aye. In the regiment, my commanders added to my duties once they kenned what I could do. They were always lookin' for men who didnae mind the rougher assignments."

"Rougher?"

"The important men run their wars from behind a desk. We're their weapons. When they find a good one, they use it 'til it's naught but rust and wear. I happen to be good with a blade. Good at stayin' hidden. A good shot." He gauged her expression, wondering if he should risk frightening her. But she didn't seem frightened. Concerned about him, perhaps, but not frightened. "Good at pain."

Still not frightened.

"I understand how to cause it, how to control it," he continued, watching her closely. "How to learn useful things, such as which divisions a French marshal might send west of Salamanca if he believed he had the advantage."

She swallowed, but she still held his hand with tender care. "Your commanders asked ye to hurt people?"

He shrugged. "They kenned if a certain man had to die mysteriously or a wee bit of information had to be pried loose, the job would get done."

"But you left the regiment. You came home."

"Aye. Couldnae continue with that lot. When ye're good at somethin', ye want to master it. I thought it best to leave before I was naught but rust and damnation."

She was taking this rather well for a lass. Her lips were pale, but she hadn't moved away from him. "Did you master it?"

"Oh, aye. Still use it from time to time, but only when necessary. Yer brother and his men created a lot of necessary."

She rubbed his forearm with her thumb. "This is why you pummel trees. You're punishing yourself for being good at killing."

"Nah. I'm givin' myself a vent because the man I want to kill is already dead. The punishment part is because I didnae see ye clearly enough." He brushed her bonnie cheek with his uninjured hand. "If I hadnae blinded myself, I would have made what Broderick did to him look like a wee skelp on a lad's backside."

She swallowed again and stared down at his battered knuckles. "What do you see clearly now that ye didn't before?"

Out of the dozen answers that came into his head, only one captured the heart of it. "My woman."

A faint smile curved her lips. She raised his hand to trail dainty kisses from his wrist to his elbow. "I want you to tup me again."

Arousal surged through his cock, rushing to meet her demand. "Bluidy hell, lass."

"But first, I want to know why ye call me Duchess. Early on, I assumed ye intended to mock me, but I no longer think that's true."

Damn it all, now he couldn't get the vision of tupping her here in the wood out of his head. He'd have to follow through or it would haunt him. "Ye *should* be a duchess," he answered. "But as ye're mine, and I cannae offer lofty titles, I call ye what ye are to me—my wife, the mother of my bairns. A woman too fine for aught that's ordinary." He shrugged. "Ye're my Duchess. That simple."

Her eyes turned soft and glowed as green as her ring. "And ye're my husband. That simple."

He drank in the sight of his woman in her bonnie green dress. Sunlight flittered through the trees above like wee birds, dappling her silk and lace. She was an angel, this woman. A regal, ethereal, delicate—

"I've an appetite to take ye in my mouth, husband."

Sweet, bloody Christ.

"Now, if ye'll be so kind as to lend me your plaid, I think I can use it to avoid soiling my knees. Dirt is devilishly hard to clean from silk."

"God Almighty."

She unwrapped his plaid with flicking motions and laid it at his feet with a saucy, triumphant grin. When his cock sprang free to greet her, she gripped and squeezed as if it gave her the purest pleasure to touch him. Then she dropped to her knees, licked the tip with a hungry little lap, and spread her lips around the head.

"Duchess."

Her groan hummed around him. Her hand gripped him at the base to hold him still for her sweet, eager suckling.

His cock was a dark, flushed stalk inside her wee, dainty white fist. The contrast between his rough, blunt hardness and her pale, delicate beauty was almost obscene. But nothing aroused him like the sight of her aroused, lambent eyes and her sweet, eager mouth. His ballocks ached to deliver what she was demanding. His cock pulsed in agonizing want.

"I'm going to come in yer mouth if ye dinnae stop," he warned.

Her moans grew more excited. Her hips moved in wee circles as she played his slit with her tongue. Why had he taught her about that? She'd used it to torment him ever since.

"Does my cock please ye, Duchess?"

Her answer was a long, agonized moan. She drew him deeper, nearly to her throat.

But he was too big for that delicate mouth to take more. And he wanted to finish inside her sheath again. So, he pulled back, gently cupping her cheek and soothing her displeased grunt with a stroke of her lips. "Easy, love. I need to tup ye now. If I take care not to soil yer skirts, will ye let me?"

Her hand clawed into his thigh. Her nipples stood out in high relief against her silk bodice. Her lovely throat rippled, and her sweet, pink tongue swiped over his cock head. "Aye," she groaned. "Just hurry."

He moved behind her and dropped to his knees. After carefully raising the back of her gown to expose her naked buttocks, he pressed her forward onto her hands. Her petals bloomed for him, pink, swollen, and glistening with her honeyed desire.

His woman *loved* taking him in her mouth.

But he loved taking her sheath—as many times as she'd allow, which was many, and in any way that pleased her, which was all of them.

Slowly, he watched his cock spreading her soft, swollen folds until the flushed stalk stretched that wee opening impossibly wide. Sinking inside her inch by inch, he savored her fluttering welcome, the spasms that were like tremors before a quake. A warning that the earth was about to move.

When he was seated as deeply as he could go, surrounded by her fire and on fire to give her more, he braced himself over her and pressed the tiniest bit deeper.

She sucked in a breath, her shoulders tensing. Shaking. "Alexander!" she gasped.

He kissed that long, beautiful neck, rewarding her for indulging him, then retreated a fraction. "Are ye tender, love?"

Her breaths came faster as she worked her hips against his. "A wee bit."

"Eight times," he breathed. "We'll have to go easier tomorrow. Ye've been hungry, eh?"

"Oh, God. Starving for ye."

He kissed her soft cheek, turning her mouth to his. He started his rhythm, keeping the ride slow and gentle. He palmed her belly and pressed with the heel of his hand to add the light pressure she enjoyed in this position. As anticipated, she went wild, bucking and thrusting her hips back into his.

"Harder," she begged. "Faster, please."

"Dinnae wish to wrinkle yer gown, Duchess," he teased in her ear. "Now, I'll take this sweet sheath as slowly as I want, and ye'll come for me like the bonnie wife ye are. Isnae that so?"

She screamed his name through gritted teeth.

He kept his pace steady and added more pressure with his hand. "Such a beautiful woman, my Sabella. 'Tis pure heaven bein' inside ye." His head was a fog of heightened lust, coiling sensation, and intoxicating enchantment. He'd known she was his from the first. But he'd had no idea how fortunate he was. His woman was nearly always wet, soft, and eager. Her sensuality stunned him every time.

Though it was obvious how desperately she wanted him to move faster, she settled in, arched her back, and patiently let him set the pace. He wanted to savor her—the rose-and-lavender scent of her hair, the richer, womanly scent of her honeyed arousal, the sweetness of her moans whenever his cockhead slid past that wee, puckered spot inside her. He liked to take his time.

But she was squeezing him hard, now, using the tightness against him. And he couldn't bloody resist her. Perhaps she did rule him. Just a little.

His cock worked deeper. Faster. Faster. He chased her satisfaction and intended to delay his own. But the sensation of being milked and spurred while she pretended wifely obedience shot him past his breaking point. His new rhythm stuttered. His seed surged upward, exploding inside her. She screamed her ecstasy and seized upon him like a proper duchess demanding to be served until she was full.

He fed her everything he had. In fairness, she fed him, too.

Late that night, as he lay with his bonnie wife draped over him in their bed, he contemplated the turns of a man's good fortune. Getting shot wasn't so bad, really. "I'm a lucky man, Duchess."

She chuckled, throaty and sensual. "Do ye suppose so?"

"Aye. I want ye to birth my bairns."

More chuckling and a dainty yawn. "If we keep havin' days like today, I've a suspicion ye'll get your wish."

He grinned, even though it was dark and she couldn't see him—and his hand hurt like it was fucking broken. He'd have to speak to Magdalene about it tomorrow. He wasn't looking forward to the lecture.

"I confess it makes me nervous," she murmured. "My mother died in childbed. Our wee brother, too."

Frowning, he stroked her naked back. "What about yer father?"

A lengthy pause. "He couldn't bear to be without her."

Bloody hell.

"In some ways, I wish he'd left us sooner. It took him a year to decide, and in that time, he spent every farthing and then some. The house had to be sold to pay debts. Nobody apart from a greedy cousin wanted to take us in. Kenneth had to steal me away until he reached his majority."

Alexander didn't enjoy hearing about Kenneth, but for better or worse, the bastard had been at the center of her life since she was wee. He braced himself and asked, "He was a lord. Didnae his title help?"

"No. Our father's disgrace followed us, and there was no estate. Kenneth was fourteen when we fled our cousin's house. He found work wherever he could. A weaver's shop. A livery stable. He wagered a bit in the beginning. Got pummeled a time or two for having such good luck. But he invested those winnings in speculation schemes. In time, he earned enough to buy the house in Charlotte Square. Kenneth was always clever."

Kenneth had been more than clever. Much of his wealth had come from a club that catered to certain perversions. Many prominent figures in Edinburgh had been caught up in his blackmail net, which was how a minor Scottish lord had wielded enough influence to orchestrate Broderick's downfall. It was also why his accommodations in the Inverness jail had resembled the finest inn, and why he would never have been punished by the courts. With judges and dukes in his pocket, Kenneth Lockhart hadn't needed to worry.

"I wish I still had something of my mother," Sabella said sleepily. "Now that I'm wed and might become a mother myself, I think about her a great deal."

"Ye didnae keep anything of hers?"

"Everything I had was in my trunks."

Bloody hell. He'd forgotten about that.

"She had the loveliest emerald necklace and ear bobs. Kenneth made certain we never sold them. He insisted I must wear our mother's jewels when he escorted me down the aisle to my husband."

Feeling a bit sick, Alexander focused on keeping his muscles relaxed wherever they touched her.

"I would have liked to have Annie's letters back, too," she said. "And the documents from Kenneth's estate. What do ye suppose a thief does with that sort of thing?"

He didn't answer. Instead, he waited for her to fall asleep. Then he left their bed and carried a lantern upstairs to the attic. Apart from dust and cisterns, it was empty—except for one corner. He removed the canvas draped over green leather with brass trim. Then he opened the largest trunk and withdrew the emerald necklace. Lamplight glinted on the faceted jewels. They reminded him of her eyes.

Next, he sifted through her belongings as he hadn't bothered to do when he'd hauled them up here. He found a neatly tied bundle of letters from Annie. Then he found Lockhart's estate documents inside a leather portfolio. A second, smaller bundle of letters fell out. When he examined them, he frowned.

The letters were unopened. And they were from Kenneth Lockhart's mistress, Cecilia Hamilton. The same mistress Broderick had dallied with, provoking Lockhart's wrathful jealousy.

Alexander hesitated only a moment before he opened the first letter. With each subsequent letter, his unease grew.

Before his death, Lockhart had married his mistress. Cecilia Hamilton was now Cecilia Lockhart. Following Lockhart's demise, she'd fled to Amsterdam, where Lockhart had sent funds to aid in his escape.

Cecilia had written Sabella to warn her about someone named Cromartie, with whom Lockhart had made a bargain. Cecilia didn't specify the terms, but it sounded like the bargain had something to do with Sabella and that Sabella would understand the context.

Cromartie believes he is owed, the letter said. *Be careful.*

Ominous and maddeningly cryptic. Alexander's gut tightened. Churned. He didn't know who Cromartie was, but Cecilia clearly saw him as a threat to Sabella, enough that she'd written to warn her.

She'd also written for another ominous reason.

Alexander cursed. He stuffed the letters back into the portfolio, slammed the trunk closed, and threw the canvas back into place. Bloody hell.

Bloody, bloody hell.

Before his death, Kenneth hadn't just married Cecilia Hamilton. He'd impregnated her. Which meant that Lord Lockhart might soon have an heir.

And Alexander might soon have to tell his Duchess how far he'd been willing to go to keep her.

Chapter Sixteen

On her twenty-fourth day as a wife, Sabella realized why there could only be one Alexander MacPherson: If all husbands were as glorious as hers, the world would grind to a halt.

How was a woman meant to get anything done? All she could think about was tupping, and when they weren't tupping, all she could think about was inventing excuses to be near him. Since he'd started growing his beard again, she could scarcely control herself. It didn't help that his muscles were noticeably larger after spending the past few weeks pounding posts, hefting stone, hauling furniture up the staircase, and building her new range.

He'd turned over the construction of Campbell's house to Adam MacDonnell, which freed up the hours he spent outside the distillery each day. But the moment he arrived home, he found her wherever she was—dusting, cooking, bathing—and made love to her as though it had been a year rather than hours since the last time.

It was a wonder he'd accomplished so much given how often she importuned him.

Sighing in blissful contentment, she carried a cup of cider outside to her braw Highlander, who was busy constructing her walled garden in the August heat. He'd nearly finished the east wall where the gate would be installed.

"I have an idea for decorating the outside, husband." She handed him the cup and watched with a long, lustful clench as he drank it down.

He wiped his forehead with his sleeve and handed her the empty cup. "Aye, lass?"

"I want that red pest's head on my wall."

He laughed.

"I'm not jesting. Let it be a warning to all intruders: Those who enter here risk imminent demise and potential stewing."

"Vicious woman."

She grinned and returned to the kitchen, where Mrs. MacBean and Magdalene were stirring up salve, soaps, and liniment on Sabella's new range. Tomorrow, the Glenscannadoo Games would draw visitors from all over the Highlands. The two women planned to sell their wares to spectators at the fair.

"How many batches did we make last time?" Mrs. MacBean scratched her shrubby head. "Seven?"

"Four," said Magdalene. "I don't think we've ever made seven."

Sabella sat down to sort through the herbs—comfrey, calendula, lavender. They were teaching her a bit, but mostly, they were arguing over quantities. That left her more time to think about Alexander competing in the loch swim tomorrow. She didn't want other ladies to ogle him, but she also didn't want to miss seeing him emerge from the loch victorious and gloriously wet. A true dilemma.

"Och, why do I keep hearin' seven? Seven batches. Seven days. Seven months. Seven …" Mrs. MacBean frowned in Sabella's direction. Her milky eye twitched. "Seven roses. Or mayhap only two upon the soil. One for the bride, one for the bud."

Sabella fingered her rose pendant. She'd found a lovely silk ribbon in the haberdashery to replace the damaged cord, and Alexander had sealed the wood with a light varnish. The finished piece was exquisite. Little wonder the old woman kept staring at it.

"Do you need more rose oil?" Sabella asked. "There's a wee bit left."

Mrs. MacBean rubbed her forehead and looked around as if wondering how she'd wandered into such a strange place. She gripped Magdalene's arm with strange urgency. "Did ye harvest enough raspberry leaf?"

Magdalene glanced at the assortment of herbs laid out on the table. "Which formulation calls for raspberry leaf?"

A befuddled blink. "We must have more. Shepherd's purse, too. Set it aside."

Frowning, Magdalene patted the old woman's hand. "Very well. Why don't ye rest, Mary. Have some tea while I finish this batch."

Mrs. MacBean shook her head then wandered outside, muttering about collecting more yarrow before spring.

Alexander entered a moment later. When he raked Sabella with a smoldering glance, she nearly melted into the chair. "Have ye any of that lamb left from yesterday, lass?"

She nodded toward the larder. "A bit. There's bacon from this morning, as well."

He kissed her temple then disappeared into the larder. When he returned, he dragged a chair next to her and sat down to eat with wolfish, eager bites.

Smiling at his hearty appetite, she poured him a cup of cider then resumed her task of sorting herbs. "Magdalene, have you decided whether you'll attend the Glenscannadoo Ball?" The crowning event of the Glenscannadoo Gathering and Highland Games was the ball hosted by the laird. Having attended the previous year with Kenneth, Sabella remembered the event as a lovely evening filled with dancing, whisky, and Highland fare.

Of course, last year's ball had ended with Annie provoking Kenneth into confessing his crimes against Broderick MacPherson. Kenneth had been dragged away to jail, and Sabella's life had spiraled into a nightmare. But that was hardly the ball's fault.

"Aye," Magdalene answered. "Dr. Cameron says we must make an appearance, as a physician's practice relies on the goodwill of his potential patients." Magdalene's cheeks were flushed from the heat of cooking, so Sabella couldn't determine whether she was embarrassed.

Initially, Magdalene had declined Cameron's invitation, concerned that she'd have nothing to wear and that others might mistake her attendance with the physician for courtship. Nora had addressed the first concern by modifying a tartan dress from another customer's abandoned order to fit Magdalene's thin frame. To alleviate the second concern, Sabella had suggested that she and Alexander attend alongside Magdalene and Dr. Cameron, removing any appearance of impropriety.

Alexander hadn't been pleased at being volunteered for duty. He'd grumbled for hours about how much he loathed "dressin' like a peacock and prancin' about like a pure dafty." Sabella had promised to reward him with *extensive* harlotry following the ball. After a hard, grinding kiss, he'd rasped, "Done."

As soon as Alexander left the kitchen to return to wall building, Magdalene observed, "I can scarcely believe he's the same man whose wounds I tended all those months. The robust appetite, the vigor. No whisky." Her gray gaze shifted to Sabella. "He's even competing in the loch swim. Remarkable."

Sabella sighed as she stabbed a sprig of lavender into an empty bottle. "Aye, the loch swim."

"You don't sound pleased."

"Oh, I am." More lavender stabbing. "So very"—stab—"pleased."

Magdalene's lips pursed in amusement as she poured her salve into tins. "It's a sign that his strength has finally returned."

"Aye. And all the ladies coming from far and wide"—stab, stab—"will have a chance to ogle that strength to their hearts' content." Stab, stab. "What could be better?"

Amusement softened into empathy. With a gentle nod, Magdalene set her pan aside and wiped her hands on her apron. "Other ladies may look, but I doubt Alexander will notice. You're the only woman he sees."

"I'm being unreasonable, I know." She started stuffing rose petals into the bottles. "But I can't help it. He's …"

Magdalene hummed agreement. "A MacPherson."

"He offered to hire maids to help me manage the house, but even the ones he dismissed speak of him with lustful longing. I can't abide having them live here. Of course, they also complained about his bellowing and impossible demands, and I haven't found either to be true. The only time he raises his voice is when I've injured myself."

"He hired those maids when he first left my care," said Magdalene. "He was still in an extraordinary amount of pain. Even a patient man's temper would wear thin."

Sabella focused on the rose petals, wincing as they bruised from the pressure. "I hate to think of it," she whispered. "I hate remembering what happened."

Magdalene came around the table to place a gentle hand on her shoulder. "It's in the past. He's healed now."

"He blamed me at first. I don't know if he still does, and I can't bring myself to ask."

Magdalene sat next to her. "Did you tell him about your injuries?"

"A little. It ... upset him." Pummeling trees might qualify as more than a wee bit upset. "We haven't really discussed it."

A deep silence fell before Magdalene said quietly, "Do ye ken what he said when he first awakened after the surgeon stitched him up?"

Sabella shook her head.

"Before he asked about Kate or Broderick, before he requested laudanum or whisky for the pain, he wanted to ken if you were still alive. Yours was the first name on his lips."

Her chest went tight. The light in the kitchen began to shimmer. She hadn't been the only one to feel it, then. That connection, that inexplicable binding.

Magdalene seemed to want to say more, but instead, she patted Sabella's hand and returned to the range to start her third batch of salve. "Hire the maids," her friend advised. "Let other lasses look their fill. I assure ye, once Alexander MacPherson has what he wants in his sights, nothing will lure him away. He's not Rannoch."

Sabella's heart twisted hard. She'd been so busy wrestling with her own jealousies that she hadn't realized how petty and self-indulgent she must sound to Magdalene. "I shouldn't be bending your ear with my nonsense," she said. "I'm sorry."

Magdalene waved away her apology, though Sabella noticed she wouldn't look at her.

After pouring oil into the lavender-rose bottles, Sabella started on the rosemary hair rinse. "Has Rannoch said whether he's coming to the ball?"

Narrow shoulders stiffened. "He's been away for the past week in Edinburgh, so we haven't spoken about it. But after he competes in the Games, I expect he'll spend his evening carousing with every lass within flirting distance. His usual entertainment."

Drat and blast, Sabella hadn't meant to dig the knife deeper. She wished she could reassure Magdalene that Rannoch's overprotectiveness showed how much he valued her, and that treating her differently from other women was a sign of respect, not indifference. But

Magdalene didn't pine for his respect, and Rannoch didn't seem capable of giving her more.

Aching for her friend, Sabella put on her brightest face. "Well, I'm certain you'll have a lovely time at the ball with Dr. Cameron." The physician was a serious, studious fellow who rarely smiled. But Magdalene could do much worse. "Perhaps you can persuade him to dance."

Magdalene cast a wry glance over her shoulder. "Or perhaps he'll recite *A Red, Red Rose* in my honor and declare his love 'till a' the seas gang dry,' hmm?"

Sabella laughed. "Not every man can be Robert Burns."

"Nor can every lass inspire poetry." She gave Sabella a sheepish smile as she poured steaming water from the kettle into the rosemary bottles. "I'm content as I am. Dr. Cameron has been quite generous to serve as my mentor. There's nothing more to it."

Mrs. MacBean returned to the kitchen with leaves in her hair and something white splattered on her shoulders. She carried an armful of yarrow. Her leather pouch overflowed with mushrooms. Looped beneath the pouch was a thorny, half-eaten stem with a limp clump of roots still attached. Huffing, the old woman piled her collection onto the table.

Sabella frowned at the pile. Was that … her rosebush? It was. Given the green in the stem, she thought it was still alive. Fingering the dirt-clumped roots, she asked, "Where did you find this?"

"Between the faery stones under the crow's nest. Those crows werenae too pleased that I interrupted their conversation, let me tell ye."

Sabella peered closer. The white splats were … oh, dear. "Aye, so it seems." She handed the old woman a towel.

Mrs. MacBean swiped at her shoulders. "They're plannin' some mischief at the quarry. I didnae ask questions. Secretive beasties." When she shook her wild hair, a small mushroom plopped out onto the table followed by a tuft of moss. She watched the mushroom roll with an unsynchronized blink. "I wondered where I put that." She stuffed the mushroom and moss into her leather pouch. "Oh, they mentioned ye, lass. Said to tell ye they'll look after yer roses if ye'll feed 'em meat scraps from time to time."

Unwinding the pouch's leather cord from around the rosebush stem, Sabella only half-listened to the old woman's nonsense. "Meat scraps. Very well."

"They also said whenever ye see 'em outside yer window, the answer is 'not today.'"

Sabella's hands fumbled on the stem, and a thorn sank into her thumb. She hissed in a breath then quickly refocused on Mrs. MacBean. The woman now turned in circles while trying to pluck another tuft of moss from her hair.

"Wh-who said that?" Sabella murmured tightly.

Another uneven blink. "The crows."

Chills chased up and down her spine. "They're birds."

"Some are, mayhap. In this glen, ye cannae be sure. Regardless, they're gossips, all. Best ye dinnae ken the things they see when we think nobody's watchin'." She blew out a wide-eyed breath. "They admire yer talent for keepin' yer gown clean whilst on yer knees, lass."

Sabella's face heated like the beeswax in Magdalene's pot. This was all a lot of nonsense. Mrs. MacBean was guessing. She had to be.

The old woman frowned down at her bulging pouch full of mushrooms and moss. "Magdalene, did Rannoch purchase the book ye wanted?"

"The one about midwifery? I asked him to, aye. He should be bringing it home with him from Edinburgh."

"Good, good. Read it twice before spring. Tell yer suitor to read it, too. He needs a wee bit more education about women." She waved a finger in a general circle around Magdalene's hips. "Lad kens about the parts but naught about how to put 'em to proper use."

Turning away from the range, Magdalene frowned. "I don't have a suitor, Mary."

"Nae the most memorable fellow, is he?" Mrs. MacBean clicked her tongue and shook her head. "Before I met Mr. Brodie, I kenned a man with a similar disposition. Cannae recall his name. Or his face. I might have wed him once." She scratched her head. "Or twice. To be fair, I mistook him for his cousin. What the devil was his name?"

Magdalene's expression lay somewhere between dismay and wry amusement. She and Sabella shared a glance before Sabella asked the obvious question: "Was it MacBean?"

"Aye! That's it, lassie! How did ye ken?"

Sabella chuckled. "Just a guess."

"A humorless fellow was Mr. MacBean. But he did ken what all the pertinent parts were for, which explains the third marriage. Cannae say the same for Magdalene's suitor, sadly."

Sighing, Magdalene wiped the sweat from her brow and poured the new batch of salve into the tins. "I don't have a suitor," she repeated, her patience now edged with irritation.

"No, ye have two. One hasnae declared his suit yet. The other never will."

Sabella intervened to spare her friend any further poking on this particular sore spot. "Mrs. MacBean, it's a warm day. Perhaps you should have something to drink."

"Och, that's how I wound up marryin' Mr. MacBean the fourth time." The old woman patted Sabella's shoulder. "Take my advice, lass. Dinnae drink a mushroom broth ye havenae brewed yerself. Also, dinnae eavesdrop on crows. Dinnae prank a man who can target ye for assassination. And never, ever mistake a goat for a horse."

Sabella stifled a grin. "Anything else?"

"Aye." She gave her a final pat. "Never tell a MacPherson what he cannae do. Soon enough, he'll prove ye wrong."

Chapter Seventeen

"I think he fancies her," Sabella whispered.

Alexander forced himself to focus on what his wife was saying. He'd been eyeing the exits in Glenscannadoo Manor's ballroom, contemplating all the possible locations for tupping. There was a grove of trees in the garden and a wee hedge maze the daft laird had installed last autumn.

Alas, he suspected there'd be no tupping until after the ball. Sabella was singularly focused on matchmaking Magdalene Cuthbert and the sandy-haired physician, Dr. Andrew Cameron—a match destined to come to naught.

He eyed his wife's gown, the one she'd worn when she'd seduced him in the wood—green silk to match her eyes and ivory lace to match her skin. By God, she was a bonnie woman. Here in an opulent ballroom surrounded by monied guests, she was in her element. She glided through candlelight as elegantly as a swan through water. Every turn of her cheek, every warm, gracious smile radiated good breeding.

This was the life she could have had, the world from which he'd stolen her.

He adjusted his noose of a cravat and swiped a glass of whisky from a nearby tray. "What makes ye think so?"

Tugging him to the right, she nodded to where Magdalene danced with Cameron and two other couples. "See how careful he is to avoid prolonged contact? He's affected by her."

"It's a reel. He's tryin' not to fall on his arse."

"I disagree."

"This isnae goin' where ye think it's goin', Duchess."

"I don't see why not." She tapped his arm with her folded fan. "You see? He grinned and she covered a smile. The signs are clear."

Silently cursing the stupidity of youngest brothers, Alexander downed his dram. "Mayhap he fancies her—"

"He does. It's *obvious*."

"—but she doesnae fancy him."

"How do you know?"

"Lass." He knew the same way everyone knew—everyone except Rannoch.

She shook her head. "Magdalene deserves to be loved, Alexander."

"Aye, she does."

"Dr. Cameron is a respectable gentleman."

Cameron was about as stimulating as unsalted rice, but Alexander didn't argue. Sabella longed to see her friend happily matched to someone who would appreciate her. Unfortunately for Magdalene, the instincts Rannoch denied were unlikely to allow it. But he couldn't explain his brother without explaining himself. Better not to invite questions.

"Did you hear their conversation about the balms earlier?" she asked.

"Aye."

"Dr. Cameron listens to her with careful attention, and she feels comfortable offering her opinions."

"They were discussin' midge bites. Hardly a grand romance."

Sabella sniffed. "I think they're brilliantly suited."

Being brilliantly suited wouldn't protect the doctor if Rannoch ever woke the hell up. But he couldn't say that. Instead, he grunted and set aside his whisky glass.

Moments later, Angus and Nora entered the ballroom bickering about Nora's gig. "That's it. I'm buyin' ye a bluidy coach, woman," Da grumbled. "That trinket belongs in the kindling bin."

"A coach is larger and requires two horses instead of one. I'd also have to employ a coachman."

"Aye. That's the point. It's safer."

"It's too costly. I'd never be able to repay ye."

Angus's glower deepened to thunderous levels. "None of this would be necessary if ye'd come to yer senses and—"

"Sabella! How lovely ye look in that color. Just as I pictured."

Beaming, Sabella ran gloved hands over the green silk of her skirts and cooed her appreciation for the dressmaker's skill.

Alexander had watched his wife dressing earlier. Her hands beneath those silk gloves were chapped and callused. She'd winced when a roughened spot had caught on her lace. Then she'd applied a second coat of salve.

He'd wanted to kick his own arse. Those delicate hands shouldn't be reddened or rough. Hiring her as his maid might have started as retribution, but he hadn't even made it through the first day before the regrets set in.

He'd all but demanded that she let him hire a proper staff, but the stubborn woman insisted on doing everything herself. Seeing her succeed at tasks no woman of her rank should have to master, watching her grow in confidence and satisfaction day by day, he battled between fury at himself and pride in his woman. But the time had come to overrule her objections. Lately, his regrets were piling to suffocating levels, and it couldn't continue.

Even old, mad Mrs. MacBean had warned him that he might lose her. "Have ye told her yet, laddie?" she'd asked ten days past.

At the time, he'd been setting posts in rock-riddled ground—frustrating work. "Told her what?"

"That she's yer bride."

Mopping his brow with a damp towel, he'd glared at the old woman. "She's wearin' my ring and sleepin' in my bed. I think she kens."

"Aye. Have ye told her the ring belonged to yer mam? That it was fashioned by yer grandfather?"

Resuming his work, he'd bitten down on his frustration. "No."

"Have ye told her what ye did to the thieves?"

His mood darkened. How did she know about that? "No."

"She cannae forgive ye if ye dinnae admit what ye've done."

If he admitted everything, she'd leave him. "Do ye have a point, auld woman, or are ye just bletherin' to plague me?"

She'd given him a pewter medallion etched with a lopsided, upside-down U. "Wear this on yer hunt. Mind the auld dwelling places. Help her tend her garden. Wily pests sneak in if ye leave the gate open."

He'd stuffed the thing in his pocket, his blood running cold. "I'm buildin' her garden, just as ye said."

The old woman smiled, but it was wistful and consoling. "That's good, laddie."

"Dinnae look at me like that."

She'd rested her hand on his arm, sadness welling in her eyes.

"Damn it, dinnae look at me like that!" he'd growled.

Her milky eye caught the light, turning whiter. Her hand gripped him hard. "Some things are written."

"No."

"Blood on yer hands. Blood on yer bride."

A denial lodged in his throat like a hot coal. But Mrs. MacBean had been right too many times to ignore a warning like this. "What do ye see?"

She'd gone silent, her eyes distant and searching. "Some things are written," she repeated in that queerly layered voice. "Some things are hidden. I'm sorry, laddie."

"Dinnae tell me ye're sorry. Tell me how to stop it."

She shook her head. "She held ye while ye bled. Now, ye'll hold her."

"Will I lose her?" His question wasn't even a breath, let alone a sound.

Frown deepening, she gazed up at him until a strange dizziness made his head swim. Then she blinked, and the feeling passed. "Some things even I cannae see."

Ten days later, he still couldn't get her words out of his mind. Urgency thrummed inside him with nowhere to aim it. He'd tried to carry on as if nothing was wrong, even dressing like a bloody peacock to please Sabella.

Now, he tugged to loosen his cravat and scanned the ballroom. When he saw Rannoch enter, he murmured his excuses to Sabella, Da, and Nora then crossed to greet his brother. "Ye're late."

Grinning at a passing lass, Rannoch replied, "Ye're lucky I came at all."

"Did ye learn anythin'?"

Rannoch had returned from a week-long delivery to Edinburgh the previous night. Before he'd left, Alexander had asked him to make inquiries with several old acquaintances.

"Cromartie was Lockhart's paid guard. A real bruiser. Fond of gin. Last anybody kenned, he disappeared the night Lockhart died."

"The same time as Lockhart's mistress."

"Aye." Rannoch surveyed the room, lighting on this female and that with varying degrees of disinterest. "Duncan thinks Cromartie accompanied her to Amsterdam. Poor lass."

"Why 'poor lass'?"

"The bruiser has a history with women. Landed him in jail once or twice." Rannoch's gaze shifted to meet Alexander's, and his disgusted fury flashed for a split second. "Let's just say lasses dinnae fare well in his care."

Alexander's gut tightened as his urgency doubled. "Any signs that he's returned to Scotland?"

"Duncan's lookin' into it. He'll send word when he kens somethin'."

Biting off a foul curse, Alexander nodded. "My thanks, brother."

Looking bored and restless, Rannoch peered beyond Alexander's shoulder. "Da came? I thought he hated the laird's peacocking parties."

"Nora wanted to attend."

"Aye, she looks happier than he does. Sabella, too. I see ye've let yer bride wear silks again." Grinning in the irritatingly knowing way only a brother could manage, Rannoch chuckled. "Before ye wed, I feared for her. Now, I fear for ye. Cannae be comfortable bein' led around by the ballocks."

Alexander glared.

"Dinnae fash. I willnae tell her how ye stare at her when she isnae lookin'."

"How's that?"

"Like a drownin' man stares at dry land."

Was he that obvious? "Ye're a daft sod."

Rannoch's grin broadened. "'Tis a shame. Seems all my brothers dance to the tune their wives play."

"The tune isnae played by either of us, ye eejit." Alexander wanted to explain that when a man found his woman, the music played on its own, and they could either let it drive them mad or dance together. But he'd be wasting his breath. Rannoch wouldn't believe him until he came to his senses. Sadly, it might already be too late.

Rannoch grunted. "Da's just as bad. I dinnae ken why he hasnae put his foot down with Nora."

"Aye. Ye wouldnae ken. Because ye're a daft sod."

Rannoch's gaze slid past a lass in yellow then one in pink before locking on the plain lass wearing violet tartan. His grin vanished as he recognized her. He stiffened. When his eyes went ice cold, Alexander wondered if there might be a brawl at the ball.

"What in bluidy hell is Magdalene doin'?" he asked softly.

Keeping his expression neutral, Alexander glanced over his shoulder. They were just finishing their reel. "Looks like dancin' to me."

"Aye, but she's dancin' with Cameron." His brother's head took on a familiar tilt, his expression a familiar hardness. Alexander had seen the same look in the mirror on a few occasions, though very rarely in Rannoch. "Why's she doin' that?"

"Same reason anybody dances. Testin' the waters, I reckon."

A deep, thunderous frown. "Nah. Not Mouse."

"Why not?"

"She's different."

"Not that different."

Rannoch glared at the dancers with fixed intensity. "She works for him. People will gossip." The reel came to a close, and she curtsied to the other dancers. "I should warn her about encouraging him. Mouse doesnae understand what men are like. Wouldnae occur to her to guard against it."

Magdalene Cuthbert had been raised in an orphan hospital. She'd served for years as a paid companion to an abusive old woman with several disreputable grandsons. She'd spent months imprisoned in the Calton Hill Bridewell for thievery. That was how she'd met Broderick. She'd also spent months nursing Alexander through his recovery without a hint of missishness about his body.

Magdalene might look like a nun, but she was far from cloistered.

Nevertheless, arguing with his brother would get him nowhere. Alexander could already see him rationalizing those troublesome MacPherson instincts. He'd done it himself a time or two. Aye, the old Rannoch was returning—the relaxed posture, the affectedly charming expression.

"Mayhap I'll stay a while." Rannoch smiled tightly at a passing maid and swiped a glass of whisky. "Keep an eye on things."

"Speakin' of which, I may need ye to watch over Sabella for a week or two."

Rannoch frowned. "Goin' somewhere?"

"Edinburgh." Alexander's gut hadn't stopped churning since he'd read Cecilia Hamilton's letter. He'd written her the following day, but she hadn't responded. For all he knew, Cromartie might have killed the lass. The bruiser might be on his way to

Scotland to "claim" the prize Lockhart had promised. He might already be here.

Blood on yer hands. Blood on yer bride.

After Mrs. MacBean's warning, Alexander's instincts were blaring an alarm so loud that he was surprised everyone couldn't hear it. He needed answers, and he needed them now.

"Duncan doesnae miss much," said Rannoch. "Ye dinnae trust him?"

"I trust myself more." He ran a hand over his beard. It itched in the heat, but Sabella loved it so much that she petted his face when she kissed him every morning. He'd pay any price for that. "I'll hire men to guard the house. Can ye handle the distillery and look in on her each day?"

"Of course." Rannoch glanced to where Magdalene and Cameron had rejoined Angus, Nora, and Sabella. Jaw flexing, he finished his dram. "Mouse enjoys their visits. I'll take her with me. Keep her … busy." He shot Alexander a glance. "Do ye really think Cromartie would track her here?"

The cold slither beneath his skin said aye. That feeling had saved him before. "I dinnae ken. But I'm nae takin' chances."

Returning to Sabella's side like a drowning man returning to shore, Alexander slid an arm around her waist. She was laughing at something Da said and nodding at something Nora said, but her hand automatically threaded through his where it rested on her hip.

His woman loved to be touched.

He kissed her temple and whispered in her ear, "Come outside with me now."

Faint pink color bloomed in her long neck and soft cheeks. Leaf-green eyes lit up with sensual awareness. A sweet pink tongue darted over her lips. With perfect aplomb, she murmured a polite excuse about getting fresh air then let him lead her out to the small hedge maze beyond the busy terrace.

Night had fallen, and the moon lit the rustling oaks and birches in a silvery glow. Stars blanketed the sky like diamond dust. Owls hooted in the faraway pines.

Sabella released his arm and dashed playfully away into the maze. Spinning in a circle, she grinned. "Are you planning to importune me, sir?"

"Aye. Thoroughly." What he really meant to do was erase all memories of French counts and random dukes. "Ye can run, lass, but I'll always catch ye."

Laughing, she skirted around the next corner. He gave her a minute or so then went in pursuit. He caught her just past the fourth turn.

She shrieked in excitement as he lifted her into his arms. Clinging to his neck, she giggled. "Who will save me? I've been caught by a wicked man."

He held her tighter, bracing her nape. The silken tendrils of her hair tickled his hand. "Nobody will save ye, Duchess. Ye're mine and always have been."

She quieted, petting his beard and running her silk-clad fingers over his lips. Moonlit green eyes roamed his face. "Always. I—I feel that too," she breathed as if only the night could hear her confession.

Suddenly, his heart threatened to explode. It expanded inside his chest, choking off his answer. Instead, he kissed her. His woman. His bride. His Duchess.

Those lips curved against his. Those hands caressed his jaw. That tongue greeted his so sweetly, he couldn't stop. He carried her the last few turns to the center of the maze where a stone bench waited. Sitting with her in his lap, he crushed her against him, trying to slow his pounding heart.

She didn't protest, merely continued petting him and raining sweet little kisses over his face and jaw. "I didn't know what to do about it," she murmured. "Ye've made me ache inside from the first, as if a crucial part was carved out of me and placed in yer hands. Do ye remember the first time I saw ye?"

He nodded.

"The desire shocked me. But it didn't feel new. It felt like … recognition."

Breaths sawed inside his chest. He touched his forehead to hers until they breathed in tandem. He wanted to tell her everything—how many times he'd contemplated abducting her from her brother's house, how many ways he'd fantasized about slaughtering Munro for what he'd assumed she'd given the man, how many nights he'd gone without sleep because he, too, felt like a part of him had been carved out. The pain had been never-ending.

"I want all the pieces of me back," she whispered. "But I also want ye to keep them so I can demand a part of ye in return."

"Ye have all of me," he said, his voice reduced to gravel. "Every part is yers, love."

She kissed him, her mouth curving against his. "Oh, I like the sound of that, husband." She nibbled his lower lip and rubbed her breasts against his chest. "Mine."

He wanted to take what was his, but he heard giggling and footsteps beyond the hedging. After kissing her as long as he dared, he resigned himself to waiting until they were home to love her properly.

It took two bloody hours to extricate themselves from the ball and drive the curricle he'd recently purchased back to his house. Unfortunately, along the way, Sabella's soft affection turned into bristling displeasure. That was his fault. He should have waited to tell her he was leaving the glen.

"Edinburgh? I shall come with you," she said as he urged the horses up the easterly road.

"Nah. I cannae afford the distraction."

She stiffened. "Is that what I am to you? A distraction."

He ran a hand over his beard. Sometimes, he wished he had Rannoch's ease with the lasses. "This isnae a pleasure trip, Duchess. My work will take me all day every day for at least a week. Mayhap two."

"A week or *two?*" She stiffened further. "I'm definitely coming with you."

"No, ye'll stay where I put ye. Which is here." His mood darkened as she withdrew her hand from his arm to her lap. "Ye willnae be alone. Before I depart, I'm hiring a staff."

"I've already told you I don't want one."

"Ye havenae any choice." He glanced down at her white gloves. "Yer hands are a disgrace."

She sucked in a breath and folded her hands together as if to hide them. Only then did he realize how his statement must have sounded.

"Very well," she said, tight and muted. "From now on, I shall refrain from touching you with my disgraceful hands."

"Bluidy hell. That's not what I—"

"I wouldn't wish to offend your delicate sensibilities—"

"Damn it, I meant—"

"—or cause you to feel disgust."

He ground his teeth. "Ye werenae built for a maid's work, woman. 'Tis well past time to hire lasses who ken what they're about."

When she went perfectly still beside him, he knew he'd erred badly. She scarcely breathed. Her hands were tucked against her middle, and her face was turned away as she gazed at the passing landscape. She didn't say a word all the way home. She didn't wait for him to help her down from the curricle. She didn't even glance at him before disappearing into the house.

He muttered a curse. While tending the horses, he eyed one of the empty stalls, wondering if she'd demand that he sleep in the stable. He rehearsed his apology a dozen times while he went in search of her. He found her in the dressing room.

She'd removed her gloves and sat staring down at her hands in the lantern light. Tears glistened on her bonnie white cheeks. She spotted him and swiped them away then quickly hid her hands in her lap. "You were right," she said mutedly. "Other lasses make far better maids." Her chin tightened and wobbled. "Hire them. Perhaps the floors will shine for once."

"Sabella," he rasped. Goddamn his black temper to hell. Crushing guilt had shortened his fuse, and she was the one who suffered. He wanted to fell an entire forest until his bones were naught but dust.

"I'm not very useful, am I?" Her voice contorted.

He crossed to the dressing table and sank to his knees before her. "Look at me."

She shook her head. "Kenneth warned me against straying outside my station. He disliked me heating my own water or tending my own roses. Whenever a rosebush died, he'd remind me how foolish I was to seek a gardener's labors when a fertile womb would gain me the world."

Alexander carefully slid his palms along the sides of her silk-draped thighs and reached for her hands. She pulled away, hiding them behind her back.

"'A stain upon your hands is a stain upon our name,'" she whispered. "That's what he always said. Perhaps he saw how worthless I'd be once that name was stripped away."

"Please, love. Look at me."

With a shuddering breath, she lifted her eyes.

He cupped her cheek, thumbing away a fresh tear. "Do ye ken who cooks the best bacon I've ever tasted?"

A blinking frown and a small shake of her head.

"You. Do ye ken how long it takes most lasses to learn what ye've learned in six weeks?"

Another shake.

"A year at least, and most start trainin' at their mother's hip when they're wee. Do ye ken how many maids it would take to keep this house as well as ye've kept it on yer own?"

A sniff and another shake.

"Four or five." He gently traced her cheekbone. "I didnae expect ye to last a day, Duchess. I thought ye'd whinge about the mud and storm back to the village in a huff. Shocked me down to my big, hairy feet when ye didnae complain, just found a bucket and gathered water from the river."

A shy, tiny smile tugged at the corner of her mouth.

"Aye, ye remember. Ye were covered in mud, exhausted, probably in a lot of pain from yer tumble. And ye were bluidy beautiful." He gripped her hips harder, dragging her chair closer. "*Beautiful,* woman. Ye've only grown more so since that day, though ye've wed a great beast who cannae manage to say what he means without flailin' like a belligerent drunkard."

"I understood ye well enough," she whispered.

"Nah. I'd walk through fucking fire to have yer hands on me."

Her brow crumpled. More tears fell. "Truly?"

"Put them on me, Duchess. I'm beggin' ye."

Trembling, she reached for his face and gently caressed his beard.

He closed his eyes, savoring her soft touch. He turned his head to kiss her palm, her wrist, her callused fingers. "When I say ye're beautiful, I mean every single part," he said hoarsely. "And when I say yer hands are a disgrace, I mean the damage done to them because of *my* stupidity. I should have hired maids before now."

"I asked ye not to."

"My purpose on this earth is to protect ye from all harm. What good am I if I cannae do that?"

Slowly, she drew him into the softest kiss imaginable. It felt like a feather stroking his lips. "Will ye help me undress?" she murmured.

He took his time with her. Often, his wife tempted him beyond all caution, resulting in a hard, driving rush to completion. But tonight, he wanted to soak in every sensation—the satiny skin painted blue and gold by moonlight and flame, the sweet scent of rose oil rising from her nape, the feminine panting as he stroked the delicate bones of her spine. She shivered as he traced each vertebra then caressed the long, lovely curve of her lower back and hips. When they were both naked, he carried her to their bed and laid her on the sheets she'd washed with her beautiful hands.

As he lay over his wife, she spread her thighs in welcome. He kissed her deeply, denying the demand pulsating in his cock until he felt that telltale wriggle in her lower half. Sabella's desire often rose swiftly. But on days when he'd tupped her multiple times, it sometimes arose more gradually, requiring more coaxing on his part.

That wee wriggle of her hips was his signal to forge on. This time, he resisted. Instead, he gathered her up in his arms and rolled onto his back. "Put yer hands on me," he demanded.

Her eyes glowed like moonlit emeralds in the dark. "Very well. But I want ye inside first, husband."

He gripped her buttocks, widening her thighs then shifted her higher to slide his iron-hard cock inside her tight, wet sheath a few inches. At her throaty moan, he sank inside a few more. "Sit up, lass."

She was kissing his neck and jaw, writhing against him, groaning with eager pleasure. Finally, he clasped her shoulders and pushed her up until she was seated astride him. In the moonlight, she was the most glorious creature. Those lovely, wee nipples were hard and demanding atop dainty breasts. That golden fall of hair tumbled to her waist. The tight, wet heat gripping his cock teased him with repeated flutters. She braced her hands on his chest, keeping her hips slightly elevated so he didn't sink too far inside her.

He'd discovered his wife could only tolerate the deepest penetration when she was in a frenzy of arousal. Her wetness told him she was close, but not quite there. He caressed her breasts and squeezed her nipples with the firm pressure she liked.

She groaned and sank lower.

He dropped one of his hands to the sweet, glistening folds just above their joining. With much gentler pressure, he squeezed her swollen nub in a pulsing rhythm.

She sank lower, panting heavily.

"That's it," he murmured. "Can ye take me?"

Nodding, she sank lower and moaned. "Alexander?"

"Aye, love."

She slid her palm to the center of his chest, her expression pained. "I don't think I can bear being parted from ye for a week or two."

He couldn't bear it either. But he had no choice. If he took her with him and Cromartie was in Edinburgh, she'd be at greater risk. It was how Broderick had nearly lost Kate. Alexander refused to make the same mistake.

He sat up and wrapped his arms around her, cradling her close. She plastered herself against him, stroking his nape and his hair, nuzzling his neck and his jaw. "I'm going to miss ye like I'd miss breathin' if I was deprived of it," he rasped in her ear. "This is how we're meant to be. Locked together, every part of me touchin' every part of you."

Her breath caught on a wee mewling sound. "Aye," she choked. "Locked together. That's it precisely."

"When you hurt, I hurt."

She clung to him with all her strength, heaving breaths rocking through her delicate frame. Finally, her palm slid over his scar. "When you bleed, I bleed," she choked.

He stroked her hair and her back, kissed her temple and her cheek. "When you're gone, half of me is gone. Why do ye suppose the first thing I do is find ye?"

She pulled his mouth to hers, tangling her tongue with his as her body began to move. The pace she set was rough, deep, and shockingly swift. It drove him to the edge of release within seconds. Unable to stop himself, he gripped her hard and drove furiously inside her until she came in a wild, gasping implosion. That was all it took. He erupted. Burying his face against her rose-scented skin, he groaned her name and filled his wife while she stroked him with those beautiful hands.

Long minutes later, she lay atop him like a blanket, her hand warming his scar. "Ye must promise to return home as quickly as ye can," she said sleepily. "I find ye … necessary, husband."

"I promise. When I'm finished with this business in Edinburgh, I'm comin' home to my bonnie wife." He held her close as her breathing deepened into sleep. Then he whispered, "Nothin' on earth could keep me from ye."

Chapter Eighteen

As August cooled into September, the glen's leafy green took on hints of bronze and gold. Rain came more often, and with it came new shades of wispy gray. The gray matched Sabella's mood.

He'd been gone for two weeks. Two endlessly long weeks. According to his last letter, he'd be gone for a third at least.

She wrote her husband every day, and he wrote her just as often, but it wasn't the same as his scent or his heat or his arms holding her. She distracted herself by organizing the household staff they'd hired before his departure—three maids, two footmen, and a curious number of strapping men to help Gavin maintain the grounds.

On evenings when Rannoch and Magdalene didn't visit, Sabella ventured into the village to dine at Joan's tavern. Somehow, cookery wasn't as enjoyable without the reward of watching Alexander eat, and she'd largely lost her appetite.

Today, she set a small bucket of fish scraps on the ground beside her replanted rosebush and began digging a small trench on either side. She'd positioned the shrub in the sunniest corner of her walled garden, hoping to give it the best possible chance to root properly before the growing season ended.

The temporary wooden gate opened, and one of the new maids entered with a watering can. "Gavin and the lads are unloadin' the new gate now, Mrs. MacPherson. Och, 'tis a braw piece. I think ye'll be pleased."

Sabella smiled and wiped her forehead with her wrist. "Splendid. Thank you, Effie." The cheerful young lass had unusual strength for such a small frame. Initially, Sabella had thought her too bonnie with her cinnamon hair and wide-set eyes. But during the interviews for employment, she'd questioned all the maids at great length about their personal attachments. Effie was in love with a lad from Aberdeen and saw Alexander as "too auld for the likes of me."

As Sabella deposited her fish scraps and refilled the trenches, the girl watered two new rosebushes Sabella had started from cuttings. Minutes later, a sweaty Gavin entered with a broad grin. "It's a grand sight, Mrs. MacPherson. Some of Adam's finest work. Care to see it?"

She gave Effie the shovel and bucket then followed Gavin out to the wagon parked in the front drive. Alexander hadn't let her see his sketched design before he'd given it to Adam MacDonnell. The wrought-iron double gate's arched top depicted a pair of swans that would kiss each time the gates closed. The swans were flanked by a pair of outward-facing crows that seemed to be standing guard. Beneath the birds, a stag's antlered head sprawled amidst latticework, as if the beastie would be forever barred from entry.

Sabella's smile deepened. That red pest's head would split down the center each time the gate opened.

Along the bottom half, the gate's swirling design paid tribute to the four seasons of roses. Two urns sprouted a profusion of vines and hips for winter, buds for spring, blooms for summer, and falling leaves for autumn. She fingered her rose pendant, noting how closely several of the blooms resembled the carving. The gate truly was a masterpiece.

Her longing for Alexander intensified until it hurt to breathe. She settled a hand over her heart to contain it. She wanted to throw herself into his arms and kiss every inch of his face, to thank him for taking such care in his design, for building her garden walls and showing her how attentive he was, even if he didn't always tell her what he was thinking.

How she loved him. So much that it pained her.

"Och, lassie! Have ye forgiven him already?"

Sabella turned to see Mrs. MacBean approaching on Bill the Donkey. Stepping aside so Gavin and the lads could carry the gate to the garden, she shaded her eyes and frowned at the old woman wearing a floppy hat and a leather apron. "Forgiven whom?"

A flare of alarm and a wary blink. "Nobody. Forget I mentioned it." She slid off the back of the donkey with a whuff. Withdrawing a small bottle from her pouch, she thrust it into Sabella's hands. "This is for the sickly stomach. Two drops in yer mornin' tea should do."

"This is for nausea."

"Aye. Now, where did I put that stone?"

"I'm not nauseated."

"Not yet. Ah, there ye are." She produced a pewter pebble carved with some kind of rune. "They like to hide things. Gives 'em a wee laugh. I dinnae mind too much, so long as the mischief doesnae go on too long." She placed the pebble in Sabella's hand. The mark looked like a Y with an overgrown stem. "Keep it with ye. Between yer bosoms is best."

"Between my …" Sabella shook her head. "Am I meant to sew it into my stays?"

Mrs. MacBean shrugged. "If ye like. There's another place ye can carry it, but I dinnae recommend insertion. That's how I lost Mr. Brodie's ring. The poor man searched for *hours* and never found it."

It took a moment to puzzle that one through. Face heating, Sabella invited her to stay for tea, but Mrs. MacBean had more deliveries to make. She remounted Bill with a final reminder, "That's strong protection, lass. Keep it with ye at all times. Dinnae forget."

Sabella watched her ride away, thumbing the smooth pewter, which warmed to her touch. The old woman might be mad. But some of the things she'd said sounded less like senility and more like sight.

She traced the whorls of her pendant, which had needed fire to reveal its true beauty. Now, Sabella couldn't imagine herself without it. Had the old woman carved the pendant knowing what it would become? Or was it simply a fortunate accident?

Annie believed Mrs. MacBean had otherworldly abilities. She'd also suggested the glen itself was rife with magic, as it "lay at the juncture between realms." Sabella didn't know anything about magic or realms or sight, but it certainly wouldn't harm anything to stitch a wee pocket into her stays.

Fetching her sewing supplies from the basket in the corner of her dressing room, she quickly fashioned a linen pocket along the center busk then sewed the pewter stone inside. It nestled comfortably between her bosoms, well below the level of her pendant. Nodding her satisfaction, she redressed in Alexander's shirt and the russet plaid she wore on days when she missed him so much that she couldn't bear it. Today was one of those days.

Just as she tucked her last fold into place, a drop of water landed on her hand. She glanced up with a frown. Water wicked in a large circle along the ceiling, with large drops forming at the center.

"Drat and blast," she muttered. "The cisterns."

Quickly summoning one of the new footmen—a sturdy young man named Clyde—she dashed up the rear staircase to the attic. The door was locked, but she hadn't yet hired a housekeeper, so she kept a skeleton key on a small loop attached to her waist. The moment she opened the door, she knew she wasn't going to like what she saw.

Water puddled nearly an inch deep beneath the farthest cistern, which lay just above their dressing room.

"Fetch the maids," she ordered Clyde. "Tell them to bring towels, mops, and several buckets. Send one of the lads to inform Adam MacDonnell one of the cisterns requires repair at once. He'll likely be at the distillery this time of day."

"Aye, Mrs. MacPherson."

Splashing through the dusty pool, Sabella felt along the piping then along the large wooden tank for obvious leaks. Her hems were soaked, but she didn't care. A leak like this could do costly damage to her ceiling, her floors, her walls. The sooner it stopped, the better.

She rounded to the rear of the cistern. There, she found the source of the leak in a seam between two staves near the floor. Looking around for anything to stanch the flow, she spotted a canvas sheet covering a waist-high stack of crates. She dragged the cloth free, wadding and stuffing it against the seeping seam. For now, it was the best she could do. Straightening with a curse, she lifted her hems and stomped away from the puddling mess.

That was when she spotted them—green leather and brass, stacked three high in the farthest corner. They weren't crates. They were trunks.

Her trunks.

The attic shrank while the trunks grew in her vision. Midday light wavered through dust motes. Water dripped, dripped, dripped.

Green leather and brass. Here beneath canvas. The canvas was dusty, so the trunks had to have sat here a long time. Weeks, perhaps months.

The air thinned. Her bones tightened, squeezing and squeezing.

Carefully lifting the lid on the nearest trunk, she felt as if her ribs were breaking again. There, atop her favorite silk pelisse, lay her mother's emerald necklace.

She covered a sob with trembling, callused fingers.

While she scrubbed his floors and burned his dinner and washed his linens, her three green trunks sat here in the attic. All her money, the letters from Annie, her mother's jewels, even the red silk peignoir and nightdress she'd purchased secretly in Paris.

The squeezing pressure tightened into unbearable pain. That pain should have crushed her. At first, it did. Then something strange happened. The pain became a burning. The burning expanded, pushing back against her bones.

She stared down at her mother's necklace, the one she should have worn on her wedding day, and the burning exploded.

Only then did she identify what it was: rage.

Rage for the woman she'd been when she'd arrived in the glen. Rage for the woman she'd become while she was here.

Rage at the man who'd betrayed them both.

Seventeen days. That was how long Alexander had gone without his Duchess. It felt like seventeen centuries.

As he dismounted outside his family's Buccleuch Street townhouse in Edinburgh, he felt every bit of seventeen centuries old. His head ached from lack of sleep. His bones ached from riding around the city hunting down Cromartie's old contacts. And everything else ached because Sabella hadn't written him for the past three days.

God, he was pitiful.

He handed his horse to a stable lad and entered through the kitchen. The house was dead quiet this time of night. Running a hand through his hair, he noticed the housekeeper had left a small tray of food and tea. Peculiar. She never did that.

With a shrug, he carried the tray upstairs to his bedchamber. He'd just stripped off his shirt and begun washing his face and hands when he heard a soft, silken swish behind him.

Instantly, he swiped the razor from the washstand and spun to face the door. His heart kicked like an enraged bull. His cock shot to full hardness within seconds. Did exhaustion cause visions?

"Sabella?"

She couldn't be real. But she moved into the light of the lantern, and he recognized her blue silk gown.

The one from her trunk.

His blood went as icy as her expression. "Bluidy, everlasting hell. How did ye get here?"

"The mail coach. Turns out I had sufficient fare after all."

The chill sank deeper. "Ye came alone?" He was going to gut Rannoch. "Ye should have waited for me to return."

"We had a leak, husband," she said softly. "It made quite a mess, I'm afraid."

He'd never seen his bonnie wife this cold. For a moment, her eyes reminded him of her brother. "Ye're angry." He set down the razor and held up his hands. "I should have told ye about the trunks."

"You should have returned them to me."

Inside, he debated how much more damage he might do by telling her the full truth. This was new territory. One wrong step, and he could lose her. "Had I done that, ye'd have left the glen and never returned. Ye'd be in London or Paris now, hostin' soirees for some soft-handed lord."

"That was *my* choice to make," she snapped. "Not yours."

"I couldnae let ye make the wrong one."

She moved deeper into the light, revealing cheeks flushed with fury. She wasn't wearing her pendant. Instead, she wore her mother's emerald necklace. Her eyes flashed a similar green. "Arrogant blackguard! Was this your revenge? To deprive me of every precious memory I have? To humiliate me and leave me with *nothing!*"

"Wasnae revenge." He took a step toward her, but she backed away with a warning hand raised. His gut twisted with desperation. "I needed to keep ye."

She shook her head in disbelief. "Did you pay the McCabes to rob me?"

"Nah. But I did repay their thievery in full once I tracked them down."

Her delicate brow flickered into a wary frown. "D-did you … kill them?"

"They likely wish I had. Australia is an unforgivin' place."

"Australia."

"An old friend from the regiment manages a hulk for convicts awaiting transportation. I asked him to offer them his finest accommodations." He smiled. "A shame.

Fourteen years' hard labor at their age might as well be a death sentence."

Her throat rippled on a swallow. "Rather a grim fate."

"Nobody robs my woman without payin' the price."

"I wasn't yours. Not then."

Again, he considered withholding the truth. But she'd likely realize it eventually. "Aye. Ye were."

She shivered, her nipples hardening visibly beneath her silk.

Perhaps all wasn't lost, he thought. Perhaps she'd forgive him more readily than he'd assumed. Perhaps her desire was the key. He reached for her.

"Touch me, and I shall carve you up like venison, you deceitful, ruthless bastard!"

On second thought, forgiveness might be a wee bit optimistic.

"I will *never* forgive you for this."

More than a wee bit, then. "Would it help if I said I was sorry?"

"You're not sorry! I can see it in your face."

He rubbed the back of his neck. She wasn't wrong.

Her eyes roamed to his naked chest and locked on the medallion Mrs. MacBean had given him. "Who gave you that?" she snapped. "Some woman, I'd wager."

He glanced down. "A woman, aye."

Her wrath grew tenfold. "I knew it. You've had your revenge on me. Now, you've found some other harlot—"

"'Twas Mrs. MacBean." He flipped the medallion over to show her the rune. "See? Naught but a wee bit of magical nonsense."

As her fury ebbed slightly, her brow crumpled. Great, heaving breaths shuddered her slender frame. Leaf-green eyes shimmered.

"I would have stayed," she whispered. "Every piece of me has been yours from the first. I would have given you everything—anything—if you'd simply asked. Instead, you trapped me. Stole from me. Lied to me."

Here it was. The fullness of the wound he'd dealt her. The sight of her tears sliced him open. He reached for her again, and she backed away, covering a sob. "Let me hold ye," he growled. "Please. God, please, lass."

She shook her head and quietly wept. "How am I to trust you?"

"Duchess."

"You hate me. That's why it was so easy for you to lie—"

"I *wanted* to hate ye." Confessing the truth might be the only way to reverse the widening chasm between them. It went hard against his grain. But it was the one thing he hadn't tried. "There are things ye dinnae ken,

Sabella. Reasons why it didnae matter that ye were Lockhart's sister or Munro's mistress."

She swayed and braced a hand against the doorframe. "I was never his mistress."

"I ken that now." Her pain drew him closer. Closer. He scented roses, her skin. When he was close enough, he lowered his head. "Ye cannae imagine the torment of believin' he'd had ye first."

She jolted. Shook. "Why should it matter?"

"It shouldnae. If ye were some other lass, I wouldnae give two shites." He rested a hand on the door beside hers. "But ye're not another lass. Ye're mine."

Her breathing shallowed. Her gaze fixed on his medallion. "Do you understand how little sense that makes? You didn't even know me before I—"

"We'd never spoken, but I watched ye." Damn. He probably shouldn't have revealed that.

"Watched me where? Why?"

He explained that, the previous December while they were hunting for Lockhart, Broderick had asked him to keep watch on her brother's house for signs of the man. Along the way, he'd observed her patterns—the lack of appetite, the careful elegance, the seclusion with only her maid for company. Her fragility had driven him to distraction. He hadn't wanted to feel anything for her, let alone obsessive desire and the driving need to protect.

"Kenneth wasn't in residence," she said with a troubled frown. "If he'd caught you watching me, he would have killed you."

"A risk, aye." For a moment, he considered keeping the rest from her. But lying and hiding who he really was had wounded her deeply. He could see that now.

"There was more to it than surveillance," he confided. "It's a bit of what ye told me at the ball—a sense of recognition. Runs in the blood, ye might say." He smiled faintly. "Da decided my mam should be his wife an hour after they met. Same thing happened with Annie's mother. 'Twas the same for Broderick with Kate, and Campbell with Clarissa." He inched closer, inhaling deep. God, it had been centuries since he'd last kissed her. "We MacPhersons have strong instincts, even if we sometimes deny them. When we find what belongs to us, we ken it straight away." He held still as she traced a fingertip over his medallion. "I fought it for months, lass. Months. Hated ye for what yer brother did, hated ye for throwin' yerself between us. Hated ye for Munro. Then, one summer night, ye fell into my hands like a ripe peach jostled from heaven's orchard. So, I claimed ye."

Her hand fell away. "You used my desperation against me."

"Aye."

"You manipulated me into thinking it was my idea to stay."

"Aye."

"When did you retrieve my trunks, Alexander?"

He hesitated. "The day after ye arrived in the glen."

Her eyes slid closed. Pain drew a deep furrow. "I told you how much I longed for what my mother had left me, how much I missed those few precious things. Yet even after we were wed, you hid them from me."

This was why. He'd known how it would wound her. He'd feared it would drive her away. And now, he watched helplessly while his worst fears came to pass.

She retreated through the doorway into the bedchamber. Crossing to the bed, she stood with her back turned, her delicate shoulders straight. "You once accused me of seeking a gilded cage," she said softly. "I didn't seek it. I was born inside it. Kenneth kept me there, ensuring I never learned to fly properly. He convinced me I had no feathers, no wings. That I wouldn't survive outside his reach. When he d-died, I wanted to die, too." The slender arms beneath blue silk rippled as she wrung her hands. "So many times, I thought how easy it would be to disappear. No more cage. No more pain."

His soul roared a denial. "Ye must never contemplate such a thing. Never. Do ye hear me, Sabella? *Never.*"

She glanced down at the wine-red coverlet, her long nape exposed and vulnerable. "I am not a bauble or a bird, Alexander. I am not a possession to be claimed." Finally, she turned to face him, her lovely cheeks wet and her dignity blazing bright. "I am a woman with a mind and a heart." She held up her hands. "These can work wonders." She flattened them between her bosoms, one atop the other just beneath her mother's emeralds. "This can love boundlessly." Her arms slipped to her sides as her eyes overflowed. "But not from inside a cage."

Her quiet grief tore him open. "Dinnae compare me to yer brother," he rasped. "I'm a blackhearted bastard, but I wouldnae cage ye."

"No, merely corner me into dependency then ensure I had no better option. You're a superb hunter, husband. When the trap closed, I scarcely felt a thing."

God, she was killing him. "What do ye want me to say? Whatever it is, lass, just tell me. I'll say it."

She shook her head, her hands spreading in a helpless gesture. Moving to the bedchamber door, she turned back briefly to answer, "Nothing. What you've done speaks well enough for itself."

Chapter Nineteen

The house looked oddly unchanged. Upon entering Charlotte Square, Sabella had expected it to be transformed.

She was different. Surely, her former home would be, too.

But no. It was the same house with the same blond stone, handsome pediment, and black painted door.

Gathering the skirts of her starling-egg-blue tartan traveling gown, she ascended the steps and knocked lightly on the door. As she waited, a light carriage rolled past followed by a heavy wagon making a delivery.

Her old neighbor had painted his door green. She glanced to the west, where another neighbor had hung new curtains on the ground floor.

No, nothing important had changed here. Only her.

A sharp breeze cut through her wool, sending gooseflesh across her nape. She brushed at the sensation. Frowning, she searched the square for signs that Alexander had followed her. He wasn't here. She rubbed it away, but the feeling persisted. She only felt that peculiar, lifting zing when someone was staring at her, and her husband was the only one who might bother.

Alexander had been gone by the time the housekeeper, Mrs. Tibbets, had delivered a tea tray to her bedchamber. His note placed beside the teapot had read simply:

Duchess,

For your safety, do not leave this house. We'll discuss the reasons why when I return this evening. Until then, know this: Wounding you will forever be my worst mistake. I'm bloody sorry.

Alexander

P.S. Would begging help?

This morning, she veered between fury and softening, heartbreak and longing. How she'd missed him. How dearly she wished she didn't love him. But she did—missed him, loved him, wanted him. From his bearded face to his big, hairy feet, she loved every piece and part.

The manipulative, infuriating blackguard.

The door opened, and a liveried footman showed her into her former parlor. "Miss Lockhart!" exclaimed Lady Whitecross, whose husband had purchased the place to please his ambitious wife. Blonde and smiling, the woman swept forward to greet her. "Such an unexpected pleasure. What brings you to town?"

While they settled in for tea on a pair of gold velvet sofas, Sabella explained that she was visiting Edinburgh with her husband.

"Husband! You've wed?"

Sabella nodded, burying her expression in a careful sip. "This summer. I'm Mrs. MacPherson, now." The strangeness of introducing herself as the wife of the man who'd been shot in this very room wasn't lost on her. Thankfully, Lady Whitecross knew nothing about that dreadful incident, nor most of Kenneth's worst crimes.

"MacPherson, MacPherson. Is he the Duke of Argyll's cousin?"

Sabella set her cup in her saucer. Lady Whitecross was quite concerned with titles, the loftier the better. "No."

"Oh. I must be thinking of the Duke of Gordon."

Sabella shook her head.

"Oh. The Duke of Dingwall?"

"I'm afraid not."

"Oh." Her smile turned brilliantly false. "Well, I'm certain he's lovely."

Resisting the urge to roll her eyes, Sabella explained the purpose of her visit—cuttings from her rose garden.

"I have rosebushes?" Lady Whitecross blinked.

"Indeed." Sabella smiled blandly. "Several rare French varieties, in fact."

"French! They must be grand. His Lordship and I have been away whilst the house was being refurnished. I haven't had time to explore the grounds."

The gardens were perhaps a tenth of an acre, hardly enough to turn around in. But Sabella didn't bother quibbling.

Lady Whitecross fluttered her fingers. "I'll summon the gardener to bring you cuttings."

"That's not necessary, my lady. If you have shears, I shall cut them myself."

She looked positively appalled. "You?"

Sabella sipped her tea and smiled. "Me."

In the end, she took cuttings from all five of her most prized varieties—three from France and two from England.

Lady Whitecross stood at her elbow waving a gloved hand in front of her bonnet-shaded face. "This won't kill them, will it?"

Sabella snipped another cane, taking care to include a good number of nodes. "No. Pruning is one of the healthiest things you can do for a rose."

"It seems damaging." She swatted at a bee. "I wouldn't enjoy having my limbs severed."

Placing a fifth cutting in her basket, Sabella stifled a sigh. Why had she never noticed how vapid this woman was? "A good prune removes ill-formed branching, increases bloom production, and encourages the plant to form deeper roots. This wee, temporary sacrifice rewards you with a more beautiful, resilient plant."

Sabella paused after her next snip. A wee, temporary sacrifice. Was that what she'd needed to strengthen her, to make her bloom?

Lady Whitecross squeaked as the bee she'd been battling dived for her decolletage. "Surely, this is what a groundskeeper is for," she complained. "I shall fetch him."

When Sabella was alone, she surveyed her old garden. Admittedly, it was crowded. She'd always loved the secretiveness of dense greenery and hidden pathways. Beyond the young trees and tall shrubbery, high walls bordered all sides, further lending privacy and a sense of safety.

But that safety had been an illusion. She'd had her ribs broken here. She'd watched from her bedchamber window, scarcely able to breathe, as Kenneth's men had carried an unconscious Alexander through the gate and into the house.

She touched the lingering leaves of her thornless Blush Noisette, a gift from Kenneth after he'd injured her arms badly enough to summon the physician. This house had been her cage, and she'd been terrified to leave it. Now, she couldn't imagine herself in a place like this.

She was different. Her roots were stronger, her blooms bolder. When the sun shined, she basked in the heat. When the rains came, she turned her face up for a drink rather than shrinking away.

Alexander had lied. He'd withheld belongings that were precious and used her vulnerability against her. But he'd also built her a garden where she could root deeply and grow to her full potential. He'd kept her planted where he wanted her, yes. But he'd also fed her in ways she didn't know she needed.

She cut one last cane and placed it in her basket. Birds cawed nearby. A soft breeze rustled the leaves of the nearest trees and dislodged a few. A sharper gust flattened her skirts against her thighs, but the light blue tartan she'd purchased from Mr. Cleghorn kept her warm without the fuss of silk.

Perhaps she *could* forgive Alexander. In time. With sufficient begging on his part. Indeed, the thought of having him on his knees sparked new shivers along her nape.

She brushed at the sensation. Then another breeze gusted, carrying a new scent. Her shivers turned chilling.

Gin.

Her stomach lurched as memories flooded in. *Vomitous, suffocating agony and heavy, gin-soaked breath. Powerful fists driving into her midsection. The fight for air. The pain. Dear God, the pain.*

Frantically, she scanned the thick foliage. She couldn't see who approached. The scent was faint beneath the damp green of the garden. But it was there.

She lifted her basket and backed toward the house. A gigantic hand slid over her mouth. A hard, massive arm wrapped around her ribcage and hauled her high against a hard, massive frame.

Panic exploded inside her as her attacker dragged her backward. It couldn't be happening again. The memories maddened her into a frenzy. *No air. No air. No air*. Thrashing blindly, she bucked and bit until she tasted blood.

"Bluidy hell, Duchess," came a growly whisper near her ear. "Next time I abduct ye, I'm wearin' gloves."

Seven hours before he abducted his wife, Alexander stood outside her bedchamber door fighting the urge to go inside. He wanted to hold her. He wanted to beg her to forgive him. He wanted to warn her about Cromartie. Hell, he'd settle for watching her sleep.

Instead, he continued downstairs to the kitchen, penned her a brief note cautioning her to stay inside the house, then headed out to meet with Duncan MacAllister at the docks in Leith.

It didn't go well.

"Aye, he has her," said Duncan as he redirected a lad carrying a rope toward the shipyard. "The bairn, too."

Alexander swiped a hand over his beard. "Christ. Do ye ken where?"

"Somewhere in the New Town. They made the crossing from Amsterdam in early August, according to the ship's captain. Finnegan found their hack driver, but the man couldn't recall which street the house was on. I've sent him to search again. Damned Irishman always was sloppy. Finn thinks Cromartie kens ye're hunting him."

Duncan MacAllister was one of the few men Alexander trusted outside of his family. He was built along MacPherson lines, big and powerful, albeit only six-foot-five. Nevertheless, his intimidating size and eerily frigid nature suited the "assignments" he and Alexander had shared during the war. Following Waterloo, the slashing scar along the right side of his face made MacAllister too distinctive to continue with clandestine work, so instead, he'd built a fortune running untaxed cargo between various ports.

He was a useful friend to have, particularly when a rat needed flushing out. Duncan knew every rodent in every port.

After Alexander had traveled to Holland and found Cecilia Hamilton missing, he'd discovered two important things: She'd recently birthed a son, and Bruce Cromartie had taken her and her child against her will, likely to control the fortune Lockhart had stashed away in her name.

Alexander hadn't found records of Cromartie sailing to Scotland, but he'd found his own letter to

Cecilia open and half-burnt inside her cottage fireplace. The place had stunk of gin.

Since his return to Edinburgh, he'd hunted down anyone who might have knowledge of Cromartie's movements—old cellmates, a half-brother living in squalor, former employers. The bruiser didn't have friends, which made him harder to track. No friends meant no favors or confidences to leave a trail. Certainly, no one had offered any useful information, apart from Duncan.

Alexander thanked his old friend, promising him a cask of the finest MacPherson whisky for his trouble. Then he spent several hours combing the expensive, elegant area of Edinburgh where Sabella had once resided. The New Town's neat, orderly streets were lined with hundreds of townhouses, any of which could be where Cromartie was hiding. Cecilia had once lived in a house on Queen Street, so he started there, but he quickly discovered it had been sold to pay Kenneth Lockhart's debts.

After hours of searching, frustration drove him back to his house in Buccleuch Street. He needed to see Sabella. Needed to hold her and feel her breathe against his neck. He needed to know she was safe.

But she wasn't safe. She was gone.

"Where did she go?" he demanded in a growl.

A wide-eyed Mrs. Tibbets stammered for a moment before answering, "Her auld residence in Charlotte Square. She said somethin' about roses."

Bloody, everlasting hell. He started for the door.

"She left ye a note, Mr. MacPherson! Ye have two, in fact."

He turned. "Two?"

The housekeeper nodded. "One from Mrs. MacPherson, and one from her sister-in-law."

"Which sister-in-law?"

"M-Mrs. Lockhart, sir."

Skin writhing like a snake's nest, he barked, "What did she look like?"

"Young and bonnie. Hair the color of lamb's fleece. I—I suspect she has a wee bairn. I heard one wailin' in the coach."

"Fetch the notes," he ordered. "Be quick."

He tore open Cecilia's letter first. It was chillingly brief: *He's been following you, Mr. MacPherson. He means to steal your wife. Kill him, won't you? – C.H.L.*

The peculiarly polite phrasing matched what he knew of Cecilia Hamilton Lockhart. Damaged by horrid abuse in her youth, the beauty had clawed her way free of her impoverished past only to land herself in Kenneth Lockhart's grasp. The lass was understandably mad.

While he waited for the stable lad to saddle a fresh horse, he scanned Sabella's note grimly.

Husband,

I take your cautions under advisement. However, I must visit the house in Charlotte Square to take cuttings from my roses. The breeds are rare, and I desire them for my collection. Further, I see no reason to waste the long journey to Edinburgh idling inside this house whilst you attend to your mysterious "business." We shall speak at dinner if you can bring yourself to arrive on time.

Your wife,

Sabella

P.S. Begging is a fine start.

Folding the slip of paper in half, he tucked it inside his pocket then pressed the heel of his hand against the ache beneath his breastbone. The rune dug into his skin, a reminder of what the old woman had told him.

Blood on yer hands. Blood on yer bride.

He raced to the New Town in record time. Slowing to a stealthier pace as he entered Charlotte Square, he dismounted and tied his horse to the fence surrounding the central green. The poor beast was heaving and deserved a rest. Swiftly, he made his way into the mews lane behind the southerly row of houses. Taking his dirk from the sheath beneath his coat, he slid along the garden wall, looking for signs of the bruiser.

He froze when he heard her voice, prim and soft as she explained the point of pruning to her daft companion.

"… wee, temporary sacrifice rewards you with a more beautiful, resilient plant."

His heart stuttered with relief. She was safe. For the first time in his life, his hands shook during a mission—his most important mission. He slumped against the wall. She was safe. His Duchess was safe.

Her companion mentioned fetching a groundskeeper and returned to the house. He could hear the faint *snip-snip* of Sabella taking her cuttings. He didn't know how to approach her. She was so furious with him that he feared she'd *snip-snip* vital parts of his anatomy. Better to wait until her departure, perhaps.

A pair of crows landed on top of the wall above his head. The wind picked up, abruptly changing direction. Then he smelled something strange. Gin fumes?

The world shrank into crystalline focus. He quickly calculated the wind direction, the proximity to the gate, their relative positions, and hers inside the garden. The bruiser was on the other side of the carriage house, mere feet from the gate. He would reach her first.

His throat knotted. Frantically, he glanced up at the crows, who stared back with bottomless black eyes—intelligent eyes.

He must climb. It was the only way.

He sheathed his dirk, eyed the ten-foot stone wall, and took a coiled leap. Grasping the top of the wall wrenched his bad shoulder with tearing force. The stones offered scant purchase for his feet, leaving his arms to bear his entire weight. His old wound blasted him with burning agony.

He didn't give a damn. All that mattered was getting to her.

Using the strength he'd built over the past two months, he pulled himself up, grateful that the birds' flapping fuss masked the noise of his ascent. He snagged the top of the wall with his boot, rolled his body over the top of the wall, and dropped silently into the garden.

The thick, dense garden. He could barely see her past all the shrubbery. She was backing toward the house, frowning in the direction of the gate. From his vantage point, he could see a meaty hand thrusting the gate open, but her view was blocked.

Which meant the bruiser's view of her was obscured, too, but not for long.

No choice, he thought. No choice. Silently, he positioned himself to intercept her retreat, covering her mouth to prevent her from drawing the bruiser's attention. Then he lifted her and glided deep into the shadows of the house.

She thrashed and kicked against him, stunning him enough that he halted to regain his hold on her. Then she bit him hard enough to draw blood.

"Bluidy hell, Duchess. Next time I abduct ye, I'm wearin' gloves."

She went utterly still, apart from labored breaths. "A-Alexander?"

"Shh, lass. We must leave."

With a jerky nod, she relaxed against him as he guided her past the inner gate leading to the fenced area around the service entrance and another leading to the square. After untying his horse, he turned to his wife. His pale, shaken wife.

She still clutched her basket in both hands.

He couldn't help himself. He kissed her. Hard and fiery, it only lasted a second. She didn't even have time to respond. But it was enough to set his heart thundering in his ears.

Lifting her onto the horse, he mounted behind her and set off at a fast walk. No need to draw more than the necessary attention. He must get her safely home. Then he'd kill the bruiser.

Simple enough.

"Something bad happened." Her voice wavered like a brittle reed. "I—I think I'm in danger."

He cradled her close, consciously releasing tension from the muscles that touched her. No need to frighten his wee wife further. "Shh. I have ye, love. Dinnae fash."

"I'm fashing, Alexander. I'm fashing hard."

He wanted to laugh, but there was no room inside him for anything but the mission: Get her to safety, kill the bruiser.

"I have ye," he repeated, kissing her temple. "Ye're safe."

She shook so badly that the horse shied. He calmly redirected the animal, routing in an indirect fashion back to Buccleuch Street. As soon as they arrived, he charged one of the lads with delivering a message to Duncan. Then he carried his wife past a concerned Mrs. Tibbets, who scurried off to prepare a tray.

He didn't set Sabella down until they'd reached his bedchamber. Even then, he had to force himself to relinquish her. She sat on the bed, her face linen-white, her gloved hands clutching the basket full of thorny stems.

Gently, he pried her fingers loose and set the basket on a desk near the window. Then he sat beside her on the bed and helped her remove her bonnet. Finally, he offered his hand.

She stared at it for a long while before sliding her fingers along his palm. She gripped. Clung. Curving into his side, she rested her forehead against his biceps. "I'm sorry I bit you."

He held up his opposite hand to the light, admiring the gouges from her teeth. "My bonnie, vicious woman. Yer fight makes me proud."

"I wasn't fighting. I was afraid."

"Of me?"

She shook her head. "Him," she whispered soundlessly.

Alexander's world shrank and darkened. "Who, love?"

"My brother's man. He struck me here." She pressed a hand over her belly. "I—I vomited on him. It made him angry, so he crushed me until my ribs broke."

Violence slithered and writhed. Every muscle twitched with it. Every fiber wanted to mete out death and pain in equal measure.

"Kenneth stopped him before he killed me." She shook her head. "But he wanted more. He smelled like g-gin."

"Cromartie broke yer ribs," he rasped, tightening the muscles in his thighs, abdomen, chest, and arms in rhythmic succession. He'd learned the trick from Duncan. It kept the violence from erupting.

"How did you know his name?"

From inside his pocket, he withdrew Cecilia's first letter. "I found it in yer trunks. This is why I've been in Edinburgh. And before that, Amsterdam."

She took the crinkled paper with trembling fingers. After reading it, she covered her lips. "A child? Kenneth's?"

"Aye."

"I should have opened it," she said.

"Why didnae ye?"

"I'd done so much mopping up after Kenneth's mess, I couldn't bear to look at any more. I simply wanted to be done with it. Done with him."

The fact that she hadn't yet castigated him for yet another secret he'd kept from her was worrisome. Either she'd forgiven him, or she was beyond feeling anything but fear. He suspected the latter. But she hadn't relinquished his hand.

A hopeful sign.

"Cromartie willnae touch ye," he promised. Moving slowly to avoid startling her, he helped her remove her gloves. "I would never let that happen."

A tiny sigh. A tiny stroke of his forearm. "I missed you."

His heart squeezed hard enough to crack stone. "I missed ye too, Duchess."

"I wish you'd told me about the trunks."

"So do I." He raised her hand to his lips. "I'm bluidy sorry."

She ran her thumb over his knuckles. "I wouldn't have left the house if I'd known about Cromartie."

"I ken."

Leaf-green eyes lifted. "No more secrets. Ye must give me a choice from now on. Even if ye think I'll make the wrong one."

He rested his forehead against hers, breathed her breath, and held her eyes to deliver his promise. "Done."

The faintest, sweetest, tenderest smile curved her lips. "Thank you, husband. Now, about that begging."

Chapter Twenty

The following morning, Sabella awakened draped across her husband's body, his cock buried inside her, hard as steel-coated stone. By contrast, not a bone in her body remained any firmer than jam.

Alexander had expressed his ardent contrition throughout the night. On his knees, with his tongue, relentlessly. Several times, she'd wondered whether she was the one being punished with tormenting pleasure. Indeed, *he* seemed ecstatic to have his head between her thighs or his mouth on her bosoms or his lips nuzzling her lower back.

But shouldn't *he* be the one begging?

"Please," she moaned now. "Deeper, please."

He slid deeper, playing with her tangled hair and stroking her naked back lazily. "Come here and kiss me good mornin', woman."

How she loved his sleep-graveled voice, his big hands, and that hard, hairy, magnificent chest that teased her tender nipples. Sliding up said chest, she teased his lips with hers and wriggled her hips. He clasped her buttocks and settled her more firmly. She groaned into his mouth as the pressure inside her grew.

"Do ye want more, Duchess?"

She couldn't focus on what he was saying because his fingers now wandered to her nape, gently kneading to soothe the sore muscles there. She was sore everywhere, of course. He'd put her through her paces. Her nipples, sensitive to every wee breath, both loved and hated him. The nub between her folds remained swollen from his suckling mouth.

But her sheath craved him. "More," she panted. "Please, more."

He pushed deeper, stretching her with the massive thickness near the root. Hissing in a breath, she drew her knees up to ease the pressure then, holding his dark, flashing gaze, she sank down to take more.

"That's it. Luik at ye shine, my bonnie Sabella. Ye put the bluidy sun to shame."

"It's you," she panted through the rippling, cascading pleasure. "Ye set me on fire. No wonder I burn brightly."

"Yer pleasure is my pleasure, Duchess."

She expected his expression to be teasing. Instead, it was stone-serious and tormented. Why hadn't she seen it before? His brow was etched with strain. His jaw flexed every time she moved. His cheeks were flushed, his big body pulsing with need. He was delaying his release to give her a tenth—no, an eleventh. Or was it twelfth?

"Alexander."

"Aye?"

"How long have ye been waiting?"

Coal-black eyes blazed like hellfire. "For you? My whole bluidy existence, love."

Sudden and squalling, a storm overtook her. The love was too much. She had to tell him. She had to let it out. "Oh, God."

"What's wrong?"

"Nothing. I just … I love you," she choked, her eyes welling. "That's all. I love you."

He caressed her cheek. "Dinnae weep."

"I can't stop it." She swiped at her cheeks. "Drat and blast."

He stretched out an impossibly long arm and plucked a handkerchief from the bedside table. "Here. Be easy. If ye love me the same way I love you, Duchess, I'm surprised ye can fit it all inside yer wee body."

Pure joy broke over her, rising like a bubble in the sun. She threw aside the handkerchief and let her tears run. Settling in to take him the tiniest bit deeper, she savored his indrawn breath and stiffening abdomen. "I can take more than ye think, husband. Now, I want *you* to take yer pleasure. No restraint."

"Nah, lass. Ye dinnae want that. Best if I control—"

"Do ye want to take me hard?"

Every muscle in his body flexed at once, including the one inside her. There was her answer.

She grinned and stretched over him like a cat, flexing her sheath to encourage a lack of restraint. "Aye, ye do," she breathed. "Tell me what ye'd do to me if I agreed to give ye anything."

His eyes blazed hotter than a forge. Veins swelled near his temple and in his neck. "Ye willnae push me past my control."

She kissed him, tangling her tongue with his while simultaneously pulsing below with subtle movements of her hips. The coiling pleasure from that small friction combined with the deep pressure and stretching fullness threatened to overwhelm her and send her into a twelfth peak. But she must discipline herself.

This man might be ruthless, but the longer she knew him, the clearer his true nature became. He loved selectively and all the way to the bone. He gave of himself without hesitation, sometimes to his own detriment. Once he'd decided to wed her, he'd worked tirelessly to fulfill her every desire. She yearned to do the same for him.

She wanted to cook him meals that would make his toes curl. She wanted to pleasure his big body until he couldn't remember a single worry. Most of all, she wanted to love him without restraint.

"Ye won't hurt me," she murmured against his mouth. "Say what ye'd do."

Chest heaving, he banded an arm across her back and rolled until he was propped above her. "I'd take ye hard, ye damned temptress."

She released a long, breathy groan. "Tell me more."

"I'd bury my cock so deep, ye'd feel me here." He traced a fingertip along the column of her throat. "I'd make ye come until ye begged me to be merciful. Then I'd put my teeth on those wee, tender nipples and make ye come again."

Dear God. She was on the edge now. A twelfth peak rolled toward her like a storm.

Dark satisfaction edged his smile as he watched her. "Come around me, Duchess. Then mayhap I'll take ye as hard as I really want to."

She came. It burst upon her, stronger for the long climb. Waves of pleasure coursed through her, though he didn't join her.

Not yet.

Instead, he watched with burning eyes. When the storm ebbed, he took. First came the long thrusts, all the way out, then circling her opening and plunging slowly back in. He spread her knees wide and pressed them higher toward her shoulders. Then came the pounding, driving rhythm of a man pushed too hard. Rough and deep, jostling and relentless, his thrusts gained momentum as he growled her name.

She reached for him, but he clasped her wrists and pinned them to the bed, holding her at his mercy. Impossibly, the desperate, furious thrusts and the friction between her exposed nub and his plunging cock shoved her closer to a precipice she hadn't believed she could find again.

Sweat dripped from his brow onto her bosom. It drew his eye, and immediately, he lowered his head to take her nipple between his teeth. Her bosoms had been sensitive of late, so he was careful, but the slight pressure sent pleasure zinging out in all directions. She arched into his mouth.

Soon, his restraint wore down to a thread. With his hips pounding mercilessly, he gritted, "Come for me again. Do it, Sabella."

She grinned triumphantly and taunted, "You first."

His eyes flared.

She had him. She bloody *had* him. Though he pinned her to the mattress and dominated her body with his, she saw the shift from a man restrained to a man consumed. He was raw, pure possession, and she held him in her wee hands. With a fury, he took her harder than he'd ever done before. She caught fire. He roared and hammered with explosive force. Pounding, pounding, pounding force.

It wasn't soft or lovely. She screamed loudly enough to wake Mrs. Tibbets. He had to smother her cries with his mouth and muffle his own against her neck. The bedframe might have been jostled loose on one corner. No doubt she'd be craving a hot bath soon to soak away the aches and irritations.

But, oh, how she loved this unrestrained man.

She couldn't stop grinning. Laughing. He groaned as he rolled them to their sides and gently withdrew.

"Bluidy hell, woman. How many times have I warned ye not to push me?"

She kissed him and petted his bearded face. "I suspect ye'll have to warn me many more, husband." A longer kiss this time. "Pushing you is my greatest pleasure."

Alexander had no intentions of introducing his wife to Duncan MacAllister. Women sometimes had a peculiar attraction to him. Something about the scar.

The problem was that none of Alexander's brothers were in town, and Cromartie must be dealt with. Alexander would happily do the killing. But he needed a trustworthy, capable man to watch over Sabella. Duncan was capable, at least.

"Does he favor pheasant?" Sabella asked as she dressed for dinner. "Mrs. Tibbets said the pheasant at the market has been quite good of late."

He raised a brow. "Dinnae ken. In my experience, he'll eat whatever ye put in front of him."

She looped her rose pendant over her head and settled it into place with a soft glance in his direction.

He didn't know what he'd done to deserve that glowing regard, but he'd take it. "Do ye have a less revealin' gown?" He gestured to the low neckline of her pink silk gown, which exposed far too much of her lovely white skin.

"Not for evening dress. I brought only one."

Glowering at the small red patch of skin along one of her bosoms, he rubbed at his nape and shifted from foot to foot. Had he been too rough with her?

"You weren't too rough with me," she chided, making him wonder if he'd asked the question aloud.

"I left marks on ye."

She grinned at him in the mirror. "And I adore every one."

He grunted.

Rising, she kissed his cheek and looped an arm through his. "Shall we?"

He grunted again.

The introduction to MacAllister didn't go as badly as he'd feared. Sabella seemed to have very little interest in his scar. She spent far more time caressing Alexander's calf with her toes beneath the table—which would please him greatly if it weren't so distracting.

"How do you like the pheasant, Mr. MacAllister?" She took a dainty bite and tilted her head in polite inquiry.

MacAllister smiled. "It's splendid, ma'am."

She sipped her wine. "Not too dry, I hope."

"No."

"Lovely."

Alexander ignored Duncan's amused glance. She'd spent the past five minutes caressing his thigh with her free hand. The other man didn't miss things like that.

"I understand you're a smuggler, Mr. MacAllister."

Nearly choking on his wine, Alexander glared at his brazen wife. Was she drunk already? She'd had less than half a glass.

"I transport goods, ma'am."

"And sometimes people, aye? A pair of elderly thieves to a prison hulk docked in London, for example."

Duncan lifted a brow at Alexander as if to say, "Do you intend to rein in your wife?" But Alexander knew there was no reining in this woman. She obviously had her own aims that she hadn't bothered to share with him.

Fingering the stem of his wineglass, Duncan smiled blandly. "I rarely take on passengers."

"But sometimes you do."

"For a price, aye."

Satisfied, she sat back with a smile. After several minutes of polite nonsense about the wine being French and the weather being difficult for sailing at certain times of the year, Sabella glanced curiously between him and Alexander. "You know, the two of you could be brothers."

Alexander balked first, but Duncan wasn't far behind. Their grumbling denials of a resemblance fell on deaf ears.

"Similarly dark, similarly tall," she insisted. "Similarly handsome."

"Pure shite," muttered Alexander. "He's three inches shorter, for God's sake."

"Liar," Duncan retorted. "Two at most. And ye're uglier by half."

"At least I didnae try to stop a Frenchman's dagger with my face."

She sniffed. "The differences are trifling. You even dress alike."

Duncan wasn't prone to glowering, but impugning his clothing was one of the few ways to offend him. "This coat was made in Paris, ma'am. The tailor once served the king."

Brightening, she leaned forward to prop her chin on the back of her hand in a rapt posture. "You *do* smuggle items from France, then!"

"I don't care for the term 'smuggle.'"

She fluttered her fingers. "Transport, smuggle. As you like."

His wife was drunk. Nothing else explained this degree of audacity.

"I didn't want to ask directly, for that would be quite rude." She dabbed her lips delicately with her napkin then leaned forward until her wee, dainty bosoms nearly rested in her peas. "What do you know about roses, Mr. MacAllister?"

Bloody, everlasting hell. Was that what this was about?

To his credit, Duncan didn't blink. He sipped his wine and contemplated the question with full seriousness. "Not much, I'm afraid."

Sabella withdrew a slip of paper from inside her bodice and slid it across the table. "I have *several* varieties of interest. Much longer bloom times. Very expensive."

Alexander trapped her hand against his thigh and gritted, "He doesnae transport plants, woman."

"But he could transport me, and I could *carry* the plants, husband."

"Ye're nae goin' to bluidy France."

"Not alone. You'd accompany me, of course." She turned to Duncan. "How difficult would it be to accommodate a forcing house?"

Duncan looked nonplussed. "On my ship?"

"Don't worry. It needn't be large. More of a cold frame, really. How might large sheets of glass fare on the uppermost deck, do you suppose?"

"Not well."

Alexander shook his head. "Ships other than Duncan's sail to France, ye ken."

"Will other captains omit certain cargo and passengers from their manifests so that I may acquire exclusive access to rare varieties for breeding in Scotland and England? I think not."

"Isnae that what nurseries are for?"

"Nurserymen." She spat the word. "Extortionists, you mean. Those diabolical blackguards steal the work of innocent hobbyists then link arms to monopolize our gardens by denying us access to important innovations. They deserve to be put out of business."

"By ye?"

She bristled at his incredulity. "Why not me?"

He paused. Indeed, why not? More and more of late, those lovely, leaf-green eyes gleamed with sharp, bold calculation and keen ambition. His uncaged swan wanted to stretch her wings? So be it.

"Very well," he replied. "I suppose ye'll need me to build ye a glasshouse." Already the plans were taking shape in his mind. They'd need a second well.

Fiery green softened into a passionate, loving glow. Her hand shifted to caress his cock through his trousers. "Oh, aye, husband," she breathed. "A glasshouse would be lovely."

He grunted, wondering how he was going to stand up without embarrassing himself.

Duncan cleared his throat.

Cheeks pinkening, she withdrew her hand. "Perhaps we should discuss our plans for dealing with Mr. Cromartie."

"Nae need."

"I daresay there is every need. He's not as dull as he appears."

"The plan is this: You stay here with Duncan. I deal with Cromartie. Simple."

"I should come with you," she said.

"No."

"You can use me as bait. It will be perfect."

"Not a chance in hell, woman."

She continued as if he hadn't spoken. "Cecilia's bairn is my blood, Alexander. The very last of it. If that wee, innocent child is in a bad way, I want to be there. I want to hold him." Her hand moved to her pendant, worrying at it. "Please. Ye promised to let me choose for myself."

Inwardly, he cursed. Never had a promise been this hard to keep. Gritting his teeth, he met Duncan's gaze. The other man's subtle nod signaled the decision was Alexander's.

After running through various scenarios in his mind, Alexander growled, "Did ye bring yer dirks?"

Smiling faintly, Duncan sipped his wine. "Ye ken better than to ask."

He glared down at his wife. "I mean to kill Cromartie."

"Oh, I know." She patted his hand as if he'd told her he intended to haul a load of manure later and might sully his shirtsleeves.

Clearly, she didn't understand. "His death willnae be pleasant."

"Nor should it be, after what he did to my lady's maid." Last night, Sabella had told him Cromartie had raped the poor lass repeatedly in the weeks before Lockhart's death. The bruiser had discovered the maid delivering Sabella's subversive messages to Munro, and he'd threatened to tell Lockhart unless the lass let him do as he liked with her. The maid had suffered in silence until after the bruiser was gone. Only then had she confided in Sabella, who'd used a portion of her brother's remaining funds to purchase the maid a cottage near her family in Perth.

Even now, Sabella's eyes flashed with cold, righteous fury. "I hope you make him beg to die."

He'd once feared revealing his ruthless nature to his angelic bride. No longer. When she felt justified in her wrath, whether toward the "red pests" who assaulted her garden or the bruiser who assaulted her maid, she was both blackhearted and bloodthirsty. He found it oddly arousing.

"Ye may come along," he said. "But ye must do whatever Duncan or I tell ye. No deviations, no delays. Ye ken?"

She nodded. "I ken."

God, he hated this down to his bones. "Very well, Duchess. Here's the new plan."

Chapter Twenty-One

They departed at dusk. Alexander hired a coach from a livery stable and assigned one of his men to play coachman for a night. He'd spent the afternoon tracking down Cecilia's hack driver for her visit to Buccleuch Street. Her address had cost him a mere two shillings. Now, they parked several houses away, positioned across the street with a full view of the narrow townhouse's front door.

A gentle hand slid over his. "Spare Cecilia any fright if you can," Sabella murmured. "I don't know her well, but we owe her a debt."

He nodded and looked at Duncan. "Ready?"

A cold, familiar smile. "As ever."

Alexander routed through a small close between a post office and a shop to approach the house from the alley at the back. There was no garden to speak of, no stable, just a wee fenced area with an open gate. He frowned. Staying hidden in the shadows, he craned his neck to peer through the rear windows. Only two were lit. The nearest one appeared to be a small dining room, perhaps for servants. The other might be the kitchen Inside, he heard a woman speaking, soft and low. He inched closer, flattening his body along the brick.

"Ye shouldnae have agreed to work for him," the woman chided. "He's naught but a hired brute. Ye ken that, right?"

"Haud yer wheesht," came a man's nasal whine. "Ye're painin' my heid with yer yawpin'."

"The money isnae his. It belongs to my son. Whatever he's promised ye, I'll double it. Help me kill him. Help me save my son, and I'll pay—"

The distinctive click of a gun being cocked.

"I said *haud yer wheesht*."

Moving his head slowly to avoid catching anyone's notice, Alexander shifted to look inside. Cecilia Hamilton Lockhart sat at the kitchen table. A teacup steamed in front of her. A brown bottle of laudanum sat near her elbow. Her exquisitely beautiful face was red and swollen along one cheek. Her lower lip was split and bleeding. Yet, she remained calm.

All except her eyes. Those were howling.

Across from her sat a weaselly, wiry man wearing a cap. The weasel slurped a bowl of soup with one hand and trained a pistol on her with the other. "If Cromartie returns and finds ye gone, who do ye think he'll come after?" The man pointed to his cap. "I'm nae dafty. I ken what's what."

Cromartie had left the house. Bloody hell. Alexander had deliberately waited until dark to make his move for two reasons—less chance of being spotted and a good chance that a gin drunkard would be deep in his cups by this time of day. No help for it. He'd have to go inside.

Making a quick calculation, he tried the service door and found it unlatched. As silently as he could, he took the passage to the kitchen, which opened behind the weasel. Though he was deep in shadow, Cecilia saw him. But not by the tiniest flutter of her pale lashes did she signal it.

"I pity ye," she told the weasel.

"Me?" he snorted and slurped. "Ye're the one sportin' bruises, lass."

"Aye," she said calmly. "But I'm not about to die."

Alexander would have used his dirk to slit the man's throat, but he didn't think Cecilia would appreciate being sprayed with blood. Instead, he stabbed through the man's wrist, dislodging the pistol. Before the weasel could scream, he wrapped an arm around the man's throat, squeezed, and wrenched until he heard cracking. The weasel went slack.

Alexander pulled his dirk free and wiped it on a kitchen towel. "Where is Cromartie, Cecilia?"

"I dinnae ken." She stared at the weasel, whose open, vacant eyes stared at his empty bowl. "H-he took my son. He has some sort of scheme in mind to steal the funds Kenneth left for us. He's hired a lass to impersonate me."

"When did he leave?"

"An hour ago. He was out of gin."

"And the bairn?"

She shook her head. "Dinnae ken. He took him somewhere early this mornin'." Her breath hitched. Shook. Her eyes screamed with hellish agony.

"Easy, lass," he said softly. "We'll find him."

Alexander went to the front of the house to signal Duncan. Moments later, he entered with Sabella, and Alexander explained the situation.

"Gin?" Sabella scoffed. "I should have known."

"Cecilia's in the kitchen, lass. She's in a bad way."

Immediately, Sabella's concern shifted to the other woman. She rushed toward the kitchen, bent on helping in whatever way she could.

That was his Duchess. One moment, she was wrathful vengeance. The next, an angel of compassion.

He turned to Duncan, who wore the same eerily neutral expression he'd always worn on a mission. "Where would a gin drunkard go to resupply?" Alexander asked.

"Depends on what sort of gin he fancies."

"He has funds."

Duncan nodded. "Let's have a look, eh?"

Upstairs, they found two bedchambers. The first was Cecilia's—several gowns draped over a drying rack, and a basket filled with blankets for the wee bairn sat beside the bed.

The second chamber was a filthy sty strewn with gin bottles. Duncan lifted one to his nose. He frowned and lifted another. "Different sources," he said. "One's from a tavern in the Canongate. The other is from a distillery near Tollcross." He plucked up two more bottles and sniffed. "These two are cheap. Ye'll find them in any public house in the city."

Alexander nodded. "Bugger could be anywhere."

"We could wait for him to return."

"The bairn mightn't last that long." He ran a hand over his beard, fighting the sick feeling in his gut. "Bluidy hell."

They returned to the kitchen to find Sabella plying Cecilia with tea and reassurances. Her eyes found Alexander's. "Anything?"

He shook his head. "Cecilia, did Cromartie say where he preferred to purchase his gin?"

The pale, bruised woman winced as her cup brushed her bloody lip. "No. We didnae precisely chat across the supper table."

"He preferred it sweet," said Sabella. "Whenever my maid smelled licorice, she would cast up her accounts."

Duncan's eyes sharpened. "Licorice. That's the distillery. There's an inn nearby that sells the stuff."

"To Tollcross we go."

By the time the coach halted outside the inn, Alexander had a new plan in mind. It involved his dirk and an empty warehouse he'd spotted near the distillery. The last piece of the puzzle was a drunken bruiser.

Duncan entered the inn while Alexander, Sabella, and Cecilia waited in the coach. When he came out a few minutes later, he tipped his hat in their direction.

"Cromartie is here," Alexander informed the lasses.

"Make him tell ye," murmured Cecilia. She rocked subtly from side to side, trembling despite the blankets Sabella draped over her and the arm she had looped around her. "After that, ye must kill him."

He lowered his head and caught the woman's gaze. "We'll find yer son. We will."

Sabella reached for him, and he took her hand in his. "Be careful," she said. "Don't get caught."

He smiled. "Dinnae fash, love. This is the one thing I'm good at."

With a tender look, she shook her head. "You're good at much more than this, husband. So much more."

He squeezed her hand and opened the door. "Dinnae leave this carriage, ye ken? We'll return shortly."

In the end, abducting the bruiser was surprisingly easy. He was a bruiser. He liked to fight, particularly when he was piss-drunk on gin. And when Duncan set his mind to provoking a belligerent drunkard, a fight was inevitable.

Cromartie was taking his second walloping swing at the air in front of Duncan's nose when Alexander entered. Alexander signaled his friend, and moments later, Duncan's fist buried deep in the bruiser's gut. Cromartie bent double and vomited. A knee to the forehead put him on the floor. One last hit to the temple put him out.

Some onlookers gaped and gasped, but most laughed and cheered drunkenly. The innkeeper scowled. "Ay! Take that rubbish outside!"

Duncan offered his apologies, and Alexander pushed away from the wall where he'd been enjoying the show to help haul Cromartie outside. They strapped the man's bulky, pig-like mass to the back of the coach then hauled the rubbish to the empty warehouse.

There, Alexander set to work doing what he was good at—delivering pain and extracting information. He didn't let Sabella watch, no matter how prettily she begged him. "Not even for a short while?" she pleaded. "I promise not to distract you."

"Ye cannae help distractin' me, woman. I'll let ye see him once he's dead. That's the best I can do."

She only pouted a wee bit before nodding. "Very well. Make it dreadful."

God, how he loved his vicious, beautiful woman. "Done."

An hour later, the bruiser begged Alexander to kill him. He'd confessed the bairn's location in the first five minutes—a cottage behind the inn with the woman he'd hired to impersonate Cecilia. Alexander sent Duncan to retrieve the boy. Then he settled into his work with grim satisfaction.

Cromartie's broad, upturned nose resembled a pig's. The bleary glaze of gin wore off after Alexander's fist broke it. The weeping began when he broke the pig's ribs one by one. The begging commenced when Alexander made his first precise cut.

When the swine blubbered for his mam, Alexander murmured, "Aye, mams are comfortin', eh? Mayhap ye shouldnae have stolen a mother's bairn from her." When the swine begged to die, Alexander said, "Aye, there are worse things than dyin'. Mayhap ye shouldnae have forced yerself on a wee maid."

When the swine pleaded for God's mercy, Alexander leaned down near his bloody, unrecognizable face. "Aye," he said softly. "God has mercy. But mayhap ye shouldnae have touched my woman. Because a devil has none."

Sabella wept as she cradled her wee nephew in her arms. "He's p-precious, Cecilia." Her heart swelled as she kissed his tiny forehead. "Do ye think he has Kenneth's eyes or yers?"

Cecilia stroked his downy blond tuft. Her sea-blue eyes were red from weeping. "They're blue for now. But they'll likely be more like yers in time."

"Mine and Kenneth's were the same."

"No," she said softly. "Kenneth's were cold. Yers arenae."

They'd found Callum Arthur Lockhart squalling at the top of his wee lungs inside a one-room cottage while an exhausted, wrung-out blonde lass shushed and rocked him to no avail. For the last hour, Cecilia had nursed her son and wept silently as she traced trembling fingertips over every inch of him.

Mr. MacAllister had sent the frayed lass on her way with a warning about those who involved themselves with refuse finding themselves on the rubbish pile. Then he'd gone to help Alexander with the aforementioned "refuse disposal."

Although she'd been keen to see the results of Alexander's work, Sabella found herself too enraptured by the sight of a loving mother feeding her bairn. Something about it felt both earthly and sacred. She'd plopped down in a chair near the cottage's window and simply watched them. Eventually, the babe had eaten his fill and drifted off to sleep. Only then did Cecilia speak a word.

"My father was like Cromartie," she whispered.

Sabella's heart lurched. She'd assumed Kenneth had been cruel to Cecilia. But a wee lassie with a father like that? "How did ye survive?"

"I did what he wanted. For him. The men who paid him."

Sabella's stomach had been queasy of late, but this nearly caused her to lose her supper.

"I … I didnae think I could have bairns. There was … damage. The physician said I'd never …"

Sabella covered her mouth, swallowing her gorge. "I'm so very sorry that happened to ye."

Cecilia nodded. A smile touched her lips. "Callum is my miracle. My reward. I dinnae ken how to be a mother. Yet, he's my son. This wee bit of hair is my hair." She stroked the white-blond tuft. "These wee, tiny fingers are my fingers." She moved her finger back and forth, showing how tightly the bairn gripped. Finally, she glanced up. "His blood is my blood. And yers, too. Would ye care to hold him?"

Dashing away a tear, Sabella nodded.

That was how Alexander found her—cradling her wee nephew, weeping and grinning like a dafty. "Oh, husband. Come see our nephew. Isn't he handsome?"

He ducked through the door and slowly approached. His sleeves were rolled up. His hands, forearms, and face were all damp from having been washed. When he reached her side, he kissed her temple then carefully drew a fingertip over the bairn's arm. That arm wagged in an uncontrolled circle.

Sabella laughed. "Cecilia believes he'll have my eyes. You see? They're already turning green."

"Aye. Like leaves in summer with sky in between."

Her heart melted. She pressed a kiss to Callum's downy head and placed him back in his mother's arms. Then she drew Alexander aside and asked, "Did he suffer?"

"Badly."

"Were you merciful in the end?"

"No."

"Is he dead?"

"Very."

She sighed. "I wish I could have been there."

"I ken." He cupped her cheek. "I might have stained my shirt, lass. Couldnae be helped."

She kissed his bare wrist. "I know a good laundress."

His reddened knuckles trailed down her cheek, along her throat, and along her upper chest to the pendant. "Seein' ye hold a bairn like that, I …" Coal-black eyes lifted and burned. "I want that with ye, Sabella. I want it very badly."

Guiding his hand from between her bosoms, which had been tender of late, down to her stomach, which had been queasy of late, she pressed his palm over her belly. Her heart lit on fire as her husband's eyes widened, heated, then shone. Those eyes asked a question.

Slowly, she smiled until her heart filled the room. Then she drew him closer and gave him his answer. "Done."

Epilogue

May 1, 1828
Eala House
Glenscannadoo, Scotland

"It means 'swan' in Gaelic," Sabella explained as Annie tossed a fiery-red curl out of her face and pulled a third loaf of bread from Sabella's ovens.

"I ken what it means. But there arenae any swans here. He should have named the house after the river. Bluidy sentimental MacPhersons."

Sabella chuckled and laid a hand on her belly to quell the wee one's frantic movements. Every time the bairn moved, she felt a need for the privy. "He offered to let me change it, but I think it's lovely."

Annie rested a hand on her own belly, which was mounding with her second child in as many years. "That glasshouse willnae be finished in time. Have ye told him yet?"

Sighing, Sabella shook her head. Alexander had promised her it would be completed before the bairn was born. "He's worked so hard, Annie. First, the glass was delayed. Then those wretched storms came. He's scarcely slept."

"Alexander would bury himself for the ones he loves. And he loves ye more than anybody."

"I know." Sabella wandered to the window to watch him working. Rain had started to pour, yet there he was alongside his three massive brothers and Annie's husband, John. "I love him the same."

Angus joined his sons, handing a hammer to Campbell and clapping a giant hand on John Huxley's shoulder. Lord Huxley was scarcely above six feet, but he was powerfully lean and strong for an English aristocrat, so he held up well beneath the force of Angus's affectionate blow. Rannoch laughed at something Angus said then tossed Broderick a shovel. Broderick, whose face was badly scarred from what Kenneth had done to him, adjusted his eye patch and shouted instructions at Gavin MacDonnell. Alexander, meanwhile, quietly worked on laying the brick for the cold frames. His hair and beard were getting long, she noticed. With the rain, he'd be soaked soon. He might have to remove his shirt.

Sabella shivered and sighed.

An old woman on a donkey rode very near the window, disrupting Sabella's view. A shrub of wild, salty hair appeared, followed by a daft, half-blind blink. "Lassie! Have ye seen my donkey? He goes by Bill."

Sabella pointed to the long-eared animal beneath her.

"Curse ye, Bill! That's the last time I take yer advice about dandelion wine, ye tricksome beastie."

Chuckling, Sabella waved her inside. Soon, they were joined by Nora, Magdalene, Broderick's lovely wife, Kate, and Campbell's equally lovely wife, Clarissa. Mrs. MacBean regaled them with tales from her youth—at least, Sabella *thought* they were from her youth. Surely, a woman her age wouldn't engage in "hoistin' a captain's sails 'til he permanently points true north" or finding "that wee, fine line betwixt a skelpin' ride and a criminal charge."

Sabella leaned over to Annie. "What is skelping?"

Annie arched a red brow. "Slappin'. If it's on the backside, it's the same as spankin'."

Eyes rounding, Sabella glanced toward the daft old woman who'd boasted that she'd "skelpt every Brodie man twice with naught but a butter churn, a cucumber, and a sack of duck feathers."

A short while later, Sabella finished stirring the onion gravy while Annie ranted at Kate about the absurd fertility of Huxley males. "I was told I could prevent conception so long as I fed Finlay from my own bosoms."

Kate started to protest, but Annie wasn't having it. "That's what yer mam and sisters said." She snorted and waved to her swollen belly. "Does this look like prevention?"

"We did warn you the effect is temporary, as I recall."

"I'm on pace for twenty, Kate. Twenty! We'll have to hire nursemaids for our nursemaids."

Sabella winced as her own bairn turned again, pressuring her back and sending pain rippling through her. She braced a hand against the wall. Breathed. Breathed.

Breathed.

Meanwhile, Magdalene and Nora discussed Nora's recent problems with fatigue and nausea, and Clarissa chatted with Mrs. MacBean about roots that might soothe a teething infant's temper.

The pain in Sabella's back and thighs worsened to a distressing degree. She staggered toward the table and lowered herself onto a chair. It helped a little, but the bairn was pressing on all the wrong places. She started to rise, thinking it was time yet again for the privy, when the pain struck with a hot, wrenching vengeance.

She doubled over. Her outward breath started as a whoosh and ended as a whimper. She sensed all the women in the kitchen rushing to help. Magdalene was the first to suggest they move her to a bedchamber, and Annie was the first to suggest someone fetch Alexander.

Strangely, Mrs. MacBean didn't say anything at all.

They helped her upstairs and summoned Effie to help her undress. Magdalene calmly took charge. Such calm competence was a great comfort. The pain was happening every few minutes, and Sabella could scarcely think. Effie arrived to help her into a loose, lightweight morning gown. She unpinned her hair and brushed it soothingly before plaiting it down Sabella's back. All the ladies crowded around her to offer bright, reassuring chatter and comforting pats.

Mrs. MacBean stood silently in the doorway, staring at Sabella's belly with that milky eye glowing white.

Sabella was about to ask what was wrong when another pain came. This one gripped her like a fist, squeezing hard enough to make her scream. Seconds later, Alexander entered like a dark storm. He was dripping. Heaving. She sobbed and reached for him. He swept her into his arms, sat on the bed, and cradled her close while pain squeezed and squeezed and squeezed.

Then it eased. She breathed against his neck, grateful for his strong arms around her. Time passed in a haze. Sometimes there was more pain, sometimes less. Always there was Alexander, supporting her back and legs, strengthening her resolve as the pain worsened. Quietly, he rocked her. Softly, he kissed her temple.

At one point, Magdalene suggested Sabella stand and walk a bit between her pains. She tried venturing back and forth to the dressing room, but the pains were coming closely together, and she couldn't manage for more than a minute or two.

During one of those minutes, Sabella insisted that Alexander eat something and change into dry clothes. "I need yer strength, husband," she said softly, stroking his beard. "That means feeding yourself. Now, go."

Minutes after his departure, she felt an ominous chill. Glancing up, she spotted a single crow perched just outside the bedroom window.

And that was when the real pain—the kind that made a mockery of the old pain—began.

Alexander wasn't certain he could do this without breaking something. To watch his wife suffer such agony made him want to howl. He rushed through a plate of venison and gravy then took a moment to wash and don a fresh set of clothes. Through the dressing room door, he could hear her screaming.

It tore him open.

He started for the bedchamber door.

"Stop, laddie." Mrs. MacBean hovered in the doorway to the corridor. She looked paler and more worn than he could ever recall seeing her. Staggering into the dressing room, she clutched his wrist and drew his arm close. Her whitish eye appeared glassy.

His heart pounded as his wife screamed. "What is it, auld woman? I'm needed in there."

Turning his hand in hers, she slowly traced a figure on his palm. Up, over, and down. Up, over, and down. "Strength, resilience, power." Up, over, and down. "These are what's needed in there." Up, over, and down. "But the fightin' must be done by her, not ye."

His frown deepened. He and his brothers had learned not to ignore this old crone's mysterious ramblings. When Sabella released a long, pained sob, he flinched and asked, "What can I do?"

"Love her, laddie. These hands were fashioned by yer *seanair*"—his grandfather—"and yer mam. Their blood is yer blood. Her heart is yer heart. Lend her what's yers."

"How?" he growled.

Up, over, and down. Up, over, and down.

"If there be two crows, she's safe," the old woman said in that peculiar, layered voice. "The wee rosebud, too. Ye'll have seven buds in all. Enough to fill yer garden." She inched closer, touching his chest with a shaking finger. "But if there be one crow, she cannae stay."

His soul roared a denial. "She must."

"Lend her yer strength. A swan can fly farther than ye imagine."

Another scream echoed, and he jerked away. Upon returning to the bedchamber, he found Magdalene soothing Sabella with cool cloths and gentle encouragement. His wife braced her hands on the bed while her head hung down between her shoulders. Her arms were trembling.

He laid his palm between her shoulder blades and kissed her temple. "I'm here, love."

At first, she didn't seem to hear him. Then her arms steadied. She leaned against his body, sweat-soaked and pain-weary.

Over the long, anguishing hours that followed, Alexander gave her what was hers—which was everything he had. He held her when she needed holding. He braced her when she needed bracing. He lied to her when Magdalene's calm façade wavered into concern. He distracted her when Mrs. MacBean's eyes reflected despair.

He kept his own agonized roar inside as he felt a warm, seeping wetness and realized it was her blood.

"Ye're so much stronger than the pain." He sat propped up in their bed, his knees raised to surround her as she lay back against his chest. "Mayhap others tried to keep ye inside a cage that was too small, my bonnie *eala*." His swan. "But ye broke free, aye?"

"Y-you broke me free." Her voice was down to nothing but raspy threads.

"Those wings needed room."

"They needed a garden," she whispered, kissing his hand. "The world is a wild land filled with cunning beasts and vicious traps, remember? You built me a sanctuary amidst the wilds, walls to protect me until I could fly on my own."

"And fly ye did."

"How I love you for that." Her voice weakened and slurred as her head lolled. "Not flying anywhere without you."

As Magdalene checked on the bairn's progress, she met Alexander's gaze, the soft gray steadying into certainty. "Time to push."

Another hour passed. Alexander didn't mark the time or glance at the clock. He watched the window across from the bed. He stared at the single crow that kept flying away as if to hunt its mate then returning when the search proved fruitless.

On the bedside table was the wooden crow carving that Campbell had fashioned for Sabella. It was a braw, intricate piece blackened by fire. From time to time as Alexander held his bleeding, anguished wife while she struggled to birth their child, he fancied that crow's wings moved. A trick of the light, surely. But he also noticed other strange things. His pewter medallion heated against his chest. His wife's emerald ring felt similarly warm, and the emerald glowed whenever the light caught it.

As a new day dawned, that emerald seemed to catch fire, and her pendant felt hot to the touch.

Sabella gritted her teeth and pushed. Magdalene and Mrs. MacBean murmured about the problems of narrow hips. They gave assurances about second bairns being easier.

But there was only one crow in the window. It flew away to hunt for its mate.

While it was gone, Alexander and Sabella's daughter was born. Magdalene immediately set to work cleaning and wrapping the squalling bairn, whose lungs appeared to be the strongest part of her. She handed the bairn to Mrs. MacBean, who gave a startled blink. The infant immediately quieted.

Alexander kissed his limp, pale wife on her sweat-soaked temple. "We have a wee lassie, Duchess," he said, wondering why his face was wet. Sweat, likely.

Sabella didn't reply. She didn't move. Had she fallen asleep?

He looked down to see blood blooming. He glanced up to find only one crow.

"No," he breathed, gathering her closer. Tighter. "Ye must stay. Ye must."

Mrs. MacBean began singing to their daughter in Gaelic, her voice layered and hoarse. Magdalene, who'd been working to stem the bleeding, clasped one of his hands and placed it gently over his wife's belly. "Gently kneading, ye ken?" She pressed his hand with the desired motions. "It will help."

He focused on holding his precious woman while she bled and fought to stay.

One crow. It flew away.

He whispered his love and praised her for the woman she'd become—powerfully strong, beautifully free.

"We'll name her Rose, just as ye wanted," he crooned, rocking his wife gently while the center of his chest burned. "Our wee Rose, who will prick all the lads with her thorns one day."

One crow returned. A wing-shaped shadow moved across his wife's beautiful white face.

One crow. A plaintive caw. A flutter. And then there were two.

Two. That was how many months it had been since Sabella Lockhart MacPherson had tupped with her husband.

Two bloody months.

This could not stand. So, on a brilliant July day, she strolled into the most popular tavern in Glenscannadoo wearing her husband's plaid draped over a light, white gown of layered cotton.

"Och, lamb!" called Joan from the other end of the bar. "Havenae seen ye in here in some time. New bairn's been keepin' ye busy, eh?"

Sabella chuckled. "Busy is one word for it."

They chatted briefly about new motherhood and sore bosoms until Sabella felt a telltale prickle along her nape. She smiled then sauntered deeper into the shadows. Pausing to let her eyes adjust, she hunted for her quarry and found him in the darkest part of the tavern.

A massive pair of boots took shape first. Then a pair of impossibly long, impossibly powerful legs. His voice, deep as an ocean, resounded with irritation. "Ye shouldnae be walkin' this far yet, Duchess. It's a long way from home."

"Magdalene says I'm perfectly fine." She swayed closer. "And the physician assures me I may resume *all* normal activities."

"Is the physician still tryin' to scrub yer blood from his trews? No? Then, whatever he says is shite."

She rolled her eyes. "Infernally stubborn man."

He downed the remainder of his cider and scorched her from head to toe with a simmering gaze. "I'll nae risk it."

"You'll have to tup me eventually."

He shifted until his chair creaked. "Not yet."

She clicked her tongue and crossed her arms. "I've a position to fill. A vital one."

"What position? Ye have a full household staff at yer disposal."

"I'm dissatisfied with the current arrangement. My husband has broken his promises."

His full-scale MacPherson scowl practically produced a thunderclap. "Never, lass. Not once."

"The glasshouse—"

"My brothers finished it before Rose was born. I said ye'd have it, not that I would lay every brick and dig every trench myself."

She sniffed in a pretense of dismissal. "Nevertheless, I must demand recompense. Help me fill the position."

He sighed and rubbed his beard. "What's the position?"

"It involves harlotry. A great deal of hard, backbreaking harlotry."

That big, long body went perfectly still. "Lass."

"Much of the work will require being on one's knees. Some things must be washed both frequently and diligently."

"Bluidy, everlasting hell."

She inched forward until her toes brushed his and her thighs pressed against the table. Then she braced her hands on the table and leaned down until their faces were inches apart. "I'm a very dirty lass, Mr. MacPherson."

He stood, shoving his chair back against the wall. "Ye always push me. I've warned ye about that."

"I'd like to offer you the position." She straightened. "I can't pay much. But there are other compensations. I'll provide the bed."

With one mighty swipe, he shoved the table to one side then wrapped a powerful arm around her waist, jerking her hard against him. "Aye, then. I'll fill yer position."

"Are you certain?" she taunted breathlessly. "You might have to get your hands dirty."

He kissed her with all the fire and tongue-tangling lust she'd been missing for two. Long. Months.

"If my dirty lass needs washin', then ye've found the right man."

She grinned her triumph against his mouth and stroked his bearded jaw. Love filled her until she could scarcely contain it. "Aye, Highlander. Ye've always been the right man for me."

Watch for the next book in the Midnight in Scotland series

COMING SOON!

MIDNIGHT IN SCOTLAND: BOOK FIVE

THE LOVE OF A HIGHLANDER

BY

ELISA BRADEN

MORE FROM ELISA BRADEN

Be first to hear about new releases, price specials, and more—sign up for Elisa's free email newsletter at www.elisabraden.com so you don't miss a thing!

Midnight in Scotland Series

In the enchanting new Midnight in Scotland series, the unlikeliest matches generate the greatest heat. All it takes is a spark of Highland magic.

THE MAKING OF A HIGHLANDER (BOOK ONE)

Handsome adventurer John Huxley is locked in a land dispute in the Scottish Highlands with one way out: Win the Highland Games. When the local hoyden Mad Annie Tulloch offers to train him in exchange for "Lady Lessons," he agrees. But teaching the fiery, foul-mouthed, breeches-wearing lass how to land a lord seems impossible—especially when he starts dreaming of winning her for himself.

THE TAMING OF A HIGHLANDER (BOOK TWO)

Wrongfully imprisoned and tortured, Broderick MacPherson lives for one purpose—punishing the man responsible. When a wayward lass witnesses his revenge, he risks returning to the prison that nearly killed him. Kate Huxley has no wish to testify against a man who's already suffered too much. But the only remedy is to become his wife. And she can't possibly marry such a surly, damaged man…can she?

THE TEMPTATION OF A HIGHLANDER (BOOK THREE)

Hunted by a madman bent on possessing her, English beauty Clarissa Meadows flees to a friend's house in the Scottish Highlands. With nowhere left to run, she accepts the protection of rough, solitary giant Campbell MacPherson. But falling for her bodyguard puts him in a predator's sights, forcing an impossible choice: stay with the man she loves or save him from the wolf she's brought to his door.

THE WICKEDNESS OF A HIGHLANDER (BOOK FOUR)

When a Highland robbery takes everything but the gown on her back, Sabella Lockhart must accept a maid's position with the man who despises her—Alexander MacPherson. Sabella is the reason he was shot, and having her sleeping under his roof and following his commands satisfies his thirst for revenge. Ruthless? Absolutely. But in a deal with the devil, he always takes more than his due.

RIGHT PLACE, WRONG DUKE (NOVELLA)

Widow Lucie Carmichael has made too many mistakes in her life, but she's not about to let the Duke of Dingwall evict her family from their ancestral home, even if that means engaging in a little abduction. Silas Northfield is not the Duke of Dingwall, no matter how much a mad Scottish lass insists he is. So, when she abducts him, Silas takes matters—and the luscious Lucie—into his own hands.

Rescued from Ruin Series

Discover the scandalous predicaments, emotional redemptions, and gripping love stories (with a dash of Lady Wallingham) in the scorching series that started it all!

EVER YOURS, ANNABELLE (PREQUEL)

As a girl, Annabelle Huxley chased Robert Conrad with reckless abandon, and he always rescued her when she pushed too far—until the accident that cost him everything. Seven years later, Robert discovers the girl with the habit of chasing trouble is now a siren he can't resist. But when a scandalous secret threatens her life, how far will he go to rescue her one last time?

THE MADNESS OF VISCOUNT ATHERBOURNE (BOOK ONE)

Victoria Lacey's life is perfect—perfectly boring. Agree to marry a lord who has yet to inspire a single, solitary tingle? It's all in a day's work for the oh-so-proper sister of the Duke of Blackmore. Surely no one suspects her secret longing for head-spinning passion. Except a dark stranger, on a terrace, at a ball where she should not be kissing a man she has just met. Especially one bent on revenge.

THE TRUTH ABOUT CADS AND DUKES (BOOK TWO)

Painfully shy Jane Huxley is in a most precarious position, thanks to dissolute charmer Colin Lacey's deceitful wager. Now, his brother, the icy Duke of Blackmore, must make it right, even if it means marrying her himself. Will their union end in frostbite? Perhaps. But after lingering glances and devastating kisses, Jane begins to suspect the truth: Her duke may not be as cold as he appears.

DESPERATELY SEEKING A SCOUNDREL (BOOK THREE)

Where Lord Colin Lacey goes, trouble follows. Tortured and hunted by a brutal criminal, he is rescued from death's door by the stubborn, fetching Sarah Battersby. In return, she asks one small favor: Pretend to be her fiancé. Temporarily, of course. With danger nipping his heels, he knows it is wrong to want her, wrong to agree to her terms. But when has Colin Lacey ever done the sensible thing?

THE DEVIL IS A MARQUESS (BOOK FOUR)

A walking scandal surviving on wits, whisky, and wicked skills in the bedchamber, Benedict Chatham must marry a fortune or risk ruin. Tall, redheaded disaster Charlotte Lancaster possesses such a fortune. The price? One year of fidelity and sobriety. Forced to end his libertine ways, Chatham proves he is more than the scandalous charmer she married, but will it be enough to keep his unwanted wife?

WHEN A GIRL LOVES AN EARL (BOOK FIVE)

Miss Viola Darling always gets what she wants, and what she wants most is to marry Lord Tannenbrook. James knows how determined the tiny beauty can be—she mangled his cravat at a perfectly respectable dinner before he escaped. But he has no desire to marry, less desire to be pursued, and will certainly not kiss her kissable lips until they are both breathless, no matter how tempted he may be.

TWELVE NIGHTS AS HIS MISTRESS (NOVELLA – BOOK SIX)

Charles Bainbridge, Lord Wallingham, spent two years wooing Julia Willoughby, yet she insists they are a dreadful match destined for misery. Now, rather than lose her, he makes a final offer: Spend twelve nights in his bed, and if she can deny they are perfect for each other, he will let her go. But not before tempting tidy, sensible Julia to trade predictability for the sweet chaos of true love.

CONFESSIONS OF A DANGEROUS LORD (BOOK SEVEN)

Known for flashy waistcoats and rapier wit, Henry Thorpe, the Earl of Dunston, is deadlier than he appears. For years, his sole focus has been hunting a ruthless killer through London's dark underworld. Then Maureen Huxley came along. To keep her safe, he must keep her at arm's length. But as she contemplates marrying another man, Henry's caught in the crossfire between his mission and his heart.

ANYTHING BUT A GENTLEMAN (BOOK EIGHT)

Augusta Widmore must force her sister's ne'er-do-well betrothed to the altar, or her sister will bear the consequences. She needs leverage only one man can provide—Sebastian Reaver. When she invades his office demanding a fortune in markers, he exacts a price a spinster will never pay—become the notorious club owner's mistress. And when she calls his bluff, a fiery battle for surrender begins.

A Marriage Made in Scandal (Book Nine)

As the most feared lord in London, the Earl of Holstoke is having a devil of a time landing a wife. When a series of vicious murders brings suspicion to his door, only one woman is bold enough to defend him—Eugenia Huxley. Her offer to be his alibi risks scandal, and marriage is the remedy. But as a poisonous enemy coils closer, Holstoke finds his love for her might be the greatest danger of all.

A Kiss from a Rogue (Book Ten)

A cruel past left Hannah Gray with one simple longing—a normal life with a safe, normal husband. Finding one would be easy if she weren't distracted by wolf-in-rogue's-clothing Jonas Hawthorn. He's tried to forget the haughty Miss Gray. But once he tastes the heat and longing hidden beneath her icy mask, the only mystery this Bow Street man burns to solve is how a rogue might make Hannah his own.

Once Upon a Midnight Kiss (Holiday Novella)

Charming antiquities dealer Andrew Farrington relies on his clumsy-but-capable private secretary, Euphemia Sinclair, to be there when he needs her. But when she travels to Scotland in search of a family heirloom only a married woman can claim, Andrew will do anything to keep this indispensable woman by his side—including marrying her before she marries someone else.

The Oddflower Series

Suitors beware: The season of wallflowers is about to begin.

The Secrets of a Moonlit Night (An Oddflower Novella)

Sinister rumors of the mysterious Half-Faced Man haunt the ruins of Northcliffe Abbey. But governess Elizabeth Nightingale knows claptrap when she peddles it. So, when the real Half-Faced Man—architect Thomas Warwick—warns her to keep her young charges away from his property, Elizabeth isn't frightened by his scars. She's frightened by how easily he sees through her disguise to the woman beneath.

TO SEE ALL OF ELISA BRADEN'S BOOKS IN ONE PLACE, VISIT
ELISABRADEN.COM

About the Author

Reading romance novels came easily to Elisa Braden. Writing them? That took a little longer. After graduating with degrees in creative writing and history, Elisa spent entirely too many years in "real" jobs writing T-shirt copy ... and other people's resumes ... and articles about giftware displays. But that was before she woke up and started dreaming about the very *unreal* job of being a romance novelist. Better late than never.

Elisa lives in the gorgeous Pacific Northwest, where you're constitutionally required to like the colors green and gray. Good thing she does. Other items on the "like" list include cute dogs, strong coffee, and epic movies. Of course, her favorite thing of all is hearing from readers who love her characters as much as she does. If you're one of those, get in touch on Facebook and Twitter or visit **www.elisabraden.com**.

Made in the USA
Columbia, SC
22 May 2024